Praise for Betty Hechtman's
National Bestselling Crochet Mysteries

"What fun—crochet and mystery."
—Vanna White, cohost of *Wheel of Fortune*

"Who can resist a sleuth named Pink, a slew of interesting
minor characters, and a fun fringe-of-Hollywood setting?"
—Monica Ferris, *USA Today* bestselling author

"A delightful addition to the mystery genre."
—Earlene Fowler, national bestselling author

"Readers couldn't ask for a more rollicking read."
—*Crochet Today!*

"Fun . . . Has a great hook and a cast of characters that
enliven any scene."   —*The Mystery Reader*

"A wonderfully woven tale . . . A well-crafted mystery that
gets unraveled one strand at a time."   —*The Best Reviews*

"Hechtman's charming crochet mystery series is clever and
lively."   —*Fresh Fiction*

Yarn to Go

BETTY HECHTMAN

BERKLEY PRIME CRIME, NEW YORK

THE BERKLEY PUBLISHING GROUP
Published by the Penguin Group
Penguin Group (USA) Inc.
375 Hudson Street, New York, New York 10014, USA

USA | Canada | UK | Ireland | Australia | New Zealand | India | South Africa | China

Penguin Books Ltd., Registered Offices: 80 Strand, London WC2R 0RL, England
For more information about the Penguin Group, visit penguin.com.

YARN TO GO

A Berkley Prime Crime Book / published by arrangement with the author

Berkley Prime Crime Books are published by The Berkley Publishing Group.
BERKLEY® PRIME CRIME and the PRIME CRIME logo are trademarks of
Penguin Group (USA) Inc.

For information, address: The Berkley Publishing Group,
a division of Penguin Group (USA) Inc.,
375 Hudson Street, New York, New York 10014.

ISBN: 978-0-425-25221-5

PUBLISHING HISTORY
Berkley Prime Crime mass-market edition / July 2013

PRINTED IN THE UNITED STATES OF AMERICA

10 9 8 7 6 5 4 3 2 1

Cover illustration by Patricia Castelao.
Cover design by Rita Frangie.
Interior text design by Kelly Lipovich.

Acknowledgments

I am so happy to be working with my editor, Sandy Harding. I appreciate her suggestions, which always seem to be right. Thanks to my agent, Jessica Faust, for all her input and persistence. Natalee Rosenstein makes Berkley Prime Crime a great place to be.

Nothing is ever wasted. Who knew the magic class with the Great Houdanni would come in handy or my experience as master magician Ricky Jay's assistant?

Thanks to Roberta Martia for all the encouragement and yarn help. Linda Hopkins once again was a wonderful help with the pattern. Her eye for detail is fantastic.

Rene Biederman, Connie Cabon, Alice Chiredijan, Terry Cohen, Clara Feeney, Sonia Flaum, Lily Gillis, Winnie Hineson, Linda Hopkins, Debbie Kratofil, Reva Mallon, Elayne Moschin and Paula Tesler are all part of my knit and crochet group. They offer yarn help, friendship and so much more.

Thanks to my muffin tasters Burl, Max and Samantha. What would I do without you guys?

1

I WAS IN THE MIDDLE OF LAYING OUT THE INGRE-
dients for my carrot muffins when the call came. It's lucky
I hadn't started mixing them, because you can't just run off
and abandon muffin batter for an hour and expect it to be
okay. I didn't even understand who it was at first. All I heard
was something about no refund on a credit card bill, the
word *retreat* and that I "better do something about it."

"Who is this?" I said when the caller finally took a breath.

"Casey, this is Tag Thornkill," an exasperated voice
responded. He could have left off the last name. I mean, it's
not like I know a bunch of Tags. Immediately my demeanor
changed from irritated at the interruption to concerned. Tag
is my current employer, or half of the pair, anyway. He and
his wife, Lucinda, own the Blue Door restaurant, which is
where I presently work. I'm the dessert chef. Tag doesn't
know it, but I also bake muffins for some coffee spots in

town using the Blue Door's kitchen. Lucinda had given her okay and saw no problem with the arrangement as long as I brought in my own ingredients.

So every night when the restaurant closes and everyone has left, I come in and bake the restaurant's desserts for the next day, along with batches of muffins for the next day's coffee drinkers.

Let me be clear from the start: I'm not one of those fancy cooking school graduates who does French pastry. I had never even thought of baking as being a career. It was just something I started doing when I was a kid. It might have been a reaction to having a mother who was a cardiologist and thought cookies only came in white boxes from the bakery.

My first experience as a dessert chef happened at a friend's bistro. He didn't care that I didn't have any formal training. The truth was in the cake. He loved what I baked and hired me. Unfortunately, he sold the bistro after six months and it became a hot dog stand that didn't offer dessert.

After that I tried law school, but by the end of the first semester, I knew it wasn't for me. Nor was being a substitute teacher at a private school. Then I tested out a lot of other professions. In other words, I worked as a temp. I did things like handing out samples of chewing gum on street corners, spritzing perfume on anyone I could get to slow down at a department store, some office work and my favorite, working at a detective agency.

My poor mother was beside herself. If I'd heard it once, I'd heard it a zillion times. "Casey, when I was your age, I was already a doctor and a mother. And you're what . . . ?" Talk about knowing how to make me feel like more of a flop. My father wasn't all that happy, either. He was a doctor,

too—a pediatrician. When I broke up with Dr. Sammy Glickner, things really hit the fan. He was my parents' dream come true: Jewish, not just a doctor, but a specialist in urology and nice. They said nice; I said bland. Well, not totally bland. He was very funny in a goofy sort of way.

But I needed a fresh start. And who better to help me with it than my father's sister, Joan Stone. Let's just say we both had the black sheep thing going. Her main advantage was she actually had a profession—actress. She wasn't an A-list star like Meryl Streep or Julia Roberts. Most of her parts were playing somebody's aunt Trudy or the noisy neighbor down the street. Her one claim to fame was she'd been the Tidy Soft toilet paper lady long enough to build up a nice nest egg before she left L.A., moved up north and started a new career.

But now back to the call.

With a nice tone, I asked Tag to repeat what he'd said.

"I was checking Lucinda's credit card receipts. There is a charge for Yarn2Go. My dear wife explained that was your aunt's business and the charge was for some kind of yarn trip." He paused as if he expected me to say something, and when I didn't, he continued. "I checked all of her later bills and there was no mention of a refund. What do you have to say about that?"

The "oh no" was purely in my head. Barely three months after I'd left Chicago and relocated to my aunt Joan's guesthouse in the northern California town of Cadbury by the Sea, my aunt had been killed in a hit-and-run accident. It was horrible. There were no witnesses, and the cops still had the case open, though it didn't look like they were going to find the driver. I didn't care that the cops, my parents and all of my aunt's friends insisted it was just an unfortunate, random accident. I didn't buy it.

Here are the basic facts. It was six thirty on a Sunday morning. My aunt never got up before eight. No one could explain, at least to my satisfaction, why she would have been out walking by the water at that hour. It was barely even light. I simply didn't buy the cops' explanation that maybe she'd taken up an exercise program and not mentioned it to me.

I mean, I was living in her guesthouse, which was just across the driveway from her house. True, we'd agreed to stay out of each other's lives, but still . . .

My aunt had left everything to me, and when I'd met with the lawyer, he'd brought up her retreat business. While Joan had still done occasional acting gigs, her real passion had become putting on these retreats that she called "vacations with a purpose." Basically all I knew about them was that they had to do with making things with yarn and she used the hotel and conference center across the street to host them. Joan had tried to explain more to me, but she got totally frustrated when I kept mixing up crocheting and knitting. I knew that you needed two things for one of them and one for the other, but not which for which. Needles, hooks, not my thing. All my creative endeavors had to do with baking.

I had told the lawyer I had no interest in continuing the business for obvious reasons. He'd looked through the papers I'd brought in and said they appeared to be for her taxes, so for all intents and purposes, the business was over.

"So what are you going to do about it?" Tag repeated, pulling me back to the here and now. I said something about checking into it when I got home, but that wasn't good enough. I could practically hear him pacing. Tag was one of those people who went around straightening pictures on the walls at other people's houses. He couldn't deal with things being out of order or unsettled. He said he wouldn't be able to sleep until it was straightened out. I glanced at my watch and saw that it was ten o'clock. I really wanted to continue making the muffins, but I knew Tag would be frantic until he had an answer, and he was sort of my boss. So I decided to run home and check. I'd finish the muffins when I returned.

Even though the restaurant was in downtown Cadbury and my place was on the edge of town, the route was direct, and a little over five minutes later I pulled my yellow Mini Cooper into the driveway. When I doused the headlights, the yard became invisible. I was still getting used to so much darkness at night. In Chicago, wherever you were, there was some light coming from somewhere. Here, on the edge of a small town that didn't allow streetlights, it really was pitch-dark.

There's something else I haven't mentioned. I had inherited my aunt's house, but after we'd cleaned out the refrigerator and I'd returned the packet of papers I'd shown the lawyer, I hadn't been able to bring myself to go back inside, let alone move into it. The space would have been wonderful. The guesthouse was basically one room. But in my mind the house still belonged to my aunt, and in some wishful corner of my heart, I thought she still might come back.

I fumbled with the keys as I headed toward her back door. A noise in the yard startled me as I pulled out the small flashlight I always carried. It was like my own personal headlight. I aimed the light around the yard and caught a deer nibbling on the petunias in one of the flower boxes. The delicate-looking creature blinked at the light but didn't seem concerned by my presence. Not really a big surprise. Deer

5

wandered around the seaside town at will, helping themselves to gardens and flowers. They really loved the small cemetery and were always lounging between the gravestones.

"No more stalling," I said out loud. In one swift move, I put the key in the lock, turned it and pushed open the door. The air inside seemed warm and a little stale. Was it my imagination or was there still a trace of my aunt's signature scent, Penhaligon's Elisabethan Rose? I couldn't help it; my eyes filled with tears at the thought of her. I flipped on the light quickly. Everything was just as it had been. She could have walked in and felt right at home. The bunch of lavender flowers she'd been drying was still hanging upside down. Her coffee mug was rinsed out and sitting on the counter.

I felt a real tug when I saw the shopping bag that the hospital had given me with the clothes she'd been wearing that morning. It had been sitting there since November, untouched since I brought it in.

"I'm sorry," a female voice said. I turned in time to see Lucinda come through the door. A quick glance at her face made it clear she'd overheard Tag talking to me on the phone about the yarn retreat charge. Her frilly pink nightgown showed through the opening in her Burberry trench coat. Only Lucinda would have thought to add a silk scarf and lipstick. "I tried to reason with him, but you know Tag. It's exasperating how exacting he is." Though the pair were in their fifties, they'd only been married a short time. They'd reconnected at their thirty-fifth high school reunion. Tag had been her high school crush. But years later she was divorced, he was widowed and they picked up as if no time had passed. Almost, anyway. Lucinda's favorite saying was "be careful what you wish for." Two seventeen-years-olds was one thing, but two people who have had years and years to develop habits and their own definitions of the way things should be—was something else entirely.

"If it was up to me, I wouldn't care," Lucinda said, closing the door and standing in the middle of the room with me. "I was so upset about Joan, I forgot all about it."

"It's got to be some kind of mistake." I hung my head. "It's my fault. I shouldn't have been such a baby. I should have come in here a long time ago."

Lucinda put her arm around my shoulder. "We'll deal with it together."

From the first time I'd met Lucinda, I'd liked her. Like my aunt Joan, she had a sense of fun, and our age difference didn't seem to matter. We were all on the same page, though visually we made an odd pair. Lucinda was smaller and lively looking with neatly styled black hair that softened her square-shaped face. She always looked put together, even in a trench coat over her nightie. I was a little rougher around the edges. Jeans, a long sleeve T-shirt and a fleece jacket was my usual attire. I had shoulder-length hair that resisted any style. It wasn't straight and it wasn't curly but went its own way. I tried to remember to put on some makeup, but it wasn't my top priority. Besides, all that sea air gave me a lot of color.

And when Joan had Lucinda taste my pound cake, she had gotten the idea of having me bake the desserts for the restaurant. I hadn't known Tag then or I would have been more flattered that he approved the idea.

Having Lucinda with me now made it easier to go through the house. We passed by Joan's bedroom quickly. The door was shut, but I knew everything was still as she had left it that fateful morning. Her toothbrush was still in the bathroom, and tufts of her black hair were still caught in the comb. I turned on the lights in the living room. Examples of my aunt's handicraft were everywhere. A colorful afghan was folded over the end of the couch. Purple irises graced a needlepoint pillow, and a soft fog gray shawl hung across a wing chair in front of the fireplace. It must have fallen off her shoulders the last time she sat there.

"All the papers are in her office," I said. We walked down the short hall. In an effort to make it seem like I was comfortable being in there, I pulled open a closet door. Yarn of every color tumbled out and bounced off my head.

"What the . . . ?" I said, picking up a ball of cotton candy pink yarn that had hit my foot and rolled off.

"It's your aunt's stash." Lucinda noticed my confusion. "That's what it's called—stash. Joan told me everybody who gets into yarn has a stash. I'd probably have one, too, at least a little one, except for Tag. He's a sweet guy in a lot of ways, but he's nuts when it comes to details. He saw I had one extra skein of yarn and made such a fuss, I said I wouldn't buy any more until I used that one."

"Skeins?" I said.

"Sorry, that's what they call these," she said, picking up a ball of yarn. "It's really a silly term. It's not like there is a universal size of a skein." To demonstrate, she pointed out a large peanut-shaped one of forest green yarn and a small fuzzy baby blue one in the mess on the floor. "Both of these would be called skeins. Go figure."

She helped me stuff everything back in the closet and shut the door before it could fall back out again.

Joan had taken the smallest of the three bedrooms and made it into an office. An adorable lion was guarding the desk. Lucinda explained it was crocheted. There was a basket of half-made things in the corner. "Those are WIPs," Lucinda said.

"Huh?" I said, picking up a forest green tube that looked like it might be on its way to becoming a sock.

"Works in progress," Lucinda said. "Don't get the idea I'm some kind of expert. Your aunt told me all of this."

As I held the tube of yarn, four silver needles slipped out and hit the floor with a pinging sound. I picked them up, examining the sharp double points. "These look like they could do some real damage." I tried to put them back the way they'd been but finally just stuck them into the yarn and put it on top of the stuff in the basket. "I have to stop getting sidetracked."

The padded envelope with the papers I'd taken to the attorney was on the desk where I'd left it. I was about to dump out the papers when I noticed a box covered in red bandanna print fabric. I lifted the top and looked inside, surprised to find that it was a file box. I'd started to push through the hanging dividers when I heard something hit the bottom with a clunk. "I wonder what this is," I said, fishing out a small black flash drive. Lucinda pointed to the computer on my aunt's desk and suggested I put it in and see what was on it.

We both watched the screen and I kept clicking on things until I got the flash drive to open and then opened a file. "What's that?" I said, looking at what had come up on the screen. It said *RIB* across the top, then *Test*. Lucinda shrugged and said it didn't mean anything to her. "We're not getting anywhere." I turned off the computer and pulled out the flash drive, dropping it back in the box.

I had a sinking feeling when I saw the tabs on the hanging

dividers. They all said something about retreats. I pushed through them until I came to one that said *Upcoming*. Inside there were several files all marked *Petit Retreat*. I opened the last one and there were several printed sheets with a bunch of questions.

"That's the information sheet I filled out when your aunt talked me into signing up." Lucinda leaned over my shoulder and looked at the page. "That's what she called it." Lucinda pointed to the heading that read *Petit Retreat*. "She said of all the retreats she put on, this was the most special. I told her I barely knew how to knit, but she said I would have a great time. Frankly, the idea of spending some time away from Tag and the restaurant sounded appealing. I love him, but our styles are just different. If he would just relax a little."

The more we looked through the papers, the more upset I felt. There were seven other people besides Lucinda who had sent in the money for the retreat. From the pile of receipts it was obvious my aunt had already paid all the expenses. "What am I going to do?"

"You can try to cancel the weekend, but you'll have to give everyone a refund. Not me, of course. I'll deal with Tag."

"With what money? Nothing personal, but I'm not exactly getting rich from baking. The house is paid off—maybe I could get a loan." I sagged. "But that would take a while." I looked at the date. "The retreat is in two weeks."

"You could go to Vista Del Mar," she said, referring to the hotel and conference center where the retreat was being held. "And Cadbury by the Sea Yarn and Supplies, and see if they would return the money."

"What am I going to say? 'Sorry, folks, for the last-minute notice but I didn't follow through with things, which my mother will be happy to tell you is my habit.'" I rocked my head with dismay. I barely knew Kevin St. John, who ran Vista Del Mar, or the mother and daughter who owned the yarn store. How could I ask them to refund the money? "There has to be another option."

"Well, you could go ahead with the retreat. Everything is paid for and arranged. All you would have to do is take your aunt's place."

"I have no idea what these retreats are. I know zero about yarn things except for what you've just told me. I don't think knowing that *skein* is really a meaningless term is enough. Joan was a master at arranging things, taking care of problems. I'm afraid my expertise is in making them—problems, that is."

Lucinda extracted one of the invoices from the file and waved the yellow sheet in front of me. "Joan hired a master teacher. Her name is Kris Garland, and your aunt raved about her. You don't have to know anything. You would just have to greet everybody and hang around for the weekend. I'd be there to help you. And Vista Del Mar is right across the street from here." She pointed to the wall of trees outside the window. When I still hesitated, Lucinda brought up the obvious. "You don't really have a choice, do you?"

I took the fabric box to the guesthouse, promising to think about putting on the retreat, before walking Lucinda back to her car. I held the flashlight as she pulled out her keys.

A red Ford 150 pickup truck slowed as it neared us and stopped next to Lucinda's white Lexus. I knew the color and make even in the dark because I knew who it belonged to. The driver's window opened and a man stuck his head out. I shined my flashlight in his face and he squinted in response.

"Hey, anything wrong?" he asked.

"No, everything is just fine," I said in a curt voice.

"Just being neighborly," he said with a smile. "I'm just down the street if you need a cup of sugar." Lucinda stared at him for a moment. I knew she was trying to process who he was. She was used to seeing him in uniform and driving a police car.

"The Cadbury police officer," she said with a friendly smile, and he nodded.

"Well, somebody's glad to see me. Night, ladies," he said and pulled his head back inside before driving off.

"I think he likes you," Lucinda said.

I threw my arms up in a hopeless manner. "I don't think he even knows my name. Not that I care anyway. Do you have any idea what goes on at his house?" Ahead we watched his taillights disappear as he pulled into a driveway. "It seems like every night there's a bunch of cars parked outside. There's loud music that seems to be coming from the garage. He never parks in it and I think it's some kind of party room. I know they say cops have to blow off steam, but he's ridiculous. Well, he can just party hardy without me."

I waited until Lucinda left, then I locked up and went back to the restaurant to finish my baking. By the time I took out the last batch of carrot muffins, I had made my decision. Lucinda was right. I had no choice but to go ahead with the retreat. She had promised to be my wingman. What could go wrong?

2

ALMOST EXACTLY TWO WEEKS LATER, I WALKED
down the driveway carrying a violet folder with the retreat
papers and a basket of muffins. I'd like to say that I was cool
and calm, ready to rise to the occasion, but my heart was
thudding so strongly against my chest I expected the red
flower on the lapel of my black Armani blazer to be bouncing up and down.

Lucinda had helped me with the clothing choice. It figured that she'd found the one thing with a fancy label in my
closet. I think everything she owned was designer. As I said,
I was a jeans and T-shirt person. What did it matter anyway?
My work time was spent alone in an empty restaurant during
the last hours of the day. Until now, that is. Now I was supposed to be in charge of an event and I was going to be
surrounded by people.

The black Armani blazer had been a gift from my mother.

It was one of those things that never went out of style and, depending on what I wore under it, could work for a variety of situations. Lucinda had found a pair of dark-washed jeans and a black turtleneck made of a mixture of silk and other fabrics. The red six-petaled flower was something we'd found in my aunt's box of completed items. Lucinda thought it was crocheted. However it was made, I thought it was lovely.

I usually wore my shoulder-length hair twisted up in a scrunchy. I don't know if there was an official name for the style, but I called it a squished-up ponytail. Nobody wants hair hanging around batter—it's too easy for some to fall in. Lucinda had talked me into getting it trimmed and wearing it pulled off my face with a headband. I wasn't so sure about the lipstick. The feel of it on my lips and the fragrance made it impossible to forget I was wearing it. At least I'd been able to talk Lucinda out of the bright red she'd picked out at Cadbury Drugs and Sundries. I thought the pinkish nude color was more me.

I could do this, I told myself. All I had to do was smile and be friendly and take care of any little problems that might crop up.

I was taking care of things, wasn't I? Hadn't I called everyone connected with the retreat? Well, almost everyone. It wasn't my fault that one of the retreat participants hadn't included a phone number or address. My first call had been to Kris Garland, the master teacher. It was hard to have to tell her about my aunt, but she thought it was a good idea I was going ahead with the retreat and assured me I had nothing to worry about—at least in the knitting department. She had it covered.

I'd gotten to the street, but my feet now seemed stuck. I

14

glanced up at the white sky. It was a Thursday afternoon in March, though you couldn't tell by the weather. Cadbury by the Sea had one climate year-round. It was cool and damp with a lot of fog. When the sun came out it was late in the day and ready to go down. What would you expect with a town on the very end of the Monterey Peninsula? Wherever you were in town, the sea wasn't far away. So much more poetic to call it the *sea* than the *ocean*. I thought the term went well with the moody feel of the weather.

Here on the edge of town, there was a certain wildness. Nobody had a lawn—just tall wild grass and lots of tall, slender Monterey pines and cypress trees whose foliage had a horizontal shape due to the constant breeze. To me those trees looked like someone running with their hair flowing behind them. Even my aunt's window boxes of petunias didn't need much attention. They got their water from the air.

Vista Del Mar was literally across the street, though from here I could barely see it through the filter of trees. The street I was standing on dead-ended at the lighthouse. It sent out its beam day and night, because once you got past the small, silky beach by Vista Del Mar, the coast became a rocky cliff with all kinds of warning signs. Danger, danger, danger— treacherous currents, killer waves and a bluff overlooking mounds of jagged rocks that jutted into the water. The Pacific Ocean wasn't very peaceful here.

Dangerous but beautiful. This area drew tourists from all over the world. The quaint charm of Cadbury by the Sea helped, too. Thanks to the town council there were no chain stores or restaurants, billboards were banned and streetlights were outlawed.

A voice in my head—maybe it was my mother's—said

something like grow up and get moving. Okay, maybe mulling over the wonders of the town was just me stalling.

I propelled myself across the narrow street and through the stone pillars that marked the driveway to Vista Del Mar. Entering the hotel and conference center grounds felt like stepping back in time. The trees were more plentiful here and the land more au naturel. I passed a Monterey pine that had fallen and been left to return to nature on its own. I followed the roadway to the main area of the hotel and conference center and a building called the Lodge. The rustic structure was built in the Arts and Crafts style. It had lots of windows looking out at the grounds in one direction and across a deck toward the boardwalk that led through the dunes to the beach on the other. All the buildings had names, and most had been built in the early 1900s. The dining hall was called Sea Foam and was just down the path. I'd never been inside, but from the outside, it appeared to be almost all windows. The Grace Chapel exterior was covered in local stones and tucked near the beginning of the dunes. The other buildings scattered around the 107 acres were covered with weathered wooden shingles and housed guest and meeting rooms.

Even though the water was obscured here by the sand dunes, I felt the ocean breeze as it sailed right through my jacket. The Armani might look nice, but my usual fleece zip up worked better with this weather.

The Lodge served as a social hall, registration and the business office of Vista Del Mar and was to be our meeting place. I was glad to go inside to the cheerful warmth of the large open room. A fire was going in the massive stone fireplace surrounded by comfortable sofas and chairs.

Kevin St. John looked up from the registration counter as

I walked in. "Don't you look nice, Casey," he said. "I hope it's okay that I call you Casey. I could call you Ms. Feldstein, if you prefer." He was the manager of Vista Del Mar, and up until the last week or so the only contact I'd had with him was when I passed through the Lodge to deliver muffins to the small gift shop that sold coffee drinks and snacks along with souvenirs. He'd always been wearing a neat dark suit and striped tie. I'd always been in jeans and a fleece.

Once I'd started baking for the Blue Door, Joan had talked me into taking samples of my muffins around to various places that sold coffee drinks, and I'd gotten standing orders from all of them. No matter how many muffins I brought in, they were gone before noon.

"Casey is fine, Kevin," I said. He flinched at the sound of his first name.

"Mr. St. John, if you don't mind. I like to set a tone," he said as I stepped up to the counter. He noticed the basket on my arm. "Ah, so you're planning to win them over with muffins." So he liked to set a tone, did he? I might have to call him Mr. St. John to his face, but in my head he would be Kevin; well, maybe Kevin St. John. He was impassive looking with a moon-shaped face and cleft in his chin. I couldn't gauge his age. The best I could come up with was that he was somewhere between my age of thirty-five and Lucinda's of fifty-four. He had seemed nice enough when I explained I was taking my aunt's place and going ahead with the retreat. "Well, just remember, I'm here to help," he said. He smiled and appeared cordial, but it felt a little forced.

I had tried to find out more about him, but Lucinda hadn't been much help. She'd lived in town longer than I had, but not long enough to know the real dope about everybody.

17

Kevin occasionally ate at her restaurant. Always alone. Her impression was that he considered himself the lord of Vista Del Mar rather than just the manager. She knew he lived in a cottage on the grounds.

"I never understood why your aunt bothered with these small retreats. For the time and energy she could have put on something larger." He examined my face for some kind of answer.

"I'm afraid I don't know much about her business. But I'm sure she had her reasons."

Kevin adjusted some brochures on the counter. "I know what these weekends meant to your aunt. I think it would be nice to honor her work and continue with the yarn events. If you would give me her mailing list, her vendors . . ." He shrugged casually. "Probably it would be best if you just gave me all of her paperwork connected with the retreats."

It took a moment to register what he was saying. "Oh, you mean *you* would put on the events."

His face broke into a broader smile. "I'm planning to do the same with the other retreats that book here. We have everything from bird watchers to quilters holding events." He gestured toward a row of photographs on the wall adjacent to us. I scanned the pictures and saw they were of various groups that had held meetings there. My eye stopped on one of my aunt with a group of women. "There will be so much more quality control when I'm handling all the arrangements instead of just renting out space."

"I suppose I could turn everything over to you. Maybe after this weekend. But right now I need to concentrate on this retreat." His expression darkened at my answer before he seemed to catch himself.

"Of course. You're right. You need to deal with what's in front of you." He started to turn away and then turned back. "One more thing. You might want to remind your charges that walking along the rocks is dangerous. You wouldn't want another incident."

"Incident?" I said, snapping to attention.

Kevin dropped his voice, and I had to practically lean over the counter to hear him. "It wasn't really connected to the last Petit Retreat. What I mean to say is that the retreat had ended with lunch and technically was over. Someone—" He stopped abruptly as a couple walked in and approached the counter, saying they had reservations.

Kevin was acting very much the host and turned his total attention to the couple. So much for the rest of the story.

"Casey, where do you want these?" I turned and saw that Gwen Selwyn, the owner of Cadbury's local yarn shop, had come in pulling a stack of plastic bins on wheels behind her. Through Joan, I'd met Gwen before. Another thing about Cadbury by the Sea—they had a rule against cute names. So instead of calling the place Darn It or Wild and Wooly, the store was simply called Cadbury by the Sea Yarn and Supplies. The reason I know is that when I first started baking muffins for the various outlets around town, I had given them names like Fourteen Carrot, A Raisin in the Sun, Plain Jane and Merry Berry. Would you believe I got a note from the town council to drop the cutesy names and just call them what they were? I thought the town took itself a little too seriously. I mean, they were just muffin names.

Gwen ran the yarn shop with her daughter, Crystal Smith. Again, Lucinda had come through with what information she knew. Gwen had lived in Cadbury all her life, but her daughter had recently moved back. Something about being abandoned by her husband who was a troubled musician. Was there any other kind? Lucinda didn't know if Gwen was a widow or divorced. Just that there was no current man in her life. She appeared very old school. Her brown hair was streaked with gray and cut short in the kind of style that needed just a little combing when you got out of the shower. I was willing to bet she'd made the long heathery gray sweater she wore. I loved the details of the etched silver buttons and generous-sized pockets. Underneath she had loose-fitting slacks and tie shoes with crepe soles. All that cool damp air had given her a ruddy complexion untouched by makeup. I had a pretty good feeling I wouldn't see her jogging in spandex or hanging out on singles' night at the Cadbury Wine Bar.

I lifted the lid on the top plastic container and looked inside. It was filled with red tote bags.

"These are for Kris Garland. I'll put the bin over here," Gwen said, gesturing toward a corner where it would be out of the way. "Just tell her where it is when she gets here." She slipped the top bin on the ground and I saw that it had a pull-out handle and wheels. When Gwen had positioned it, she came back to the other one and headed toward the gift shop.

"I'm putting some yarn and supplies in the gift shop. We always do that during the retreats. Not just for the retreaters, either. It seems like the other guests see people working with yarn and suddenly they want to make something, too. We sell a lot of yarn here."

I followed behind her, and when she got into the gift shop, a corner had already been cleared for her wares. She set out a pile of what I now knew were skeins of yarn. They were ordinary looking and basic colors. At the end, she took out a handful of royal blue yarn that had other colors mixed in. The texture seemed to change, and I couldn't help myself, I had to touch it. I was surprised at the softness and the name of the color. It was called Dr. Blue's Wild Ride. Luckily the town council wasn't into yarn or they'd have made her change the name to just "Blue."

"Crystal insisted I bring this yarn," Gwen said, referring to her daughter. "She says we've got to move with the times and stock all the new weird yarn they're coming out with. But give me a nice worsted-weight gray wool any day," she said as she finished putting the last skein of Dr. Blue's Wild Ride on the pile. Just before she left, she reminded me they'd be all ready for the yarn tasting.

"Yarn what?" I said.

"Don't worry about what it is, Casey. We'll handle everything. Just make sure you get all the retreaters to the store Saturday afternoon." She pulled her empty bin toward the door and disappeared.

"Are those muffins for us?" the young woman behind the gift shop counter asked, interrupting my thoughts.

"Sorry, Louise," I said, shaking my head. "They're for my group." I glanced at my watch nervously. I had come over early because I wasn't sure exactly when the retreaters would arrive. I barely knew Louise, but she listened patiently as I told her about the yarn retreat situation.

"I had to call them all and break the news about my aunt and then tell them I was taking her place. Well, that is all but the one who had no contact information." I didn't mention that I had secretly hoped they would all cancel when they heard. None of them had.

Louise motioned toward the window, and I saw the Vista Del Mar van turn in to the driveway next to the Lodge.

"That's probably your people coming from the airport," she said. I took a deep breath and headed into the great room.

Three women were just coming through the door. All had some kind of bag with yarn sticking out of it. They were definitely mine. But who was who? I had made up a file with the incomplete schedule I'd found and the information sheet each of them had filled out. Joan had scribbled in a note at the top of each sheet. I tried reading them over to see if I could match the names with the faces in front of me.

I guessed that the younger woman with the frizz of blond curls was Bree Meyers. The hint—she had on a gray hooded sweatshirt that said *Serrania Elementary Woodland Hills*. My aunt had written in "frazzled mom" on top of her sheet. Bree had her cell phone wedged between her ear and shoulder and seemed totally preoccupied with her conversation as she ran her suitcase over the foot of the older woman next to her without even looking up. She stopped when she got to me, and when I mouthed "Bree?" she smiled and nodded before continuing with her call.

The woman with the run-over foot barely seemed to have noticed the accident. She had a distracted, unhappy expression. On top of the page for Olivia Golden my aunt had written "needs care." The woman with the reddish hair framing an almond-shaped face seemed to fit that description. I smiled at her and held out my hand. "Olivia Golden?" It took a moment for her to come into focus. I expected her to smile and shake my hand, but she barely acknowledged me. The only positive was that I'd been correct again in determining who she was.

I didn't get a chance to try to figure out who the third woman was. I just caught a blur of her dark wavy hair and animated face as she rushed up to me and stuck out her hand. "Edie Spaghazzi. It's like Spaghetti, only different. We all flew up from Burbank on the same plane." She pulled back her offered hand and threw her arms around me. "What am I thinking, shaking hands? We yarn people are huggers. I'm so glad to be here. Thank you, thank you for not canceling the retreat. Your aunt would want you to go on." She stopped long enough to take a breath and lower her gaze in respect. "It was so terrible what happened to her. She can never be replaced. You have big shoes to fill." The moment for my aunt ended as Kevin St. John came out from behind the long dark wood registration counter.

He took a step back as she rushed toward him.

"It's so good to see you again. It's so wonderful to come back here. What a great place for a retreat. It's like taking a step back in time, Kevin." She waved her arm around the place before leaning in close to him and dropping her voice. "How's the social life? Dating anyone?" She actually stopped and waited for an answer.

He was obviously part of the old school where the customer was always right. Though I'm sure he didn't like being called Kevin or being asked personal questions, he simply put on a smile, maybe just a little forced looking, and said how nice it was to have her as a guest again.

Lucinda arrived as the hotel manager made his way back behind the massive counter that separated the business part of the room from the guest area. I think I heard something like a sigh of relief from him once he was back in his domain.

"I'm here and ready for a great weekend," my friend said as she stopped next to me. She made looking good seem so easy. The peg-legged black pants, pale coral scooped-neck top and black knit hoodie were perfect for the occasion. I was guessing it was all Eileen Fisher. Her tan leather suitcase had a Hartmann label. Even though her house was just a short drive away, she'd opted to stay on the premises. She knew if she stayed home, there would be one crisis after another with Tag or the restaurant and she wouldn't be able to enjoy the long weekend.

"Oh, I know who you are," Edie said, grabbing Lucinda's arm. "You own the restaurant, the one in the converted house. The Blue Door, right? Your food is so great. After the last retreat, we stopped at your place for dinner. Do you remember me?"

Lucinda chuckled and rolled her eyes. Before she could say something, Edie burst in, "If anyone asks, I was alone, okay?" Edie dropped Lucinda's arm like a brick when she looked through the window and saw a white SUV pulling into a parking slot. "It's Kris," she squealed. I wondered how she knew, but then I saw the decoration on the back window. The ball of yarn with the needles sticking out looked hand done. Underneath were the letters KWRBK. Before I could ask, Edie recited, "Kris Would Rather Be Knitting." And then to make herself seem even more in the know, she announced that Kris had driven there from Santa Cruz.

Edie was waiting by the door when the master teacher came in. "Kris, see, I came again. How could I miss one of your fabulous classes? I don't think the rest of them know what a treat they have in store." Edie waved her arm toward the rest of us but didn't take her gaze off the curvy woman with highlighted shoulder-length brown hair. Just as I was admiring the way Kris had draped the cream-colored shawl over the olive green linen pants and robin's egg blue long shirt, Edie hugged her and got her bracelet tangled in the shawl.

No matter how glad Edie was to see her, I was more glad. Now that she was here, I could just let the master teacher take over. It had been particularly hard telling her about my aunt. She was especially fond of Joan and kept saying she wished she'd known sooner and regretted that she hadn't realized something was wrong when Joan hadn't answered her emails.

"I'm sorry," Edie said, carefully trying to untangle herself. "I wouldn't want to ruin your trademark shawl."

Even though we'd met on the phone, I introduced myself to Kris. "We're just waiting for a few more," I said.

She nodded and said, "I know."

Bree had finally hung up her phone and joined the group. "If it's Emily Dotson, you can forget it. She backed out at the last minute," Bree said before introducing herself to everyone. "We signed up together. We belong to the same knitting group. It's called the Ewes." She spelled it out and then made sure we understood it was a play on words. Bree took a big sigh and glanced around the small group. "This is the first time I've ever gone anywhere without my kids. It's the first time I've gone anywhere alone." When she got to the word *alone*, her voice cracked. "Emily and I were going to share a room—"

"And you've never stayed by yourself in a hotel room," I said, completing her thought. Her blond curls bobbed as she nodded her head.

Edie threw Bree a dismissive glance. "Your kids will be fine and so will you. My kids are grown and on their own, but it was always nice to get away from them and my husband for a few days. Be glad for a room to yourself. The bathroom will be all yours." Edie spoke to all of us. "You have no idea what a great weekend you are in for. I've been to two other of these Petit Retreats and they are the best." She sucked her breath as if she'd just thought of something, and her eyebrows knit in concern. She grabbed my arm. "You ought to tell them not to go walking along the rocks by the water. It was too sad about Amanda."

"Who is Amanda?" I said, opening the folder. I could tell that Kevin St. John was listening from the other side of the counter. He seemed perturbed.

Edie pushed the violet folder shut in my hands. "You won't find anything about her in there. She didn't sign up for this retreat. She couldn't because she's dead."

A collective gasp went through the group, and Edie continued, saying she just thought we all should be aware of the danger.

"What exactly happened?" Olivia said.

"I don't know. I'd been home for almost a week after the last retreat when Joan called me and told me that Amanda had died, that she'd fallen off the cliff over by the lighthouse. Joan wanted me to talk to the cops." Edie's eyes grew sad as she said my aunt's name. "She thought I might be able to help."

Olivia seemed impatient. "Why would you be able to help the police if you didn't even know what happened?"

26

"I might have been the last person to see her alive, "Edie said. "I hung around after the last retreat was over. I was, uh, meeting someone." Edie stumbled over her words. "That doesn't matter. I saw Amanda late that afternoon. She said she'd been over at Joan's. I thought she was showing off that her relationship with Joan was more than just from the retreats." Edie stopped for a beat and then plowed ahead. "Amanda wasn't very friendly. She kind of blew me off when I tried to talk to her and said she was going to watch the sunset. The last time I saw her, she was heading for the beach," Edie said.

Kris seemed stunned. "I had no idea something happened to Amanda." She directed her comment at Edie. "I wish you had more details." Anxious to please Kris, Edie dredged up a tidbit about the dead woman and said she was found holding some yarn.

I heard Lucinda clear her throat, and when I turned, I saw that she appeared uneasy. "I wasn't going to bring it up," Lucinda began. "I didn't want the retreat to get off on the wrong foot, but since Edie brought it up—" She hesitated a moment, and I urged her to continue. Lucinda had gotten her information from the newspaper and also from the way information traveled around the small town: word of mouth. "Amanda Proctor was a computer programmer from Silicon Valley, and they thought she'd gone for a last chance to spend some time along the water before heading inland. It seems like she had walked down to a spot near the lighthouse to knit and watch the sunset. She must have gotten too close to the edge and slipped. There's quite a drop there and rocks below." Lucinda stopped talking and seemed to be measuring her words. "I think the lesson here is that you shouldn't go walking alone."

Kris tried to step in and change the subject, but no one listened. Bree's face had drained of color, and she said, "Oh my gosh, tell us the rest." Lucinda looked to me again for approval, and I told her not to hold back.

"If Amanda hadn't been alone, someone could have called for help when she fell and maybe saved her. The waves had slammed her body between the rocks, and they didn't find her for several days."

Kris stepped into the middle of the group this time and intervened. "It's was very sad what happened, but let's try to concentrate on something positive, like what a great weekend we're going to have."

Bree still looked stunned. Her mouth had fallen open and her eyes were wide. "I'm not going anywhere near the water."

3

THERE WAS STILL NO SIGN OF THE LAST THREE
retreaters. Bree had moved over to the sitting area in front
of the fireplace. She'd taken out her computer tablet and was
hovering over the screen, talking. Concerned, I stepped
behind her to see what was going on. These days you never
knew if someone was nuts and talking to themselves or if
they were talking on a cell phone. Okay, she wasn't nuts. A
little boy's face took up almost the whole screen, and it was
obvious she was video chatting. Bree appeared upset.

"Maybe I should come home now," she said. Now there
were two boys in the picture, jumping up and down, but the
video image was distorted and kept stopping the action,
making them look like they were momentarily floating in
the air.

"Yes, Mommy, come home," one little voice whined.

"Daddy gave us dog food sandwiches for lunch." The

other boy stuck his face close to the screen and made faces for the camera.

"Don't listen to them. It was a joke. Everything is fine." A nice-looking man with tousled dark hair had stepped into the picture and held the little boys off to the side.

"But, but this place is kind of creepy and somebody died here," Bree said, sounding strangely just like her own kids.

"It'll be fine, hon. Go on and have a good time," the man said in an encouraging voice. He signed off, and I stepped away quickly, not wanting to be caught eavesdropping.

"You might as well get Bree, Olivia and Edie registered," Kris said, snagging me.

"I'm first." Edie was in my face before Kris got the last word out. There was really nothing for me to do beyond escort her to the registration counter and move off to the side.

I had never paid much attention to the area behind the counter before. Now when I looked I was surprised to see a wall of dark wood pigeonholes with room numbers below each. It went along with the old-time atmosphere of the place, as did the actual keys that Kevin St. John was handing out. No plastic cards like most hotels used these days.

"Can I have two keys?" Edie said. Of course she didn't leave it at that but went on to explain how she always liked to keep one in her pocket, just in case.

The manager just nodded and turned back to take the second key off the hook below one of the pigeonholes. He offered her directions to the building that housed her room as he handed it to her.

"Don't be silly, Kevin," she said. "I know this place like the back of my hand." I expected him to dismiss her and go on to Olivia, who had followed us to the counter, but he continued to talk to Edie. I'm sure dropping his voice was deliberate, and I only heard bits and pieces, but he said something about wanting to talk to her over the weekend since she'd been a regular at the retreats. He wanted her input for something he had planned.

"I'd love to help," she said, breaking in before he finished. And she definitely didn't drop her voice. "It would be a shame for the retreats to end. You should take them over. I can give you a lot of information." She glanced over her shoulder in my direction. "I'm sure she means well, but she certainly isn't like Joan."

As if I didn't know that already.

But there was no time to feel bad, because there was a commotion at the door as a man came in. He was clutching a briefcase to his chest and trying to pull his suitcase through the door as it banged against it. Was he one of our retreaters? It didn't seem likely. He looked like the definition of Mr. Businessman with his neatly trimmed light brown hair and blazer over nice slacks along with slip-on shoes with tassels. The pale yellow dress shirt and striped tie finished the look.

Apparently Kris didn't agree with my assessment and went right up to him. "You must be Scott Lipton," she said in a friendly voice. When she held out her hand, he shrank back and then glanced around furtively. His cell phone began to ring. He dropped the briefcase and let go of the suitcase as he dove in his pocket for it. As he answered, he started to walk toward an empty corner of the large lobby-like room. I caught the beginning of his conversation as he passed.

"Yes, I landed. I know it's lousy that they're having the

sales meeting on the weekend. No, no, you shouldn't jump on a plane and come up here." There was more conversation, and he kept smoothing his hair with his hand with short, nervous strokes. Finally he hung up, and when he approached the registration desk, I introduced myself.

"I thought someone named Joan was in charge," he said, looking confused. Scott had been the one person I hadn't called because there was no contact information for him. I got ready to explain about Joan again.

Before I could start, Edie rushed toward him and threw her arms around him.

"Scott, you're here. Welcome." She turned to the rest of us. "I'm the one who got Scott to sign up for this. I found him in the yarn department at the Super Yarn Store in Chatsworth. He has a problem and I knew this retreat would be just perfect for him."

Was it my imagination or was Scott wincing more and more as she continued? "I'm afraid she was mistaken," Scott said. "I'm here, but I'm not really part of your group." Edie opened her mouth, but Kris stepped in and shushed her.

I heard a car door slam outside and a flurry of conversation. I couldn't hear any words, just the tone, and it sounded like squabbling. The door opened and two women walked in, continuing to fuss. My immediate reaction was that they were related. They both had the same cascade of brown hair, had a similar lean body shape and gestured with their hands in the same manner.

I looked at the sheets and found the one that had two names—Melissa and Sissy Patterson. I remembered that they were coming from Fresno, and I had just notified one of them about the change in the retreat. My aunt had written in "mother and daughter weekend, need some space" on the top of their information page. Kevin St. John seemed to be handling registration of the other retreaters without my help, so I went over to greet the new arrivals. I hoped Kris would join me, but she had gone off to the side and was on her cell phone.

Squaring my shoulders, I introduced myself, and fortunately Melissa and Sissy stopped mid-squabble. Although I knew it sounded corny, I told them they looked like sisters instead of mother and daughter. Melissa, the mother, loved it, but her twentysomething daughter seemed horrified.

"This weekend was her idea," Sissy said, jabbing her finger in her mother's direction. "I'm just letting you know I'm here under duress."

Olivia overheard and nodded in agreement. "I second that emotion." She held up her key. "I'm going to my room," she said. "Don't expect me at any of the sessions. This trip was a gift." Everyone started saying something about it being nice, but Olivia shook her head. "It was to get me out of town."

I traded looks with Lucinda. This was not what I'd expected at all. I thought the group was going to be much happier to be here. So far only Edie seemed enthusiastic about the weekend.

I was glad when Kris rejoined us. She seemed undisturbed by all the problems. "It's always hard at the beginning. We all need to let go of the outside world and give ourselves over to the retreat. Me included." She caught Olivia before she left and pressed a workshop schedule on her. "Please, at least come to the first session. Then if you don't want to continue, no problem."

I couldn't tell from Olivia's expression if she'd agreed or

not. I handed her one of the individually wrapped muffins from my basket before she headed for her room. I was going to say something to Lucinda, but now she was on her cell phone. She was shaking her head and waving her hands around as she spoke. When she hung up, she shook her head with dismay a few more times. "It was one of the waitresses, telling me that Tag had just instructed everyone on the correct way to place a coffee cup on the table. He's tried that before, but I was always there to stop him. She said he was following them around and adjusting the cups so the handles pointed to the right." She sighed and looked toward the door. "Maybe I should go back there. Just to check on things," she said. But her voice sounded halfhearted and it wasn't hard to convince her to stay.

"If you go back once, you'll be doing it all weekend, and what kind of retreat will that turn out to be?"

Lucinda straightened. "You're right. Besides, I really need the time away from Tag or I might kill him." She looked around furtively. "Oops, I hope no one heard me. It would sure blow the fairy-tale image." She was referring to the story printed on the Blue Door menu that told how the couple had met up again after so many years and moved to Cadbury by the Sea to follow their dream of owning a restaurant.

Kris handed out schedules to the rest of the group and suggested everyone take their things to their rooms and get situated before the first session. Everyone but Scott took a muffin. He had registered on his own and was out of the building before I could offer it.

Once they had all left, I went back across the street to my place. My plan was to come back for the first session and make sure everything was going smoothly. Then I figured Kris would take over for sure. I'd only need to be there for meals and to take everybody to the yarn tasting. Kris would probably handle the evening events, because they were yarn related. And then the weekend would be over and I'd shut the door on my aunt's business.

As soon as I got back to the guesthouse, I pulled out my laptop and fired it up. After hearing the story about Amanda and how she slipped off the rocks, I was curious to see what I could find out. It only took a few clicks to locate the story in the *Cadbury by the Sea Herald* archives. It mostly repeated what Lucinda had said, although there were a few more details. Kevin St. John was quoted as saying he noticed a Prius parked on the Vista Del Mar grounds for three days and none of the guests had claimed it. Cadbury PD had run the plates and found it belonged to Amanda Proctor of Sunnyvale who, according to the manager, had checked out on Sunday.

There was even a mention of my aunt. She was the one who suggested that Amanda might have gone for a walk. Apparently Amanda did some kind of technical work and liked the release she got from working with yarn and spending time in nature. Joan knew because Amanda had come to every retreat my aunt had put on.

I sat back from the screen, thinking that two people connected to the retreats had died. Was that a coincidence or something more?

I looked at my watch and calculated the time difference in Chicago. Frank would be in the office. Since he was a private investigator, I was curious to see what he thought.

And with that I punched into my phone the number of

the detective agency where I'd temped. "Feldstein!" Frank said when he heard it was me. "Where are you?" He didn't wait for an answer. "I had more temp work for you, but when I called I got a disconnect notice."

I gave him the short version of where I was and what I was doing, and as I spoke I heard a protesting squeak from his chair. Frank resembled the Pillsbury Doughboy more than James Bond. His office chair reclined, and he always seemed to be pushing its limits.

"Baking desserts and muffins and a yarn retreat? What's a yarn retreat?"

"Knitting," I said, trying to make the answer as basic as possible. "That's kind of why I called. I need some advice."

Frank chortled. "Feldstein, you want knitting advice from me? I'm not Miss Marple."

I read him the article about Amanda's death and then told him about my aunt Joan's hit-and-run accident. "So, what do you think?"

"About what? Are you asking if I think they're connected? In a word, no. Sorry about your aunt and that woman, but sounds like it was just bad luck for both of them. Don't get your underwear in a knot over it. Let it go." I heard him chuckling. "Feldstein, I just can't see you with a bunch of knitters." Then he hung up.

"You and me both," I said to myself.

4

BARELY AN HOUR LATER, I WAS BACK AT VISTA DEL Mar waiting in a small building called Cypress. It consisted of a big room that could be divided, but we had the whole thing and it was to be our meeting room for the weekend. I was early and gazed out the windows toward the dunes that ran along the edge of the Vista Del Mar grounds. The area was in the process of being reclaimed, and the sandy area was off-limits to people. But it was okay for the two deer I saw wandering among the Menzies' Wallflowers with their bright yellow petals, the Beach Sagewort and the Mock Heather before disappearing in a stand of tall bushes.

You couldn't tell that it was afternoon by the color of the sky. It had been white since dawn. It was hard to tell it was spring, too. Year-round it was always like this, chilly and damp. I was grateful for the inviting fire crackling in the comfortable room's fireplace. A long table was set up with chairs around it. In the corner there was a sink and a counter. A coffee and tea service had been brought in. I added a plate of fresh butter cookies I'd baked while I stopped home.

Kris and Edie arrived together. Kris did a little shiver as she walked in and pulled the cream-colored shawl around her more closely. Edie trailed her talking a mile a minute. I envied Edie's cappuccino-colored sweater. It looked cuddly and warm.

"At least you two showed up," I said. "I'm not so sure about the others."

Kris nodded with a knowing smile. "This group seems a little more difficult than the ones we've had in the past," Kris said. Something in her manner made me feel that even though this group was a problem, she'd be able to handle it. I supposed it came from being a teacher and getting used to being in charge. I had never gotten the hang of that position when I was a substitute teacher, which was probably why I left that job.

"Yes, but Joan would have known what to do with them," Edie added.

"I'm sorry," I said. "I'm doing the best I can." I didn't want it to happen, but my voice sounded a little warbly and I had the desire to leave—well, run away. It had only been a few hours and it was clear I was already a flop. I literally had to hold on to the seat of the chair to keep from bolting.

Kris threw Edie a dirty look and turned to me. "I'm sure Edie didn't mean that the way it sounded. You're doing great. Giving out the muffins was a wonderful idea." She glanced toward the counter and saw the plate of cookies. "And you brought more sweets. It's a nice touch."

"Thanks for the pep talk. But Edie's right. My aunt would

have handled things better," I said. My comment caused Edie to gush about how sorry she was and how thoughtless her comment was as she rushed over and hugged me.

"Don't worry about this group," Kris said. "I've worked a lot of retreats both big and small and everyone comes around. Besides, I have something up my sleeve."

I felt relieved at Kris's confidence and wished I had even half of it. But then she was an expert at knitting. Realizing she was only a few years older than me, I asked her how she'd earned the title of master teacher. She seemed flattered at my interest, and while we waited for the others to show up, she told me her background. She practically had to put her hand over Edie's mouth to keep her from chiming in.

"I learned to knit when I was in high school," Kris began. "Then I needed a job with flexible hours when my kids were small, so I got a job in the local yarn store. I seemed to have a knack for helping the customers with their projects. By chance I heard the instructor had bowed out of teaching an advanced knitting class in the extension program of the local community college. Sometimes you just have to seize the moment," Kris said, explaining that even though she wasn't exactly a master teacher then, she talked her way into getting the class. "I kept learning more, and pretty soon I was teaching classes around the Monterey Bay area. I began to sell some patterns to yarn companies, and suddenly I had a career. I'm afraid master teacher sounds better than it pays, though. Doing the retreats really helps out. When I met your aunt, she had been using Gwen Selwyn from Cadbury Yarn to do knitting classes for her retreats." It seemed like she was going to end there, but then she continued. "Let's just say I made the classes more contemporary. Joan particularly liked putting on these Petit Retreats because she got to be one of the participants."

So, now I had the answer to Kevin St. John's earlier question about why my aunt had opted for these less-profitable events. I didn't want to say anything, but if he took over, it was very likely that this was the last of the small gatherings.

"She's just being modest," Edie said. "She's also won all kinds of awards and ribbons. She's like a superstar of knitters." Kris flushed at the description but seemed to like it.

Lucinda came in and looked at the empty room.

"I was beginning to wonder if you'd given in and gone back to the restaurant," I said to my friend as she pulled up a chair.

"No way." She glanced at the other two and cringed. "I didn't mean that the way it sounded. I love Tag and the restaurant, but even fairy-tale couples need some time apart." She looked at the empty table. "Where is everybody else?"

"The others didn't exactly seem happy to be here," I said. "What am I going to do if they all suddenly want a refund because Joan isn't here?"

"Don't worry, they'll come," Kris said in her perky cheerleader voice. "And if the past is any example, you'll see—I'll win them over."

Bree arrived next. She sat down and laid her cell phone on the table. She took off the hooded gray sweatshirt with the school name on it. Underneath she had a navy blue long-sleeved T-shirt, a hot pink shirt that peeked below the hem and jeans. Olivia marched in and sat down with a thud. It was as if she wanted everyone to know she was there under protest. Melissa and Sissy were fussing as they arrived. Melissa was concerned that her daughter wasn't warm enough in her rolled-up jeans and short-sleeved T-shirt. Sissy kept insisting she was fine even though I caught her shivering.

Scott came in last, hung by the door and kept his eye on the window. What was he so afraid of? Or maybe the question was who?

Kris welcomed the group again. Scott finally sat down, but at the far end away from all of us. Bree's cell phone began to beep loudly, and she held her hand up apologetically.

"My boys got some app on their game gadgets that turns them into walkie-talkies. I have to take this. It'll just be a moment." She headed outside and started pacing up and down in front of the window while she talked. Judging from her body language there was trouble at home. Maybe now the kids were claiming their father wanted to feed them kibble for dinner?

Edie got up and went to stand at the head of the table with Kris. "You guys are going to be so happy with this workshop." The repeat retreater pulled out her smartphone and flipped through a bunch of photos and then held it up. "This was the last retreat." She walked around the room and showed each of us a number of photos. "Don't they look like they're having a good time?" she said, flipping through them again herself. "Oops, I didn't mean to show these," she said, gazing down. I strained to see what she was looking at. Even though it was an odd angle, the first photo was of a man in a baseball cap with the sunset behind him, and the next one was of Kevin St. John talking to Gwen Selwyn, the yarn store owner. Edie moved to the head of the table. "I've got to get some shots of this group." She got us all to gather around the retreat leader and snapped several pictures.

When Edie sat back down, she flipped through the photos

on her phone again. She seemed to stop on one and stared at it for a long time. She looked up at Kris and started to say something but stopped herself, which I found amazing after her verbal Olympics.

"Thanks for sharing the pictures," Kris said, and Edie almost bowed. "I know if Joan were here, she'd tell us to get started."

Scott stood up. "Is anybody going to tell me what happened to Joan Stone? She's the reason I'm here." He pointed at Edie. "You sold me on this retreat. You said that Joan put on these amazing weekends."

Kris's expression became somber. "I'm sorry. I thought Casey had told everyone. Joan was killed in a hit-and-run accident a few months ago."

My automatic response was to say that I didn't buy that it was an accident and give the reasons. But I kept it to myself this time. It wasn't their problem; it was mine.

Bree returned appearing drained, her blond hair even frizzier from the dampness in the air. "You don't really think my husband gave them beer and said they could stay up until midnight, do you? How am I going to get through this weekend?" she said, slumping into one of the chairs.

"You could start by turning off your cell phone—and your mommy brain," Edie said.

Olivia seemed oblivious to all the fussing and was staring off in space.

"One of the great things about a retreat is leaving everything behind," Kris said in a pointed manner. "Let's all put away our cell phones." She demonstrated by picking up Edie's and making the screen go dark. "I want you all to just focus on being here and immerse yourself in the wonderful weekend we have planned." She nodded toward me to indicate I was part of the *we*.

"Let's get started," she said.

"But we don't have anything to work with," Lucinda said. "The instructions said we didn't need to bring anything."

"Well, I have something," Bree said, dropping a blue tote bag that said *Serrania Elementary School* on the table. She began to pull out some yellow yarn and a couple of needles so long they looked like fencing foils.

Olivia began to fumble through her purse. "I have something, too. I always carry a little project just in case." As she pulled out a plastic bag with multicolored yarn and the same kind of silvery double-ended needles I'd seen at my aunt's, a pill bottle came with it and rolled across the table. The ever-eager Edie grabbed it before it went off the table. She read the label.

"Sleeping pills? You won't need those here. The sound of the waves will lull you to sleep. Just open your window and—"

"My sleeping issues are none of your business," Olivia said, snatching the bottle back and putting it in her bag.

I watched all this thinking I should do something. Joan would have stepped in and said something funny to break the tension. All I could do was glance at the door and think about making a hasty exit. But Kris had made me promise to stay through this first session.

"I said not to bring anything, because I have everything you need," Kris said, opening the plastic bin Gwen Selwyn had dropped off. She took out a tomato red tote with *Petit Retreat Three* on it in yellow letters. I was relieved that she'd found them. In all the fussing, I'd forgotten to point them out.

43

Edie's eyes lit up. "This is it, you guys. Wait until you see what Kris has for you. She's a genius at this." Edie started to ramble on about some kind of special yarn and circular needles, whatever they were, and the first Petit Retreat. Kris put her fingers to her lips in the universal shush gesture.

"Edie, you're absolutely my best cheerleader, but you're going to ruin the surprise," Kris said in a friendly voice. "First, let me explain my philosophy of a retreat. I believe it's the time to push the envelope, broaden your horizons and overcome obstacles." She picked up a tote bag and handed it to Bree. "You all filled out questionnaires when you signed up for the weekend. They were passed on to me. That's how I know that Bree is most comfortable being part of a group." Kris urged her to look inside her tote bag.

Bree began to unload the contents onto the table. She stopped when she got to two balls of yarn. I had never seen anything like them. Each was multicolored and not the usual fuzzy texture that I thought of as yarn.

"They're made from recycled saris," Kris said. "No two skeins are the same. The scarf you make is going to be unique. No one in the world will have another exactly like it."

Bree didn't seem pleased with the prospect. "Then we're all going to be making scarves out of this, this sari stuff?"

"No," Kris said. "Only you."

"But the Ewes always make the same project together. How will I know if I'm doing it the right way?" Bree sounded a little frantic.

"Don't you see that's exactly why Kris gave you the yarn she did?" Edie said. "You need to break out of the conformist box you're in."

Kris threw Edie a pointed look. "I wouldn't have said it

quite that way. Bree needs to experience her individuality." She picked up another of the tote bags and handed it to Olivia.

"I didn't fill out any questionnaire," Olivia said, checking the contents. She extracted an orb of fuzzy purple yarn with bits of jewel-toned metallic highlights that blended nicely with her pink velour pants and matching zippered jacket. When she looked at the label, her face clouded. "Cashmere?"

"You might not have filled out a questionnaire, but somebody did for you. It was clear from it that you'd always only used inexpensive yarn and right now you needed something luxurious and special."

Olivia felt around the bag. "There are so many skeins."

"You're going to be making a shawl. And when you finish it, every time you wrap it around yourself, it'll remind you that you're special."

Olivia seemed unimpressed. "Save the heartwarming stuff for the others. It'll take more than some fancy yarn to get me past this weekend."

"Let me be next," Edie said. She turned to the group. "I've been on two of these special retreats before, and Kris is like a mind reader. You should have seen the things she came up with for the others."

Kris gave Edie a broad smile. For all of her chatter, I was glad that at least one person was enthusiastic about the retreat.

"Oh my. Just what I wanted!" she exclaimed, taking some wiggly things out of her bag. "Turbo circs," Edie said, as she put the metal needles with cables between them on the table. She looked at the instruction sheet. "Fabulous. I'm making two socks at the same time using both of the circs."

Betty Hechtman

Was she speaking a foreign language? What were *circs*?

"I'm not much of a knitter," Lucinda said, taking her bag. Instead of inspecting the contents, my friend let Kris tell her what was in it.

"Yes, I understand that you are just a fledgling knitter and that you only know how to knit," Kris said, and then I stopped her.

"Excuse me, but what you just said doesn't make sense," I said. Coming to my friend's aid made me feel useful. For a moment, anyway. Why were they all laughing at me? Edie rolled her eyes so many times she must have made herself dizzy.

"Kris, do you want to explain or should I?" Edie said, smiling.

I was glad when Kris took over. She explained it in a way that made me feel less stupid. How was I supposed to know that while it was called knitting, there were actually two different kinds of stitches? It got even more confusing. If you only did the knit stitch, it was called the garter stitch, and if you knitted one row and purled the other, it was called the stockinette stitch. Yikes.

Lucinda knew how to do the garter stitch, which actually meant she knew the knit stitch. The scarf she was going to make required her to learn how to purl. Kris lost me when she said Lucinda would actually be doing the seed stitch, which was to alternate between knitting and purling in the same row. It made me dizzy, but the main thing was Lucinda seemed happy with it.

Kris went back to the bin and extracted two bags, announcing the mother-daughter team was next. Besides their constant fussing, the most notable thing about them was

46

their hair. Both women had the kind of hair I would have loved. The long, wiry curls had so much volume, they almost stuck out sideways. I guessed the color would be called something like chestnut. Only Melissa's had a few silver hairs mixed in. Kris approached the pair, and Melissa reached out for both bags. Kris dodged her reach and made a determined effort to hand each woman her bag.

Melissa watched as her daughter began to search through her bag, setting out the contents on the table. Sissy took out several skeins of light blue wool, a pair of needles and an odd-looking hook. "Cables!" the young woman exclaimed after reading over the pattern she'd taken out. "I've always wanted to make something with cables, but I was afraid to try."

"You never told me," her mother said. "Well, we can work on them together this weekend." Melissa began emptying her bag, but her expression sagged as she took out needles and two peanut-shaped skeins of yarn, one black and one white. She glanced over the paper pattern. "Oh," Melissa said in disappointed tone. "A houndstooth-patterned scarf." She turned to Kris. "Don't you think it would be more efficient if Sissy and I worked on the same pattern?"

"No," Kris said with a smile. I think everyone got it but Melissa. Giving them different projects was the plan.

Scott kept scooting his chair closer and closer to the exit with each tote bag Kris handed out.

"I think I've changed my mind," Scott said, getting up. He was still dressed like he was going to a business meeting and seemed very tense.

"Scott is a closet knitter," Kris announced. "Even his wife doesn't know." She stepped next to him. "There's

47

nothing to be embarrassed about. Knitting for men is hot now. That woman who wrote the *Stitch and Kvetch* book wrote one just for men. It's called *Knitting for Man Hands*. You know, some people believe that sailors created knitting."

She pushed the tote bag into Scott's hand. He ran his free hand over his neatly trimmed hair in an upset gesture. I could identify with his longing glances out the window. I knew he wanted to run. He set the bag on the table and looked inside. I heard him gasp and understood why when he took out two bloodred knitting needles. They were as thick as broom handles. The yarn was also thick and red. But as he handled the needles, a dreamy look came over his face.

"You've never made anything big, have you?" she said, and he shook his head.

"I only made things that would fit in the briefcase."

"Not anymore," she said, pointing out the sheet with a pattern in his bag. "You're making a lap blanket." She ran her hands through the supply of yarn, which clearly was too much to fit into his briefcase. "Why don't you just cast on the stitches. Give the needles a trial run."

He glanced back at the rest of us. "You all think I'm weird, don't you? If my wife knew, or my boss—that would really be bad. I don't want regional manager of the Sandwich King franchises to be my last stop on the ladder. If my boss saw me knitting . . ." The dreamy look had vanished and was replaced with one of anguish as he held his forehead and stood up.

Everyone at the table forgot about their own issues and was supportive, saying they thought it was great that he knitted. He didn't seem convinced, and I wasn't sure what he was going to do. His head kept swiveling back and forth between the door and the tote bag. I surprised myself by stepping in. Me, the person who could most understand his desire to take off, suggested he stay.

"I personally don't get the pull of knitting, but it certainly means something to you." I gestured toward the chair, and to my amazement, he listened and sat down. With a sigh, he began happily working with the yarn.

My job here was done. I pushed back my chair and prepared to get up. They were all starting on their projects and certainly didn't need me around.

"I'll be going, then. Don't forget there is coffee, tea and fresh cookies on the counter," I said. "I'll rejoin you for dinner."

Kris touched my arm to stop me. I was surprised to see that she had another of the tote bags in her hand. "Your aunt told me that she really hoped you would take up knitting. I know you have difficulty sticking with things and that you're totally green in the knitting department, but I think if you try it, you may find out it helps with all the aspects of your life."

Yeah, right, I thought, *it would really help fix my life.* If only it were that easy. But I had to admit I was curious to see what could be so fabulous about fiddling around with needles and yarn. I found myself reliving Scott's moment of looking back and forth between the door and table.

"Don't worry, we'll all help you," Lucinda said. "The nice thing about being in a group like this is we all support each other."

"And don't forget me," Kris said. "I'll be here all weekend to help all of you."

I ventured a look inside my bag. There were a bunch of small balls of yarn in different colors. There were also several pairs of needles and then two packages of the most beautiful yarn that changed colors from rust to muted shades of beige and brown.

Along with the yarn, there was a clear plastic pouch. There were a bunch of things that looked odd to me, though I figured the rest of the room knew what they were.

Finally I found a little burgundy ruler type thing with a slot in it and a bunch of holes. I noticed something written in gold along the top. *Compliments of Kris Garland's Retreat in a Box.* "What's this?" I said, holding it up.

Edie started to explain that it was to measure gauge, whatever that was, but then noticed the writing on it. She had a similar bag of tools in her tote. She pulled out the ruler, read it over and started to wave it around. "Wow, you actually did it," she said to Kris. She turned to the rest of us. "You have no idea how exciting this is."

Kris beamed with pride. "Edie's right, it is very exciting and an absolute savior. I don't know what I would have done if this hadn't come through." Her expression had become serious as she said the last part, but she gave her head a little shake as if to get rid of a bad thought and her round face brightened. "Starting in a month or so, kiosks will be in yarn stores offering the same thing you've all just gotten. A custom-designed project that broadens the customer's horizons, pushes the envelope or shows them how to make something they've always wanted to accomplish." She explained that a customer would use a touch screen to answer a questionnaire that gave the key to their skill and their desire. The perfect project would then be chosen for them.

A supply list would be generated, including yarn, instructional DVDs made by Kris, written instructions for the project and all the necessary tools. "And then the store clerk would put everything together in a tote bag similar to what you got and present it to them," Kris said. Her whole face grew more animated as she talked about the project. Enthusiasm danced in her blue eyes. "This is my chance to take a step up and join the movers and shakers in the yarn world. And have some breathing space. Being a single parent with two teenagers gets expensive." Then she caught herself and apologized, saying the weekend was supposed to be about the group, not her.

"And to think it all started here," Edie said. "It was the last night of the first Petit Retreat. At dinner, I think. Who was it who brought up the Retreat in a Box idea? What a fabulous meal. Chicken Piccata made with local lemons, and salad with those baby greens. I think there were scalloped potatoes, too."

I think we were all grateful when Kris stepped in and stopped Edie from going on with her rambling monologue before she got into the details of the dessert they'd had. Kris suggested we all get started on our projects.

I needed the most help. I was absolutely starting from scratch. My kit included a whole stack of printed instructions, but I was glad when Kris personally helped me. She decided it was best to cast on the stitches for me and then showed me how to do the knit stitch. In no time, I had the hang of it.

"Don't worry about a thing," Kris said. "You're just going to be making practice swatches at first."

The time flew, and before I knew it, Kris was telling us

to pack up. I had managed to complete a number of rows on my first swatch and found out that *circs* was short for circular needles. Not that it seemed likely I'd have anything to do with them. But I thought my stitches in the golden yellow yarn looked particularly nice. I got a lot of congrats from the rest of the group as we stopped working. Kris told us just to leave our tote bags in the room and only work on them during our workshop time when she was there to help. "I'm sure you all brought some of your own projects to work on." Everyone nodded but me.

Lucinda and I walked back to the dormitory-style building she was staying in. I had to admit, I was stoked. I was enthralled with that little piece of yarn material I'd made. I couldn't wait to go check out the yarn and needles at my aunt's house. Lucinda laughed. "Joan would be so happy to see you've caught the bug."

"Bug?"

"The yarn bug. Once you try it, there's no going back," my friend said.

5

WHILE MY GROUP WAS GETTING READY FOR THE evening meal, I went across the street and checked out my aunt's stash with new eyes, though in my head, my mother's voice was groaning that I'd just picked up another diversion. But now the dinner bell was ringing and I left my house and headed toward the dining hall.

I'd never been inside the Sea Foam dining hall before. It was built in the Arts and Crafts style, similar to the Lodge, and had the same old-fashioned feeling.

A hostess greeted me as I came in and punched my meal ticket. I was happy to see Lucinda waiting for me. The huge room was filled with round wood tables, and I suggested we snag one in a corner.

"The food is cafeteria style," Lucinda said, gesturing toward the back. I noticed she had freshened up her appearance with new makeup and a patterned silk scarf that blended with her apricot-colored top. There was just the slightest wrinkle of distaste to her nose as she looked over the menu of meatloaf and mashed potatoes. Not exactly the gourmet fare they served at the Blue Door.

Edie was the first to come in and, no surprise, she was talking to someone. She and the tall man in a baseball cap stopped for a moment before separating. Her troubled expression quickly brightened into an upbeat smile as she saw me. The temperature was dropping, and she'd replaced the sweater I'd admired with a blue fleece jacket.

She stood with me and helped wave our people over as they came in. Only Scott declined the invitation and chose to sit at a table nearby instead. I bet his tablemates had no idea the conservatively dressed man had a knitting project hidden in the briefcase at his feet.

"Let him be for now," Kris said as she pulled out a chair. She had cute features and the kind of round face that would probably never look old. Whatever lift Olivia had gotten during the workshop session had evaporated, and she was back to looking sour as she snagged the seat next to the knitting teacher. Lucinda and I sat together.

"Baby steps," Kris said. "At least he stayed and knitted in front of us. And it's just the beginning of the retreat."

Lucinda took the basket of bread off the lazy Susan in the middle of the table and went around using the tongs to put a piece on each of the bread plates. "I can't help it. I'm used to being in a restaurant," she said with a shrug.

Bree arrived with a sagging canvas bag and deposited it on a chair. She sat next to Olivia, pulled the bag on her lap and started going through it. I saw her computer tablet sticking out of the top. "I promised I'd read the kids a story later," she said, showing the book behind it. "Thank heavens they have Wi-Fi in that Lodge building. I can't believe this place has no phones or TVs in the rooms. What is it, from the Dark Ages or something?"

"Vista Del Mar was built before phones were common and TV even invented. I think it adds to the romance of the place. It's like stepping away from everything," Edie said. She was a little too perky, too enthused about everything, and was beginning to get on my nerves. She glanced across the large room, and I saw that her gaze stopped on the man in the baseball cap, but only for a second. Then she put all her attention on our table. She rolled her eyes as she stared at Bree. After setting the canvas bag out of the way, Bree had absently taken Olivia's slice of bread and was in the process of cutting off the crusts. She buttered it and cut it into triangles.

"Thanks, I guess," Olivia said, picking up one of the pieces.

"Oh my gosh. I'm sorry." The young mother blushed with embarrassment. "I see bread and go on automatic pilot. My kids hate crust and I make what I call a puzzle." She demonstrated by moving around the triangles. "They love to put the pieces back together before they eat them."

"You need this weekend," our leader said with a smile, and I suggested everyone get their food. It might have been a little heartier fare than the Blue Door served, but it smelled delicious.

I was glad for the dinner. When it came to muffins or cookies or pie, I was your girl. But regular food? I was embarrassed to admit that I lived on frozen entrées.

Dinner was a success. The only problem wasn't even really a problem. Olivia thought someone had taken her purse, but it was located under the table. She seemed to be looking for things to be upset about. As we got up to go, Kris made an announcement.

"I thought it would be nice if we all met at the fire circle and had a toast to Joan's memory. I've ordered some wine." Edie offered to tell Scott, and we agreed to meet in half an our.

"Do you think I should have done the wine thing?" I said to Lucinda when we got outside. "Maybe I should offer to pay for half of it." Lucinda suggested I let it be.

It was inky dark outside, with only low-watt lights dotting the road that wound through the grounds. The waves sounded loud now that the tide had come in, and the air smelled of wood smoke. I followed Lucinda to her room so she could pick up a jacket.

"Wow," I said when she'd opened the door. I hadn't seen the accommodations before. Her room was on the first floor of a building called Sand and Sea. I understood Bree's comment now. The room had none of the usual amenities of a hotel. There were two narrow single beds, a dresser and a radio. The bathroom was the size of a closet, with only a stall shower.

"The point is the rooms are really just for sleeping," Lucinda said. We'd passed a living room area as we came in. A cozy fire was going in the fireplace, and there was plenty of comfortable seating.

When I'd come back for dinner, I'd left the Armani jacket and gone with my usual green fleece zip up. As Lucinda and I found our way through the grounds, I was glad I'd made the change.

The fire circle was located just before the dirt morphed

into sand. A glass barrier stopped the wind, and a number of benches were arranged around a crackling fire going in a pit in the center. The only other light came from a lone floodlight.

"This is just like camp," Lucinda said as we joined the group. Her comment seemed rather funny, considering her designer outfit. As if anyone would wear that Eileen Fisher outfit to camp. Lucinda and I were trying to decide whether to sit or stand when Kevin St. John stepped out of the darkness. It must have been the firelight making weird shadows on the manager's face, but he looked kind of sinister. He was carrying a tray of glasses. I guessed it was red wine, but in this light it looked almost black.

He set it down, and everyone went to help themselves. Lucinda and I got glasses and found seats close to the fire. I was surprised to see that Kevin St. John had stayed and was joining the toast. The breeze made the flames dance as Kris held up her wine.

"Thank you, Joan, for starting this great tradition of yarn get-togethers in this beautiful place. You will be missed." Kris nodded, and everyone began clinking glasses before taking the first sip.

"Don't you think you should mention Amanda?" Edie said as she glanced in the direction of the water. The small woman shuddered, and I didn't think it was from the chill air.

Kris seemed at a loss, but Kevin didn't. "That's not the same. Joan put on the retreats. Amanda What's-her-name was just a participant," Kevin said.

Edie didn't give up and mentioned that Amanda had been to every retreat Joan had put on. Kris agreed that Edie had a point and raised her glass again. "Also, a toast to our fallen retreat member, Amanda Proctor."

With the toasts done, the group spread out and someone knocked over their glass. Kevin appeared with another bottle of wine and began refilling glasses. When he got to me, he stopped.

"I saw that you went home for a while. Did you have a chance to look for your aunt's papers?" His voice was friendly but persistent. I had no doubt that he remembered that I had said I didn't want to deal with it now. I just said no.

"Oh no, the boys' story," Bree said, holding her refilled glass. With her sweatshirt and frizzle of blond hair arranged by the ever-present breeze, she looked like she could be at camp. "I can't read it after a glass of wine. If I slur a word, they'll think their mother is a lush."

Olivia set down her untouched glass and put her hand on Bree's arm. "Will you stop, already? They'll live without the story. Or your husband can read to them."

Even in the dim light I could see that the young mother's face was still tense. "But I have to tell Daniel," she said, pulling out her cell phone. After the call, she let out a big sigh and picked up her refilled wineglass.

Scott moved in from the edge of the group, and Bree made room for him. "It's so dark, no one can see you're with us," she said. It was true; just a row back from the fire everyone was shrouded in shadow. Lucinda and I moved closer to the warmth and light. Just when I was enjoying the moment, Kevin St. John stopped next to me. "One of your charges is drunk. You better handle it."

When I turned, I saw that Edie was almost next to us, struggling to stay standing. "This wine really got to me," she said, falling against Lucinda. "I think I'll go to my room," she slurred. There was some discussion about letting her go on her own. Olivia had gathered her things and was starting to leave when Edie fell against her. I started to ask Olivia for her help, but she took Edie's arm on her own.

"I'll take her," Olivia said. "I'm ready to call it a night anyway."

The rest of the group hung around and finished their wine and then scattered, leaving Lucinda and me alone by the fire.

"Well," she said, setting down her empty glass. "You made it through the first day."

"Something has been bothering me since the toasts," I said. "Somehow it didn't register until then." I mentioned how two people connected to the retreats had died. "Isn't there something about things coming in threes?" I said to Lucinda with an uneasy smile.

6

MY ALARM WENT OFF EARLY FRIDAY MORNING. I started to shut it off and go back to sleep, thinking it was a regular day and I didn't have to be anywhere until my night baking time. Then I remembered the retreat and threw back the covers.

I dressed quickly and went across the street. The clouds were particularly heavy, and the grounds seemed even more untamed than usual. The damp, chilly air made me want to curl up in front of a fireplace and drink hot chocolate.

I heard the clang of dishes and a low hum of conversation as I approached the dining hall. When I opened the door, I was greeted by the comforting scent of breakfast food— something cooked in butter, a touch of a maple syrup, a hint of the sage in sausage links, along with an overtone of freshly brewed coffee.

My stomach gurgled in response. How nice to have another hot meal.

Lucinda waved me over to the same table from the night before. Most of the group had beaten me there.

How did my friend always manage to look so put together? I'd hastily pulled on a pair of my better jeans and a turtleneck, and topped it with a black fleece jacket. My hair had gotten smushed overnight, so there'd been no choice but to neatly twist it up with a scrunchy.

We all exchanged greetings as I sat down. Lucinda pointed to the lidded cup at my place. "It's a cappuccino. I can't seem to stop with the restaurant stuff," she said with a smile. "I figured you'd need a little jolt to start the day." Bree had a plate of untouched food. She looked drawn and tired as she clutched her cell phone to her ear. Not that it made any difference in their ability to fuss, but Melissa and Sissy were on either side of her. Sissy seemed unhappy with her mother's food choices. Lucinda explained that Kris was off getting her food.

Scott was sitting at another table talking to the person next to him. At least he was dressed more casually than the business wear he'd had on the day before. Lucinda leaned in close to me. "I think Kris has her work cut out for her. It's pretty obvious those projects she handed out are supposed to evoke a change in the person who works on them." Lucinda chuckled. "Except for me. I've just avoided purling because it feels awkward."

"Good luck with me, then," I said, rolling my eyes. I'd be the first to admit that I had a problem sticking with things. My job history was proof of that. Did she really think that doing a little work with a pair of needles and some yarn was going to change that?

Kris set her plate down across the table. "Where are the others?" she said, noting the empty seats.

"Here's Olivia," Lucinda said, pulling out the chair on the other side of her for the new arrival.

Olivia still had the distracted stare. The soft gray warm-up suit went better with her mood than the happy shade of pink had. She did give Lucinda a small forced smile as she accepted the seat. "I need coffee," she said, reaching for the carafe on the lazy Susan in the middle of the table and pouring herself a cup.

I asked how she'd slept and Olivia shook her head. "The good thing about sleeping pills is that they knock you out. The bad thing is you feel out of it in the morning." She picked up the coffee and began to drink it as her eyes half closed.

"Everyone is here but Edie," I said. "Well, Scott's here, but not exactly here," I said, giving him a wave when he looked up.

"Maybe she decided to sleep in," Bree said. She'd finally gotten off the phone and had begun to eat her breakfast. At first it was stop and start while she kept asking if anybody needed anything, then finally she settled in to eating. "This feels strange," she said. "At home, it seems like I'm always jumping up to get something or wipe up something that got spilled."

Kris smiled. "Enjoy, Bree. No guilt, either. I'm sure your boys are fine." Kris turned to me. "We didn't get a chance to talk yesterday. What do you think of knitting now that you've had a little time for it to sink in? When I handed you the bag you had that deer in the headlights look."

"I wasn't expecting to be a participant," I said. Kris's smile broadened.

"That was obvious."

"It would be great if I could make something like that," I said, touching the kimono-style knitted sweater she was wearing. It was a tweedy-looking brown and flattered the blond highlights in her wavy hair.

Kris laughed. "Don't defeat yourself by taking on more than you can handle. For now just stick to practicing knitting and then work on the scarf. There's nothing like finishing your first project to give you confidence." She turned her attention to the rest of the table. "Joan always said these small retreats were life changing because you were pushed out of your comfort zone." Kris glanced toward Scott at the next table. "With some people it's harder than with others."

I finally went to get my food, but the entire time I ate my pancakes, I kept looking toward the door expecting Edie to come in and make a stir.

"I'll just call her and ask if she wants me to make up a plate for her," I said, taking out my cell phone and the list of numbers. There might not be phones in the rooms, but these days, you could reach people anyway. I was disappointed when her phone went right to voice mail.

"I wonder what's up with Edie," I said.

"That wine really went to her head," Melissa said, sounding judgmental. "She's probably hungover and shut off her phone."

"I hope she gets up in time for our morning session," Kris said, setting down her coffee cup.

"Is there a problem?" Kevin St. John seemed to have appeared out of nowhere. As usual, the manager of Vista

De Mar was dressed in a dark suit, crisp white shirt and conservative tie. His short dark hair didn't have a single strand out of place. His formal dress clearly set him apart from the guests and the rest of the staff. I thought that was his plan.

Kris twisted in her seat and acted as spokesperson. "One of our retreaters is a sleepyhead," she said with a smile. "No problem."

Kevin eyed me. "I was thinking, if you'd rather turn things over to me now, I could step in and handle the rest of the weekend," he said in a tone that was supposed to sound helpful, like he was throwing me a life preserver, but to me felt like it was just one more nudge from him to get hold of my aunt's business. I smiled, thanked him and declined, all the while acting as if I thought he was doing a kindness. Not a surprise, he wasn't happy with my answer.

He addressed the group. "I want you all to feel welcome and cared for here. We want repeat guests," he said, taking out a handful of papers. "If you wouldn't mind filling out some questionnaires about what you'd like to see in future retreats?"

His smarmy smile was annoying and, I knew, fake, because it didn't show in his eyes. He was going ahead as if I'd already turned over my aunt's files. I didn't like his manner, and maybe there was something else. When somebody else wants something you have, you tend to hold on tighter. I surprised myself by putting up my hand to stop him from handing out the papers.

"Why don't you wait until the end of the weekend," I said. "I want my people to focus on the here and now."

Kevin's face clouded. "Well, of course, you're right," he

said. He slipped the papers out of sight and with a nod wished us a good morning and moved toward the exit.

Had I really stepped up to the plate and said *my people*? I watched Kevin go. I was sure he'd only appeared to give up.

"THE FIRE FEELS GOOD," KRIS SAID AS THE GROUP reconvened in the Cypress meeting room. It was just as we'd left it the previous day. Someone had gotten a cheery fire going in the fireplace and brought in a fresh coffee and tea setup. I was surprised to see a black cat looking in the window. It was uncanny how its yellow eyes seemed to lock onto my gaze. A moment later it was gone. Scott came in last, looking around as he did. His eyes darted over the group as he edged toward his seat. Something like a sigh came out of his mouth as he picked up the huge red knitting needles and began to work them. Then he looked up to see if we were watching him. His eyes narrowed when he saw Kris approaching.

She gave him a supportive pat on the shoulder, and he let out his breath. "Sorry. I'm just so nervous about doing this in front of anyone," he said, continuing his knitting frenzy as he talked. "If Edie hadn't found me hiding out in the yarn department of the craft store . . ." He lowered his head, seeming to feel guilty. "I told my wife I was buying some art supplies for my daughter. Do you have any idea what it's like to keep your yarn stash in your car?" He began to unload and explained that he only knitted in his car or when he was on the road. It was difficult when he flew because he was always afraid the security people would take his needles out of his carry-on and make a spectacle. "It really helped when

Edie let me come over to her place and knit. I told my wife I was taking a class to relieve my stress, which was sort of true. It only lasted for a few afternoons. Something about her husband not being happy with her having a man over."

Olivia stared at her knitting as if she was seeing something else. The conversation was flying past her unnoticed. Lucinda had picked up the work she'd started. She seemed nervous as she began to move her needles slowly and deliberately.

Melissa's eyes flew skyward as her daughter began to work on her scarf. She seemed about to grab it out of her hand, but Kris stepped in and stopped her. Bree had her phone on the table. I could see a picture of her children, and every time the screen went dark, she did something to make the picture return. I supposed I should be glad she'd settled for just looking at a photo instead of talking to them. Her eyes widened as she looked at the balls of sari yarn. She picked up the little work she'd done. She looked at the work of the people on either side of her and seemed dismayed, remembering their knitting project was nothing like hers.

"How am I supposed to know if it looks right? I have nothing to compare it with," she said.

While Kris reassured her, I kept looking toward the door, expecting Edie to come rushing in, talking a mile a minute about why she was delayed. I had to admit I missed her exuberance. Scott glanced toward her tote bag and the pair of circular needles. "Where's Edie?"

I tried to call her again and got her voice mail. "Maybe I should go to her room," Kris said, getting up.

"No, it's my job," I said. It was an automatic response, and once again I surprised myself.

Lucinda set down her work and pulled her Burberry jacket on. "I'll come. I need to get something from my room anyway."

Kris, Lucinda and I headed up the path to the weathered-looking building called Sand and Sea. A fire glowed in the fireplace of the living room area, but the overstuffed chairs were all empty. We went down the hallway to where all the rooms but Kris's were located. A housekeeper's cart was in the middle of the dark wood hall, and the door to one of the rooms was open. Lucinda directed us to Edie's room at the end of the hall.

I walked ahead and knocked loudly on her door, but there was no response. I tried again with the same result. Lucinda caught my hand before I went to knock again. "Maybe they can help," she said, gesturing toward the two women in gray uniforms pushing the cart in our direction.

I explained the situation, and one of them walked up to the door and rapped loudly. "Housekeeping," she said. When there was no answer, she pulled out a key and stuck it in the lock. When the door swung open we all looked in. What we saw made us gasp.

7

THE CLUSTER OF COP CARS AND AN AMBULANCE seemed out of place in the rustic setting of the conference center when I went outside. My legs still felt rubbery as I went down the few steps of the stoop at Sand and Sea's back entrance. The gloominess of the day seemed the perfect backdrop for the gloominess I felt. What was I supposed to do now? I know what I wanted to do. I wanted to go up to Kevin St. John and hand over my aunt's retreat file and say, "It's all yours." Then I could flee across the street to the guesthouse and pretend none of this happened.

But a voice in my head, probably my aunt Joan, told me to pull myself together and deal with the situation. I just couldn't get the picture of Edie out of my mind. I'd been the first one to go into the room, while Kris and Lucinda hung behind me and the housekeeper took off.

Edie was lying in her bed on her back. Her eyes were closed

and she almost looked like she was sleeping, but for the red ooze on her face, and on the bed. It barely registered that she was still in the print top and pants from the night before, because my eyes went right to the light glinting off the double-pointed steel knitting needles sticking in her chest. I heard someone letting out a shriek and then realized it was me.

Kris already had her cell phone out and was calling 911. Lucinda stepped forward, saying she knew CPR, but then winced at the idea of doing it under the circumstances. Despite having two doctors as parents, the limit of my abilities was to check Edie for a pulse, but her neck felt cold and still.

The cops and paramedics had arrived almost simultaneously. It was all a fog to me now, and I just recalled that Kevin St. John had led them down the hall toward us and then hustled the three of us back while the paramedics went ahead, carrying in some kind of rescue equipment.

"Good luck on that one," I said under my breath, hoping I was somehow wrong. I felt a strong arm take mine and steer me down the hall. It didn't register who'd grabbed me until I heard the voice. It was the same one I heard whenever the red truck drove by my house and the guy who lived down the street called something out the window. It was my neighbor, Mr. Party Guy Police Officer.

He didn't let go or stop until we reached the living room area. "You'd better sit down," he said, pointing me toward one of the overstuffed chairs. I started to object but realized he was right. I ought to sit down, before I fell down. I felt like my bones had dissolved and there was nothing holding me up. "Take a deep breath," he ordered.

I had never thought about it before, but part of a cop's job was dealing with people in my position. He seemed very good at it, but then I suppose all those parties he gave sharpened his people skills. I followed his command and felt some of my strength return.

"Thank you—" I peered up at his badge, trying to make out his name. My aunt had probably told me what it was, but I didn't remember. "Officer Mangano," I said, reading the blue letters.

"You can call me Dane," he said. He was still standing and was holding a clipboard with some papers on it.

"Dane?" I said. "Like in Great Dane?"

His serious face cracked a smile and he nodded. "I've gotten that one more than a few times. What can I say? It's obviously appropriate."

"I'm glad to see you're modest," I said. Was I really thinking about his name and his cocky attitude just after encountering the body of someone in my group? Maybe it was an effort to distract myself from the situation.

"So, it's Casey Feldstein," he said, taking out a pen and beginning to write.

"You know my name?" I said, surprised.

"And a whole lot more," he said, making eye contact. "This is a small town, and I'm a cop. Besides, I like to know who lives around me. I know you bake the desserts for the Blue Door and supply muffins for a number of coffee spots." When I seemed surprised, he chuckled.

"It was kind of an accident how I found out. I had the late shift one night last fall and noticed lights on and someone moving around in the Blue Door long after closing. It looked pretty suspicious." He cocked his eyebrow. "Luckily I checked with Tag Thornkill before I called out the SWAT team." He glanced down at the clipboard. "Everybody thinks cops like donuts. Me, I'll take a good muffin anytime, and yours are outstanding."

I had a feeling that this little interlude was just an effort to make things seem more friendly before he got down to business.

"Do you want to tell me what happened?" he said.

"I don't know what happened." I explained that when Edie hadn't shown up, the three of us had gone to see what was wrong. "Where are they, anyway?" I said, looking around the empty room for Kris and Lucinda.

"We like to get the facts from people individually. They're being questioned by some of my associates in other locations." He was acting all official now and encouraged me to go on about Edie.

"What do you think happened to her? She couldn't have gotten that way on her own," I said. Dane didn't seem that happy with my answer.

"That's not for me to say. Lieutenant Borgnine does the investigating, and the medical examiner will determine how she died."

"But you must have some kind of gut feeling," I said. "From your experience."

"Actually, we don't get many suspicious deaths in Cadbury," he said.

"Aha, so you think it's suspicious." I waited while he blew out his breath and shook his head at my persistence.

"I'm supposed to be getting information from you," he began. "But it's pretty hard not to think it's suspicious with those rods sticking out of her chest," he said. "How about we get back to you talking. Could you give me the basics? The victim's name. Your connection. I'm just after the facts.

Lieutenant Borgnine will want to talk to you later." He tapped the pen on the clipboard. "One thing, though. Lieutenant Borgnine won't be happy with your answering a question by asking one."

I shrugged off his comment. "They're not rods," I said. "The things sticking out of Edie are knitting needles."

"At last, you gave me something I can write down," he said with mock annoyance. "So now that you've started . . ." He waved his fingers for me to keep rolling.

I think he got more than he bargained for. Once I'd answered his questions about Edie, I kind of babbled on. I told him about the weekend and my aunt's business and how I'd just wanted to get through the weekend and shut it down forever. He nodded a lot, but after the information about Edie, he didn't write anything down or maybe even listen.

I know it was the chicken's way out, but I was relieved when he said Lieutenant Borgnine would notify Edie's husband. Dane examined my face. "Good, your color is coming back." He gestured that he was done and held out his arm to steady me as I stood up.

"Remember, my door is always open if you need a cup of sugar or want to join the party," he said with a wink.

I just bet it was.

I'd lost track of time and was surprised to hear the bell clang announcing lunch. I didn't know what had happened to Lucinda and Kris, and I thought about the rest of the group we'd left in our meeting room. I hoped they'd had the sense to go to the dining hall.

I walked around to the front of the building and started down the slope. Ahead I saw Kevin St. John standing next to his golf cart. He didn't look happy.

He waited until I was next to him to speak. "The whole Sand and Sea building has been put off-limits for the present. Your people won't be allowed back in their rooms until—" He faltered. "Until they finish investigating and remove the body."

I looked behind me and saw that yellow tape was being wound around the perimeter of the building in a discreet manner. "It shouldn't matter to our many guests who are staying in the other residential building. I'm just telling anyone who asks that the yellow tape is caution tape closing off the area while we take care of some broken steps." He mentioned that the cruisers and the ambulance had all entered the grounds with no lights or sirens and had parked out of sight around the back of the building.

His mouth twisted in distaste. "In all the years I've worked here, we've never had a suspicious death on the grounds. I've alerted the Delacorte sisters and they are very disturbed. We all agree there needs to be someone with a steady manner and experience handling your group." He didn't say it, but it was obvious he thought I lacked both qualities. "The sisters suggested that I step in and take over your duties."

The Delacorte sisters were the owners of Vista Del Mar. They were the last surviving members of the family who'd owned just about everything in Cadbury by the Sea. There had been a fleet of fishing boats, a cannery to handle their catch and lots of land. They'd sold off the fishing boats, and the cannery had long since closed and been turned into a shopping mall. The land had been subdivided and turned into plots of houses. Neither woman had married or had any children. Unless something happened to change things, all their holdings would be left to a charity in town.

My aunt Joan had gotten to know them. Apparently, they'd been impressed to meet the former Tidy Soft toilet paper lady; they had sparked on her idea to put on yarn craft retreats, encouraged her to use their conference center and offered her a very reduced rate. I'd met Madeleine and Cora Delacorte only in passing and then again at my aunt's funeral.

He was offering me an out, and I should have jumped at the chance, but instead I said, "No," and folded my arms. "If the Delacorte sisters are so set on me giving up, let them call and tell me themselves."

Kevin made a tsk-tsk sound. "Do you even realize what you have to do now? You have to save the weekend for your retreaters. Manage to make it a success when one of their own died on the first night. I thought you'd be relieved to be able to walk away." The manager looked down and shook his head as he tried to shoo something away. The black cat I'd seen before sauntered across the path.

"Well, I'm not relieved by your offer nor do I want to walk away. Now, if you'll excuse me, I have to find my people." I walked away in a huff, as if his suggestion was totally ridiculous. Thank heavens he wasn't a mind reader or he would have known how uncertain I was.

When I got to the dining hall, I found Bree, Olivia, Melissa and Sissy huddled around one side of a round table. None of them had their food, and they were staring at me as I approached the table.

I felt a pang of guilt that I had even considered abandoning them.

"What's going on?" Olivia said, for once seeming to be in focus. "Mr. St. John came to our meeting room and told us we couldn't go back to our rooms before lunch."

"And I thought I saw a police car," Bree said with a worried look. "Where are Kris and Lucinda?"

I stepped close to them and took a deep breath. "I'm very sorry to announce that Edie has died."

"How?" Melissa asked with a gasp.

"I'm not sure, but the cops are calling it suspicious." I tried to sound reassuring, but it didn't work.

"You mean, she was murdered?" Melissa said with another gasp.

Kris and Lucinda came across the large room slightly apart but caught up to each other before they got to the table. Kris sank into a chair with a heavy sigh, and Lucinda grabbed the seat next to Bree.

"I told them about Edie," I said. "Or at least the basics." I shared what I knew, which it turned out was more than either of them.

Kris appeared all in. "The last thing I expected this weekend was to get questioned by the police."

Lucinda had managed to freshen her lipstick and comb her hair and seemed the least discombobulated of the three of us. "Poor Edie." She shook her head sadly. "She was so excited about being here." She pulled out her cell phone. "I better call Tag and tell him I'm okay."

Bree shrieked and then took out her phone, saying she ought to do the same. "It'll probably be all over the news and my family will be worried."

"Are you going to give us any details?" Melissa said, sounding upset and worried. She'd pulled her abundance of curly hair into a ponytail to get it off her face.

"Mother, can't you see they've all had a shock," Sissy said, her voice full of reproach.

"Melissa is right; we need to tell you what happened," I said. I waited until Bree finished her call and then explained how we'd found Edie. They all cringed when I mentioned the double-point knitting needles.

"Who would want to kill Edie?" Bree said.

"Let's see," Lucinda said, "by my account, though I don't think she realized it, she managed to insult just about everybody."

"I think she meant well, but she did have a way of sticking her foot in her mouth. She even upset the manager of Vista Del Mar," I said before explaining how uncomfortable he'd looked when she brought up his social life.

Bree started to push her chair back. "Well, I suppose that's the end of the retreat." She sounded relieved. "It's fine by me. I didn't sleep a wink last night. There were all these creaks and groans in the building all night long and the bed was lumpy. Did I mention that I've never stayed in a hotel room by myself before? Frankly, I don't think I've missed much. My boys will be glad to see me coming home. I can just imagine what I'll be coming home to."

Kris put out her arm to stop her. "No plans have been changed yet."

Olivia shrugged. "Even if the retreat ends, I'm staying. There would be nothing but trouble if I came back early." I waited for her to add to her statement with some kind of explanation, but Olivia just stopped talking. I wondered if we'd ever know what was bothering her so. She was pleasant looking when she let go of the upset expression, and gave off a vibe of someone solid and dependable.

"I suppose Sissy and I could move into one of those cute bed-and-breakfasts in Carmel and finish our mother-daughter weekend there." Melissa had taken a cup of coffee and started to push it away as if she was getting ready to depart.

"Thanks for consulting me," Sissy said in an annoyed tone. "Didn't you hear what Kris said? There aren't any plans to end the retreat yet." The mother-daughter argument was all too familiar. Is that what my mother and I sounded like? I vowed right then never to argue with her again, at least not in public.

"I was just trying to handle the situation," Sissy's mother said before pulling the cup back in front of her and refilling it. "What about Scott?" We all checked the room and Sissy pointed to a faraway table.

I went over to tell him the news. He saw me coming, and as soon as I got close to the table, he jumped up from his seat and drew me by a tall window. His brow immediately went into furrow mode as soon as he heard, and for a few moments he didn't speak. Then he said, "I suppose the media will be here. These days everything goes national. You have to keep me out of sight." He slumped in distress. "My wife thinks I'm in San Francisco. And my boss can't hear me being listed as part of a knitting retreat." He went outside, shaking his head. Did he even care about Edie?

When I got back to the table, Tag Thornkill had just arrived. He must have jumped in his car as soon as Lucinda called. As always, he was dressed in neat perfection. But then everything about him was neat perfection. Lucinda looked upset, and Tag stood in front of me.

"Lucinda really needs to come home. Everything is off at the restaurant without her there." He looked down in a dejected manner. "The staff just won't listen to me." A moment later, he'd raised his head and leaned toward the table to straighten the place setting next to me before rearranging the salt and pepper on the lazy Susan in the middle of the round table. "And now with this terrible incident . . ."

"Do you want to leave?" I said to Lucinda.

"No," Lucinda said a little forcefully, then it seemed to register that she was in public. She turned toward Tag. "Honey, you go on back to the restaurant. I'm sure everything will be fine without me. Besides, Casey needs me right now, don't you?" she said, turning toward me with pleading eyes.

"Yes, of course. I need Lucinda here now more than ever," I said. Tag appeared disgruntled but finally left. As soon as he neared the door, Lucinda undid the place setting he straightened and took the salt and pepper shaker off the lazy Susan, and when the saltshaker spilled some of its contents, she left it there.

I felt like rolling my eyes. Poor Edie was dead in her bed and all anyone could think about was their own personal troubles. Well, maybe I was guilty of that, too.

I thought of what Scott had said about the media. Would the story make its way all the way to Chicago and my parents? I had considered not mentioning the retreat when they'd done their weekly call to try to convince me to move back to Chicago and the sort of life they thought I should be leading. But I'd caved and told them about it.

"I don't know why you have to tie up the loose ends of her business," my mother had said before going into her usual reminder that when she was my age, she had a profession and a family and, oh, I had neither. And now there'd been a murder in the middle of the weekend. I pictured her seeing the story online. What would the headline be? *Knitter Needled to Death.*

78

8

LUNCH ENDED AND NO ONE HAD EVEN GOTTEN their food. I managed to get everyone to go directly to our meeting room without passing the Sand and Sea building. I didn't want them to see the yellow tape around it or realize they couldn't go to their rooms.

"C'mon everyone," Kris said, standing at the end of the long table. "Pick up those needles and focus on your work." She was trying to sound cheery, but I could hear the effort in her voice. Kris and I had agreed that the best thing to do was to keep things going according to schedule. The problem was everyone was staring at Edie's spot and her tote bag.

"Edie was so excited about working with two circular needles," Bree said. "And now she'll never get to make two socks at the same time."

"Among other things," Olivia said under her breath. She picked up the needle holding the rows of lacy purple stitches and checked them over before taking the other needle and beginning on the next row. I was amazed at how effortless she made it seem.

When Bree saw that Olivia had started to knit, she picked up her work, but her manner was totally different. She fretted about the yarn, grumbling that it seemed to keep changing colors and textures, and held up the portion she'd already done in front of Kris. "Is this the way it's supposed to look?" Poor Bree wasn't doing well at all at making something one of a kind.

The large red plastic needles slipped out of Scott's hand and hit the table with a loud noise, making the whole group jump. "Sorry," he muttered, retrieving them and beginning to knit. As soon as he did the tension around his eyes began to soften. I know it was a sexist thought, but it still seemed strange to see this conservative business-type man with his close-cropped hair, pressed khakis and oxford cloth shirt knitting with those huge needles. For a moment he seemed peaceful, then he set down his work and looked around the group. "Have any of you seen any news media around here?" He didn't wait for them to answer. "If you do and they ask you any questions about who is here, don't mention me. Don't even mention there is a man in your group."

"Scott, your secret is safe with us," Lucinda said. She picked up her knitting with gusto. Her individual plan called for her to make a swatch with alternating stitches of knits and purls before she started her actual project. She showed off what she'd already done. The first thing I noticed was that both sides of her work looked the same.

Sissy seemed to have completely lost herself in her kit. She'd done several rows in the golden yellow yarn and was poring over the directions as she picked up the metal hook with a rather sharp point.

"What's that?" I said. Sissy looked up, but before she could answer her mother had stepped in.

"It's a cable hook," Melissa said to me before turning toward Kris. "I'm sure your intentions were good, but my daughter and I really should have had the same project. Neither of us have done cables, but if we were working together, I could help her."

"Mother," Sissy said in a tired tone. "I can figure this out myself. And when I do, I'll show you how to make cables." Sissy had a triumphant little smile.

"I can learn to make cables on my own. I was knitting when you couldn't even hold a spoon," Melissa said, her eyes flaring. Kris got Melissa to pick up her two colors of yarn and go back to working on her houndstooth scarf.

"I'm glad to see some things are going along as usual," I said to Kris as we both watched the mother and daughter try to tend to their own knitting.

"Casey, do you need any help?" Kris asked. Oops, I'd been caught. I'd been preoccupied with watching the others and hadn't even taken the pair of bamboo needles out of the bag. Now on the spot, I took out the needles and started to work on my swatch. The others might be able to knit and do something else, like talk, but for me it was a totally engrossing activity. And hardly relaxing. As I began to poke the right needle through the loop on the other needle, my shoulders immediately tensed. Or maybe they were tense to begin with after what had happened with Edie.

Just as I got halfway through the row, the door to the room opened and Kevin St. John walked in accompanied by another man. They stepped to the head of the table and stopped next to Kris as she moved aside.

"I'm sorry to interrupt your session," the manager said to the group. The expression on his round face was at odds with his words. I don't think he was sorry at all. It was just another example of Kevin St. John displaying his authority. "This is Lieutenant Theodore Borgnine of the Cadbury by the Sea PD. He'd like to talk to you."

Lieutenant Borgnine reminded me of a bulldog. He had almost no neck on a fireplug-shaped body. His short, stubby graying fringe hinted at the full head of hair he must have had once. In place of a uniform, he wore a pair of gray slacks and a herringbone sports jacket that seemed a little mis-shapen. It was pretty clear he wasn't interested in being a fashion plate.

"I want you to know that we have the situation under control. Sorry, but we've had to close off the whole Sand and Sea building." I cringed as he said it. So far I'd managed to keep that information from my group. He seemed immune to their looks of discomfort as he continued. "As soon as we're finished with our investigation, we'll be opening it up so you can access your rooms." He surveyed the faces around the table. "I will be wanting to talk to each of you separately. And I have to ask something else of all of you. I see a number of you are from out of town, and I'm sure the shock of what's happened to one of your group has made some of you want to change your plans and return home immediately. But I'm requesting you all stay put for the entire weekend."

It wasn't so much what he said but how he said it. The emphasis on certain words made it clear that while he said he was making a request, he was really ordering everyone not to leave. It was probably something they taught at police school. "Ms. Feldstein, we'll start with you."

This wasn't our first meeting. He'd been the one to investigate my aunt's accident. As I followed them to the door, I looked back at Kris and she gave me a reassuring nod that all would be well in my absence.

Kevin walked out with us but left us at the fork in the road and went back to the Lodge building. Surprisingly, it seemed like business as usual on the grounds. A group of birders were heading toward the walkway through the dunes. A family hiked up the hill toward one of the residence buildings that wasn't blocked off. The black cat was walking behind them.

"Is he yours?" I asked. They didn't seem aware of who I was referring to at first. Then the woman saw the cat.

She shook her head and said that he looked like a stray. As they walked on, the cat wandered off into the brush. I'd never had a pet. My parents blamed it on the fact we lived in the Hancock building and had no yard. The downtown Chicago high rise probably wasn't the best place for a pet, but I still had always wanted one. I wondered if the cat was hungry.

Lieutenant Borgnine seemed impatient with my concern about the cat and urged me on to a meeting room near the entrance to Vista Del Mar. There were a bunch of chairs with desks on the arms and a table in the front. No fireplace or anything to make it cozy. I shivered partly from the chilly air inside and partly from the thought of being questioned.

He gestured for me to take a seat as he leaned against the front table, holding on to his position of authority. He took out a pad and paper and asked for my name and address more as a formality.

"So, Ms. Feldstein," he said as he scribbled it down, "still baking for the Blue Door? The wife thinks your apple pie is the best. And still doing the muffins?" It was more of a statement than a question. Here I was all tensed up to be grilled about Edie and he was discussing my baking. What was that about?

"Those muffins with the berries are the best."

"Oh, you mean the Merry Berries," I said, and his expression darkened.

"No, I mean the ones with the berries in them. No cutesy names in Cadbury. We call things what they are." Lieutenant Borgnine held his pen poised to write. "So, you've taken over your aunt's retreat business?"

"Have you gotten any leads on her accident?" I said. He seemed surprised by the question and not happy with it.

"It's an open case. We're still looking for the driver," he said curtly.

"But what if it wasn't an accident?" I said. I was about to bring up my evidence, but he cut me off.

"I understand you're still upset about your aunt. But you have to leave it to the professionals. Now let's get down to Edie Spaghazzi." He wanted to know everything I knew about Edie, but mostly who might want to kill her.

I mentioned she was a no-show at breakfast and that I'd tried to call her but had gotten her voice mail. "Did you find her cell phone?" I asked.

Lieutenant Borgnine did a double take. "I'm the one asking the questions. How about you just tell me about Mrs. Spaghazzi," he said.

"Okay," I said, sort of giving up. He started writing as I explained I'd really just met Edie. He pushed me to tell him more about her personality and if I thought she had any enemies. I started to shrug off the question about enemies, but I hesitated for a split second. Lieutenant Eagle Eyes picked up on the change in my expression and pressed me until I explained. "Like I said, I didn't know her very well, but she seemed to stick her foot in her mouth a lot. I don't think she meant any harm."

"But what you're not saying is even if she didn't mean any harm, she stepped on a few toes."

I nodded in agreement with his statement. He asked for specifics, but offhand I couldn't remember any. "Sorry, but everything is a bit of a jumble in my mind right now." He didn't seem happy with my vague answer and started to ask about my dealings with her.

"Like I said, I barely knew her," I said. I explained I was simply tying up the loose ends of my aunt's business with this retreat, which I suspected he already knew courtesy of Kevin St. John.

Then his questions began to make me uneasy. "This retreat you're running has to do with knitting, right?" I nodded. "And there were knitting needles stuck in the victim's chest." He looked at me intently. "Do you have any idea where they came from?"

I said they were probably Edie's, but he just looked at me and said, "Maybe, maybe not."

"Lots of people have knitting needles. Just go look at Cadbury Yarn. They have all kinds. Or in the gift shop." I explained that the owner of local yarn store had left supplies for sale there. "Gwen Selwyn said when guests saw the retreat people knitting, it seemed to make them want to knit, too."

"Like some kind of virus," Lieutenant Borgnine said.

"Not exactly. It's supposed to be enjoyable and relaxing."

"Let's just get down to it," he said. "Who in your group has those steel double-pointed needles?"

"You think it was someone in my group?" I said. I was surprised and defensive and said it couldn't possibly be one of them. They all seemed so nice. He rolled his eyes.

"Sometimes something happens to nice people and suddenly they're not so nice." He looked at me. "What about you? Do you have some of those sharp needles?"

"Are you kidding? I barely know how to knit," I said, trying to avoid a direct answer. But he was good and picked up on it.

"So, you're saying you don't have any needles like that?" he said. Something in his voice made me uneasy.

"You don't honestly think that I—"

"Just answer the question," he said, interrupting.

What I did next did not please him. I'd learned something when I'd done temp work at the detective agency. As much as Lieutenant Borgnine was trying to assert his authority, I wasn't really under any obligation to answer his question or stay there.

"That's really all I have to say," I said, getting out of the chair and heading for the door.

9

"DON'T YOU SEE? THEY THINK ONE OF US DID IT,"
Bree squealed. I'd just walked back into the meeting room
and told Kris that Lieutenant Borgnine was waiting to talk
to her. As Kris headed to the door, she stopped when she
got close and dropped her voice.

"I did the best I could to keep them knitting and calm,
but I'm afraid the natives are freaking out." Kris looked
back as Bree continued.

"What if it is one of us?" Bree looked around at the group.
"And then one by one we start disappearing. Like that Agatha
Christie story." She jumped up. "I don't care what that police
guy says. I'm leaving." She made a rush toward the door Kris
had just gone out of.

"If you leave, it's going to make you look guilty," Scott
said. The sound of a male voice startled us. "If I were a cop
and one of this group bolted, I'd chase after her."

Bree looked stricken. "What would my boys do if I went to jail?" She started to cry. All the commotion made Olivia stop thinking about whatever seemed to be continually on her mind and she went over to Bree to comfort her, though with a few prickly comments.

They all wanted to know what Lieutenant Borgnine had asked me and seemed apprehensive about their own turn with him. Even Lucinda seemed worried.

"Do you think he's checked up on us already?" she said, rocking her head with concern. "Tag doesn't know, but I have a few outstanding parking tickets." Poor Lucinda. Tag would definitely throw a fit about unpaid parking tickets. In his detail-oriented world, you never left anything like that hanging.

"Isn't Tag your husband?" Scott said. "If my wife had a few parking tickets I wouldn't have a conniption fit."

"You don't know Tag," Lucinda said. Scott still seemed confused, and Lucinda tried to explain that Tag had been an engineer, and everything he did had to be perfect, just so. Every *i* dotted and *t* crossed.

Olivia had gone back to working on her knitting. She seemed to go off in her own world again and looked lost in her stitches.

"Didn't Edie say something about a romantic story with you two on the cover of the menu at your restaurant?" Melissa said. "Something about high school sweethearts who reconnected?"

I heard Lucinda suck in her breath. No way did she want it out there to anyone besides me that their ending wasn't totally happily ever after. "Forget I mentioned anything," Lucinda said.

"So are you going to tell us what that cop asked you?"

Sissy said, seeming agitated. "I'd like to know what to expect." She stopped and swallowed.

"I think we should be questioned together," her mother said. "Sissy, you're likely to say the wrong thing."

Sissy flashed her eyes. "Me say the wrong thing? You wrote the book on that. When you came to school with me in third grade, didn't I tell you not to say that I hated math? And what did you say, first thing? 'Miss Quinn, my daughter hates math.'"

"You're not going to bring that up again," Melissa said. She looked at the rest of group and rolled her eyes. "So, I made a mistake. It was how many years ago?"

Lucinda interrupted before their fuss could escalate. "You know, Casey did some work at a detective agency. She can probably wrap this case up before the cops figure it out."

It was my turn to suck in my breath, and suddenly I regretted that I hadn't been more specific about my duties to Lucinda. I'd just been a temp and was either a detective's assistant or an assistant detective, depending on your point of view. Most of my work had been tracking down people on the phone. In the month I'd worked there, I'd gotten quite good at getting information on people. But the closest thing to actual detective work I'd done was taking over a surveillance when one of the PIs had a toothache. It hadn't turned out well. Just my luck I'd been dressed in a bright red top that day. The subject had noticed me sitting in the car and took off out the back door.

I didn't think that qualified me to figure out what happened to Edie. I was about to try to tone down what Lucinda had said, but Bree jumped in. "If you're going to investigate Edie's murder, you have to realize it wasn't me. I don't think it was any of us."

"But who else is there? Who even knew Edie besides us?" Melissa said. She nudged Olivia and urged her to join the discussion.

"To start with, there was a guy sitting at the table with me last night. I saw him talking to her when she went to get her dinner," Scott said.

"What were they talking about?" Bree asked.

Scott shrugged and blew out his breath. "Probably nothing important. I forgot that Edie picked up people wherever she went. You all know how I met Edie," he said. "She found me in the yarn department of a craft store. She figured out right away what was going on. I tried to act like I was just playing with the yarn. I tossed the skeins I was holding back into the bin they came from like I was playing basketball. But then she saw the needles I was holding. Edie wasn't one to mince words. She looked at me and said, 'You're a closet knitter aren't you?' Right away she told me about this retreat and said it was just what I needed."

"Didn't you say you went to her house to knit?" I asked.

"Hey, I see where you're going. No, I didn't have something going on with her. I only went there a few times."

Kris came back in the room and saw that the only one knitting was Olivia.

"How was it?" I asked, and she shrugged.

"He wanted to know what I saw and what I knew about the group." She looked around at everyone. "He asked me to send Scott in."

Reluctantly, the one male member of the group got up and headed toward the door. "You didn't see any media people around, did you?" he asked Kris.

She shook her head and he left.

And so it went. When Scott came back, Bree went to talk to Lieutenant Borgnine. Lucinda went after her, and no matter what any of us could say, Melissa and Sissy went together. I'm sure Lieutenant Borgnine was thrilled about that. Olivia was the last one to go.

By then the group had realized they'd missed lunch. Lucinda called Tag and talked him into having the cook whip up some treats.

Just as Olivia returned from talking to Lieutenant Borgnine, Tag arrived with the food. The Blue Door was known for using as much local food as possible. Tag had brought thin-crust gourmet pizzas with fresh mozzarella cheese, tomatoes they grew behind the restaurant, garlic from Gilroy, artichoke hearts from Castorville and olives from Paso Robles. I knew the vegetables in the chopped salad came from a local farmer's market that sold produce grown in the Salinas Valley and the dressing was made with olive oil from a boutique grower in Carmel Valley. He'd brought a selection of fruit—raspberries from Watsonville, strawberries from Oxnard, grapes from Delano—and a selection of cheeses from a small producer in Point Reyes Station.

I think Tag was happy to have a reason to come back to the conference center so he could see Lucinda and make sure she was all right.

"Let me help you with that," Tag said. Sissy was trying to cut her own piece of pizza with the tool lying next to it, and it was clearly driving him crazy watching her struggle with it. She gave him a dirty look, no doubt reminded of her mother. Finally, Tag couldn't take it anymore.

"The pizza has already been cut into exactly equal-sized pieces." He took another spatula, picked up one of the perfect little rectangles of pizza and deposited it on her plate. Lucinda came over just in time.

"Tag, honey, thank you for bringing this feast over," she said, giving him a hug. Everyone else added their thanks. "But don't you want to get back to the restaurant? The waitstaff is probably setting the tables all wrong."

Tag's face clouded. "Do you really think they are? You're right. I better get back there."

When he left, Lucinda rolled her eyes and turned to me. "I love him, but he drives me crazy. I must have told you how he started going around with a ruler making sure all the plates were the same distance from the edge of the table. He said he saw some English butler doing it on a TV show." Lucinda rocked her head with disbelief.

Kevin walked in and sniffed the air, then saw the food. "Nobody cleared this with me," he said. He pulled me to the side. "Vista Del Mar does all the food service on the premises."

I started to argue. The gift shop certainly didn't get their food from the Vista Del Mar kitchen. I made their muffins. And what did it matter anyway? We'd been through a shock and missed our lunch. As soon as I said something about talking to the Delacorte sisters, he backed off and turned on his heel.

I left the group to eat and went outside where I could get some privacy. I pulled out my cell phone and called Frank. He was probably going to freak. He hadn't heard from me in months, and suddenly I was calling him every day.

"Feldstein?" Frank said. "Again? What's up now?"

"I was hoping you could help me with a situation."

"Okay, Feldstein, I knew you were leaving something out when you called before. What kind of mess are you in?

Need a background check on a guy you met online? Take my word for it—he's probably married and a deadbeat besides."

"I love your take on people," I said. "I don't need a background check, and for your information, I meet guys the old-fashioned way, in person." I brought up the retreat and told him what had happened. As soon as I said the word *murder*, Frank made a noise, and even though I couldn't see him, I pictured him leaning back in his reclining office chair, shaking his head.

"Feldstein, you're in charge of a group and one of them is murdered the first night? How could you let that happen?"

"It isn't like I planned it," I said with an edge creeping into my voice. "And now, the thing is, they kind of think I'm going to investigate and find out who did it." I paused while I got to the uncomfortable part. "But, well, I'm not sure how to proceed."

Frank laughed, and I heard his chair squeak in protest and knew he must be trying to recline farther. He had this habit of leaning back to the extreme, and one of these days, he was going to push too hard and the whole thing would break. I knew it sounded ridiculous, but I always pictured that when the chair broke it would somehow catapult him into the air, which would have been quite a sight.

"We mostly stick to getting the goods on cheating spouses, and catching insurance cheats—skiing when they're supposed to be on crutches. But I suppose I could give you a few pointers." He stopped for a moment. "You carrying these days?"

"Carrying? You mean do I have a gun? Not even close. All I have is a flashlight."

"Ooh, that's really going to scare someone. What are you

going to do? Shine it in their eyes?" I heard the chair make more noise as Frank readjusted himself. "Here's the deal, Feldstein. The cops aren't going to be happy with you for interfering. They will probably think you're trying to make them look bad, which, incidentally, you are. So, it's best if they don't know what you're up to. Though you do have an advantage. If there's some cop you can flirt with, you might be able to get some inside information."

"There's something I didn't mention, Frank. I have to solve the whole thing by this weekend."

"Geez, Feldstein. That's a lot of pressure. Okay here goes." He began to outline what I should do, beginning with finding out as much as possible about the victim. What about the murder scene? Was there a struggle, forced entry? My head was starting to swim. Frank stopped for a minute and laughed. "I hope you're writing all this down, Feldstein." He had a point, so I started taking notes. Whether I'd be able to read them or not later was another question.

"Here's a real hint, Feldstein. Go for the people closest to her, like her husband. That's most likely who did it," Frank said. "Kind of a lot to do, huh?"

"Well, now that you mention it, yes," I answered before he threw in some more things to consider. How was I going to find out her time of death or who saw her last?

"By the way, how exactly was she offed?" he said. When I mentioned the knitting needles, I heard him make a *yuck* sound.

"Stabbed with knitting needles? I thought it was just sweet little old ladies who knitted. Who knows anymore?"

I tried to tell him about each person in the group, but he was already getting impatient.

"Feldstein, just concentrate on the big three. Means, motive and opportunity. Who had the needles, who wanted her dead and who doesn't have an alibi. Oh, and it's a good idea to take notes." Before I could say anything, he was getting off the call. "Got to go. Keep in touch. And if this yarn thing doesn't work out, I might have a couple of weeks for you next month." With a click he was gone.

I tried looking over my notes and groaned. If only Frank hadn't talked quite so fast. Words here and there stood out, but most of what I'd scribbled was illegible. Uh-oh. But he had made me think about the murder scene. I sat down on a bench at the edge of the walkway and started to write down what I remembered. The door was locked when we got there. I remembered that because the housekeeper had used her key to open it. Edie was lying on the bed, but I wondered if she'd struggled with her killer. Then I drew a blank. What had I gotten myself into? My brief experience working for Frank certainly didn't prepare me for this, nor did reading all those Nancy Drew mysteries when I was growing up.

Oh no, had I just gotten myself into another situation I'd flop at? The list of my career attempts floated before my eyes. I had a million reasons why I'd left each one, but other than the temp jobs that were only supposed to last a week or two, the truth was I had failed.

I could almost hear my mother's voice, saying, "Casey, when I was your age, I was already a successful doctor and a mother, and what is it you're doing now? You're handling a yarn retreat when you know nothing about yarn and now you're going to solve a murder, too?"

I thought of just leaving it up to the cops. It was their business, after all. But that's what I had done with my aunt's hit-and-run, and where had it gotten me? Lieutenant Borgnine claimed they were still looking for the driver, but I knew they really had given up on it.

I looked through the window into the meeting room, where everyone seemed to be occupied eating and talking. I shivered thinking that one of them might be a murderer. Hadn't Lieutenant Borgnine wanted to know who had those double-pointed needles? I wasn't about to tell him Olivia had some or that there were some at my aunt's. I suddenly wanted to make sure my aunt's were still there.

It would only take a few minutes and no one would miss me. I ran across the street and up the driveway.

I had the key ready, but as I put it into the lock, the door pushed open. In all my rushing in and out did I forget to lock it? I caught the hint of my aunt's rose-scented perfume still hanging in the air and felt a moment of deeply missing her. I walked through the house directly to the office and to her knitting basket. I noticed a ball of dark blue yarn on the floor. Had I done that when I was there last? I rustled through the works in progress in the basket, looking for the sock with the four double-pointed needles, and came up empty. Then I dumped the whole basket and frantically started rummaging through all the balls of yarn with needles stuck in them, and the projects they were connected to. I finally found the ball of forest green yarn, and the knitted tube, but the slender, sharp needles were missing.

I had a sinking feeling as I remembered how much I'd handled those needles. My fingerprints had to be all over them.

10

MY MIND WAS A MISHMASH AS I WALKED BACK INTO the meeting room. There was all that Frank had told me, and then finding the double pointed needles missing from my aunt's. I tried to keep myself calm. I would sort it all out later. For now I needed to take care of my group.

Lucinda and Kris were clearing up the food while the rest of them hung around, seeming at loose ends.

"We're supposed to have a break now before the rest of our workshop time," Olivia said, looking at the schedule. "It must be okay for us to go to our rooms by now," she said as she gathered up her purse.

"No," I said a little too sharply. I'd just passed Sand and Sea as I'd come back. The yellow tape was still up and a police car there. A white van had just pulled up, and a man was pulling a gurney with a plastic bag on it out of the back. There was no marking on the van, but I was sure it was

Edie's ride to the morgue. Not what I wanted the group to see.

"Taking a break is a great idea," I said with as much false cheer as I could muster. "What the schedule was supposed to say was that we'd be taking a group walk. After all the sitting, moving around is a good idea." I was making it up as I went along, but at the same time, it did seem like a good idea.

Melissa glanced toward the window and the white sky. "It looks kind of cold out there."

"Are you nuts? It's maybe in the upper fifties," Sissy said, grabbing the opportunity to disagree with her mother. "I think a walk is a great idea."

"It's not cold," Lucinda said. "It's brisk." To show her support, my friend was already pulling on her Pendleton fleece jacket. Then she leaned in close and whispered, "What's up?"

"There's too much to tell right now," I said. I wanted to explain about my conversation with my old detective boss, Frank. And, of course, the break-in at my aunt's house and the missing needles. By now I was certain I hadn't left the door unlocked and whoever had taken the needles had broken in. But a bunch of whispering between us would seem suspicious, so I just quickly told her about the van outside the Sand and Sea building and she got it. I stepped away from her and waved to the group to follow me as I pulled open the door.

As soon as I got everyone outside, Kris separated herself from the group. "I'll meet you all back here," she said.

"Oh," I said, surprised. "I thought the whole group would stick together."

She pulled me aside. "My responsibility is really only

for the knitting sessions. When I've done this retreat before, I had meals with the group, but your aunt handled all the other activities. Under the circumstances, I'm trying to do whatever I can, but with Retreat in a Box coming out so soon, there are some things I have to take care of." She repeated the whole idea of kiosks in yarn stores with a computer program that was supposed to replicate our experience of having a customized project and the tools and supplies to do it with. She repeated that the official name was Kris Garland's Retreat in a Box and it was clearly her baby. She pointed to the laptop peeking out of her bag. I told her about Sand and Sea still being off-limits and the van. "I was going to the social hall anyway. Need that Wi-Fi." She waved to the group and wished us a nice walk.

I heard some more grumbling about the cold when I rejoined the group. "Do you really think this is a good idea?" Melissa said, pointing at Bree. "That sweater isn't going to keep her warm."

"Mother, I'm sure Bree can take care of herself," Sissy said.

Melissa made a disgruntled sound. "Maybe, maybe not."

"She's got kids of her own. I'm sure she knows to put on a sweatshirt if she needs one."

Thankfully Bree had been beeped by her kids and didn't hear the conversation going on about her judgment or she probably would have had a fit that anyone had questioned her mommy skills. But Melissa's point about her clothes was well taken. I noticed Bree shiver. I took off my fleece jacket and handed it to Bree. She protested a little, then gratefully accepted it.

"Good work," Lucinda said, catching up with me. I tried

to hide a shiver as the damp breeze cut through my cotton turtleneck.

"Better me than her. She has enough to be upset about without being cold on top of it." I tried to hide another shiver, but it was a lost cause. "We'll stop by my place. I have a whole selection of fleece jackets." It occurred to me that if the killer really was someone from our group, I might be able to kill two birds with one stone. Maybe I could ferret out who had taken the double-pointed needles from my aunt's. That someone was probably also Edie's killer.

The group trailed behind Lucinda and me as we followed the winding road through the grounds of Vista Del Mar. I had taken the long route, pretending it was about giving them the scenic tour, but really it was all about missing the whole area around the Sand and Sea building.

We were almost to the edge of the grounds when I heard the whine of a golf cart and Kevin St. John pulled up next to us.

"Off to somewhere?" he said. He looked at my jacketless state and made a tsk-tsk sound. I didn't bother explaining I was going to pick up a jacket but begrudgingly told him we were going for a walk.

"Will you be leaving the grounds?" he asked. It was really none of his business, but I was caught in an awkward spot and didn't want to make a scene, so I just nodded. I expected some kind of admonishment but was surprised by what he said. "I've managed to keep the news people out of Vista Del Mar, but I can't keep them off the street outside. If they stop you, please be discreet."

The black cat made another appearance. "Shoo," the

manager said in an angry voice. "If I find out someone on the kitchen staff is feeding that cat . . ." He didn't finish the threat but glared at the fluffy animal, who had chosen to sit down in the middle of the narrow road and stare back at Kevin St. John.

"Then it doesn't belong to anybody?" I said.

"I don't think so. But it walks through the grounds like it's Julius Caesar or something." The manager made another attempt to get the cat to move, by driving the golf cart toward it. With a whip of its furry tail, the cat took off, and the golf cart continued down the winding road.

I heard Scott making upset noises, and when I turned he'd put the hood up on his hoodie and pulled it so his face was lost in the shadows. "You wouldn't know it was me, right?" he said.

"No, you just look like you're about to knock over a liquor store," Olivia said.

I led the group to a small metal gate in the fence. We left the grounds of Vista Del Mar behind and came out on the street a distance from my house. I knew everyone in the group was aware that my place was somewhere across the street, and I hoped whoever had taken the needles from my aunt's would tip their hand by knowing exactly which house. I huddled with Lucinda quickly and told her to hang back.

"First stop is my place to get a jacket," I said, setting the trap. I took a slow step toward the street. Suddenly Scott plowed ahead almost in a sprint and stopped in my driveway. I was stunned, to say the least.

We all caught up with him, and I was looking at him directly, or thought I was; with the hoodie up it was hard to tell. "So, you know this house is mine?" I began. I was about to bring up the missing needles when it all came unraveled.

"We all know which property is yours," Melissa chimed in. "Edie pointed it out, bragging about how your aunt had invited her over after the last retreat."

"Oh," I said, suddenly deflated. Lucinda came up next to me and gave me a supportive nudge.

"You tried," Lucinda said.

"Anybody else need a jacket?" I said before going in. When I returned wrapped in a thick layer of beige fleece, I led them back to the street.

"Do you have a destination in mind?" Lucinda asked.

"Well, there's the cemetery," I said. "Oops, bad idea." Even with the sweet deer that hung out there, the rich green grass, the quirky headstones and the view of the water, did I really want to remind everyone of death, which in turn would make them think about Edie? "Let's go to the lighthouse."

The street that ran in front of my place was called Lighthouse for good reason. It led right to it. As we headed up the street we passed the last of the Vista Del Mar grounds, which from here looked like it was all trees and slopes covered in tall golden grass. On the other side of the street, the landscape was a little tamer, though not by much. The cottage-size houses had ivy ground cover instead of lawns and were surrounded by trees that had grown of their own accord. Here and there a spot of color showed in a window box of impatiens. The clouds were beginning to melt, and there was a hint of blue sky.

The street made a little curve, and the lighthouse came into view. I did my tour guide bit and explained its history.

Personally, I didn't think it looked like any lighthouses I'd ever seen. They were always shaped like a cylinder with a light on top. The Cadbury by the Sea Lighthouse was set back from the shore and looked like someone had stuck a cylinder into the top of a house. But despite how it looked and where it was, apparently it functioned just fine and was the longest continuously operating lighthouse on the West Coast. Since 1885 it had been keeping ships from wrecking off the rocky coves at the end of the Monterey Peninsula.

Bree seemed to be feigning interest in what I was saying. Lucinda was polite. I knew she'd heard it all before, probably many times. Scott was keeping his distance from the group, so much so that a passerby might not have even realized he was with us. Melissa and Sissy were arguing about something, and I'm pretty sure it had nothing to do with the lighthouse. In other words, my spiel was pretty much for nothing. I checked to see if maybe I'd captured Olivia's attention, but she had gone on ahead and was crossing the street that ran between the lighthouse grounds and the water.

Sunset Avenue made a loop around the lighthouse before snaking along the coast. On the other side of the street a narrow strip of land ran along the rocky cliff. I couldn't see the waves, but I could hear them hitting the rocks below. Olivia stopped next to a weathered bench facing the water.

"Is that where it happened?" Bree asked, pointing to the little slip of land Olivia was standing on.

"Yes," I said in a low voice, realizing this destination wasn't any better than the cemetery. "Amanda must have been sitting on that bench, knitting and looking at the water." It didn't seem like the most peaceful spot for the activity, but there was something mesmerizing about the rhythm of the waves and the salty breeze. "I heard she lived inland. Maybe she just wanted to get in a little more time by the sea."

"But how did she go over the edge?" Bree said with a shudder.

"I don't know. Maybe she heard a harbor seal or something and went to have a look and . . ." This time both Bree and I shuddered.

By now Olivia had walked to the edge of the unprotected bluff. I didn't know much about her other than she had brought sleeping pills with her, seemed upset about something and the trip had been a gift to get her out of town. Was it my imagination or was she teetering on the edge? Without hesitating, I ran across the street and grabbed her from behind, pulling her back. As I did, I caught a glimpse of the waves rolling over the piles of rocks nestled against the base of the cliff.

When I let go, she looked at me as if I was crazy.

"What are you doing?" she said, straightening the cream-colored fleece jacket she had on over her velour pants. Either I was wrong or she was trying to cover up what I'd stopped her from doing. Either way it was an awkward moment. The rest of the group caught up with us, even Scott, hidden in his hoodie, and we all stood watching the waves lash against the rocks below.

As I stood there, something else I knew about Olivia suddenly popped into my mind. In all the confusion I'd forgotten until that moment that Olivia had walked Edie back to her room and must have been the last person to see her alive.

11

KRIS WAS KNITTING AT THE LONG TABLE IN OUR
meeting room when we got back from the walk. Everyone
was glad for the cozy interior, and there was an instant run
on the coffee and tea service.

I hung back and let them all go first. As Olivia approached
me, I noticed she'd gone from appearing distracted to looking upset. "I just want you to know that what you think you
saw was wrong," she said.

"It would help if I knew what was on your mind," I said,
glad that we were out of the earshot of the others.

"Right now it's being a suspect in Edie's murder," she
snapped. "Someone told Lieutenant Borgnine that I insisted
on taking Edie back to her room." Olivia glared at the group
as they brought their drinks to the long table. "I said I was
just trying to be helpful since her room was down the hall

from mine, but that cop acted as if it was some kind of plot so I could kill her."

So, I hadn't been the only one who'd remembered that Olivia had escorted Edie to her room. I thought Lieutenant Borgnine had handled it wrong. Instead of accusing her outright, he should have tried to pump her for information first and then accused her. I considered trying to find out how Edie had been when Olivia left her. But I'd learned something during my work for Frank. If I started questioning someone on the phone and I hit a sensitive spot and they got all angry, the chance of getting any useful information was gone. I suspected the same was true of Olivia right now.

Kris rapped on the table to get everyone's attention. "Let's try to get back to work on your projects." The low hum of conversation stopped, and they drifted toward the table.

As Melissa passed Olivia and me, she stopped. "I heard you talking," Melissa said, her face squeezed in distress. "It was me. I'm so sorry. But I didn't imply you had anything to do with Edie's death. He asked me what I remembered about that night. I told him that I'd had some wine and was feeling a little fuzzy around the edges. I mentioned that you seemed upset about something and that you'd offered to help Edie back to her room."

Bree's phone began to beep, and we all jumped at the sound as she quickly answered it, while mouthing *sorry* to all of us. "Mommy is in the middle of something," she said in into the phone in a singsongy voice that was almost as irritating as the loud chirp the phone made.

Scott had dropped his hoodie as soon as he came inside and slid into a chair. He grabbed his giant needles and happily began to work on the red lap blanket. Lucinda couldn't help herself and was checking cups to see if anyone needed a refill of coffee or tea.

As Bree tried to end her call, Sissy stepped between Melissa and Olivia. "Mother, how could you tell that cop that Olivia killed Edie?"

A gasp went through the group, and Bree clicked off her call without even saying good-bye. Melissa looked like she might cry and repeated that it was a misunderstanding. Kris rapped on the table again.

"Our whole schedule has gotten off track, and I understand that what happened to Edie has us all on edge, but I think you should turn those energies into something positive. We only have limited time together." She gestured toward the array of yarn and projects on the table, but no one moved.

During my stint as a substitute teacher I'd had to deal with lots of unruly kids and had discovered the best way to get a handle on the situation was to ask for their help. I thought the same strategy might work with this group.

I went over to the table and picked up the swatch I'd been working on. "You all know how to knit, but I'm just a struggling beginner. This may sound stupid, but what do I do now? How to I end the swatch?"

It worked, and suddenly the whole dynamic of the room changed. The people who were standing found their seats as everyone looked toward my dangling piece of knit material. They had all become a team to help me.

"I can certainly help you with that," Olivia said, taking the swatch from me. She did some fast work with the needles and one of the stitches was hanging off the side.

"It's no good to do it for her," Melissa said. "Remember

Betty Hechtman

that thing about giving someone a fish or teaching them to get their own." She took the swatch from Olivia and handed it back to me.

Kris sat back and seemed glad to let them take over. Melissa told me to knit another stitch and then slip the first one over it and off the needle. I was clumsy as I followed her directions but was able to do it, and now there were two finished stitches hanging off the needle.

Scott looked up from his work. "That's it. Keep going. Now knit another stitch and do the same." They all watched as I moved across the row. Lucinda gave me a thumbs-up and a pat on the back when I got to the end.

Unfortunately, as soon as I'd finished binding off my swatch, Sissy brought up Edie again. "Do any of us know what happened to Edie—like how she died?" Sissy glanced around the table. "I tried asking the cop who questioned me, but he kept saying, 'I can't give out that information yet,' no matter what I asked him."

"He told me the medical examiner has to investigate and determine the cause of death. The best I got was that she died under suspicious circumstances," Lucinda said, shaking her head with disbelief. "I could have told him that." Suddenly all eyes were on her, and Olivia asked why she was so sure. So far the three of us who'd found Edie hadn't mentioned the knitting needles sticking in Edie's chest or the red stuff all over the place. Lucinda caught herself and said it just looked fishy to her, but she didn't remember why.

Kris seemed exasperated. "You're getting distracted again. Please, all of you, let's get back to knitting. I'm going to help Casey learn how to pick up a dropped stitch." She

108

walked around the table and leaned in close to me. "We need to keep their minds off of Edie."

It worked. At the mention of dropped stitches, they left the discussion of Edie and all started sharing their stories of stitches they'd lost and how they'd fixed them. Meanwhile, Kris had me start a new swatch.

When I'd knitted a bunch of rows and was in the middle of one, Kris had me stop. In order to fix a dropped stitch, you had to drop one and then keep knitting. Doing it by accident apparently wasn't hard, but doing it on purpose was another story. Kris told me to push one of the loops off the needle without knitting it first. Since I knew this was going to make a problem, it was hard for me to do. As I hesitated, Kris said, "Drop it, Casey."

Then the others joined her, and pretty soon there was chant going of "Drop it, Casey." When I finally nudged the loop off the needle, they all applauded. It was certainly the first time I'd gotten a round of applause for making a mistake.

All their eyes were glued to my little swatch as I followed Kris's directions and kept knitting more rows and watching the fallen loop slip farther and farther down.

Kris finally held up her hand and told me to stop. "Now the fun begins," she said, handing me a metal thing with a hooked end. "You'll fix it with a crochet hook." She gave me some story of it being like a ladder as she pulled the loop up through the first missed row and then turned it over to me.

Give me a dessert gone wrong anytime rather than this. I could do wonders to a lopsided cake, with buttercream frosting. Cookies that crumbled got mixed with melted butter and became pie crust. But this—I was sweating by the time I wove that loop through all the rows and finally put it back on the needle.

Somehow my learning how to pick up a stitch served as a catalyst to the group and they all picked up their projects without another word about Edie. I suggested that since we'd missed a lot of our workshop time, we go through to just before dinner. It seemed like everyone had reached a stumbling block and needed Kris's help and they were glad for the extra time with her.

As for me—now that I'd learned how to cast on, knit, bind off, and fix a dropped stitch, Kris pushed me to start my real project. I held up the directions that had been in my tote bag. There was a picture of the finished scarf. "This is way too complicated. The scarf has bands of different colors," I wailed.

Kris smiled indulgently at me, held up a skein of my yarn and pointed to the name of the pattern. "It's called *It Only Looks Complicated.* Casey, check out this yarn. See how it changes into different colors? The yarn makes the stripes for you."

"Really?" I said, viewing it with amazement. "If only it could knit itself, too."

Lucinda was the only one who chuckled.

Kris stood over me while I clumsily casted on the stitches and began the first row. She went into her cheerleader mode. "Yay, you've got it. Now just keep going," she said, giving me an encouraging pat before moving on to Sissy.

Toward the end of the workshop, I ducked out to check on what was happening with the police investigation. The sun had finally come out and was making shadows from the trees limbs. Everything looked normal from a distance, but when I got closer I could see that the yellow tape was still strung around the perimeter of the building. I walked around to check the back of the building and saw there were still a police car and the white van there. The back door of the building opened, and two men brought out a gurney with something dark on top. I shuddered when I realized it was a body bag and Edie zipped inside. I couldn't help but remember how excited she'd been when she arrived at Vista Del Mar. Who would have guessed this was the way she was going to leave?

Once they'd loaded the gurney inside, the van pulled away and slowly drove down the narrow road.

"What are you doing here?" Lieutenant Borgnine said, startling me as he came from behind.

"I wanted to see if my group could get in their rooms." I gestured toward the yellow tape. "When is it coming down?"

"Miss Feldstein, as long as you're here, I'd like to talk to you again," he said, totally ignoring my question. "Maybe this time you won't be so uncooperative. You know I could take your abrupt departure before as an effort to hide something." He let it all sink in for a moment before continuing. "You didn't mention that the victim was falling down drunk and had to be helped to her room, nor did you mention the party who did the helping." He paused a beat. "Is there anything else you'd like to tell me?"

As he was talking, all I could think about were those needles missing from my aunt's, which seemed awfully likely to be the ones stuck in Edie's chest. But I wasn't about to volunteer anything.

12

I GOT BACK TO THE WORKSHOP JUST AS THEY WERE finishing up. The only positive thing about my run-in with Lieutenant Borgnine was that I was there when he released the murder scene and Sand and Sea was once again available to the residents. He had tried his best to squeeze information out of me, and I had done my best to get information from him. We were both losers.

When I worked for the detective agency, Frank had always said my job was to get information, not give it. I was pleased that I'd learned my lesson well.

"Are you sure we can go back in our rooms?" Bree said, her brows knit in worry. I nodded, but just to be sure, I said I would accompany the group to the building. Only Scott went off on his own.

I went inside first and checked it out for them. A fire had been laid in the living room area, and everything seemed normal. The only hint that anything had gone on was that several housekeeping carts had been arranged to block off the end of the dark wood hallway where Edie's room was located.

Once I gave the all clear, they filed in. Kris thanked me before heading upstairs. The rest went to rooms on the first floor. I'd hoped to get a chance to talk to Lucinda, but she was already on the phone with Tag, and I gathered there was another dustup at the restaurant. I'd have to catch up with her later.

The afternoon was waning as I walked away from the Sand and Sea building. The brief bit of blue sky had been replaced by a thick layer of white clouds. I let out a sigh of relief as I headed down the slope through a sea of tall golden grass. How had my aunt managed these weekends? But then she hadn't had a murder to contend with.

Finally, now that I had a moment alone with my thoughts, I went through my phone conversation with Frank. He'd given me so many things to think about, and they were all more or less a jumble in my mind. Who had motive? Well, that was easy, since Edie seemed to be in the middle of everybody's business. Who had opportunity? The obvious person was Olivia, since she had walked Edie back to her room. The thing was, it seemed almost too obvious. Who had means? Assuming the murder weapon was my aunt's knitting needles, it had to be someone who knew they were there. But why go to the trouble of getting those particular needles? What could set them apart? The only reason I could come up with was it was a way to get needles with fingerprints on them that weren't the killer's. As an afterthought, I remembered some of the fingerprints were mine . . .

I had hoped for a cup of coffee in the meeting room, but when I'd gotten around to checking the container, it was lukewarm and almost gone. This had been a long day, and there was still dinner and a night knit get-together to handle. I needed a jolt of caffeine.

By now I'd passed the main driveway that served as the entrance and exit to the grounds. Ahead the road narrowed and ran past the Lodge. With the dining hall just a short distance beyond, I thought of this area as being the heart of Vista Del Mar. The hotel van had pulled in front of the double doors of the social hall, and several people were getting out with their bags, no doubt to check in.

I followed them into the building, hoping the gift shop was still open with its coffee wagon. The large room was busier than I'd seen it since the beginning of our retreat. It was filled with guests who had finished their afternoon activities and were waiting for dinner. Though somewhere in the white sky the sun was still up, all the lights were blazing inside.

Four people were having a table tennis tournament at the back of the large open room. A family was gathered around the pool table preparing to start a game. The couches and chairs in the sitting area were all full, and the one TV in the whole resort was tuned to the news.

I glanced toward the window that overlooked a large deck on the opposite side of the building from where I'd entered. I was surprised to see heat lamps and a crowd of people. When I looked closer, I saw Kevin St. John bringing out bottles of wine. This seemed more elaborate than the impromptu toast we'd had the night before. Kevin filled the glasses on a tray, and one of several uniformed servers picked the tray up and started to circulate through the crowd. I watched as a woman took a glass and set it onto one of the posts along the railing. A moment later, the woman next to her hit the glass with her elbow and sent it tumbling. I don't know how Kevin St. John managed it, but within a moment he had replaced the glass on the post. I supposed there was a lot of breakage with outdoor events, remembering I'd heard a crash of glass at ours.

A waiter carrying a tray of some kind of appetizers headed for the door to the deck, and I asked him what was going on.

"It's a welcoming party for the guests of an upcoming wedding."

"You have weddings here?" I asked, and he rolled his eyes.

"Are you kidding? Mr. St. John wants to put on every-thing here. Next it will be funerals." The man suddenly realized what he'd said and looked around to make sure no one had heard.

"Don't you mean he rents out the space for them to use and offers accommodations for their guests?"

"No, he's added wedding planner to his title," the man said. "He wants complete control of everything that goes on here." He nodded to me and said he better start serving because he wanted to keep his job.

I was going to head for the gift shop and my coffee when the television screen caught my eye. The scene changed from the Channel 3 studio to an exterior shot. It only took me a moment to recognize the street that ran between Vista Del Mar and my house. I stepped closer as the field reporter began to talk. The shot grew wider, and I recognized Kris.

I was practically standing in front of the screen now, trying to hear what they were saying. All I heard was something about a retreat.

Suddenly the channel changed, and when I turned, I saw Kevin St. John with a remote control in his hand. He stepped closer to me. "Just in time," he said, discreetly looking at the people in the area to see if they had heard. They barely seemed to notice that he'd changed the channel to an old black-and-white sitcom. "You don't know the work that has gone into keeping the police investigation on the down low." He stood a little taller and had a self-satisfied smirk. "But I managed it. I bet if you were to canvass almost everyone in this room, they would have no idea that someone died here this morning." His expression grew stern. "And I'd like to keep it that way."

I almost saluted and said, "Yes, sir," before he turned on his heel and walked away. I really needed the coffee now and made my way to the gift shop with my fingers crossed that they were still brewing. I smiled when I got my first whiff of the pungent scent as I walked into the small shop built into the back of the building.

At least Louise, the girl who worked the counter, was happy to see me, for a moment anyway. She looked at me expectantly. "Did you bring muffins?" When I held up my empty hands, her expression drooped.

"You don't know how many people came in here asking for them. Somebody heard from somebody else that we sold these fabulous locally made muffins and they couldn't wait to try them. All I could offer them were these," she said, making a face as she showed me a shiny muffin in cellophane. When I looked at the ingredients it read like a shopping list for a chemistry class.

I apologized and again explained the retreat and that I'd be back baking Sunday night. "That long? My customers aren't going to be happy," she said, wide-eyed.

"You just made my day. I had no idea my muffins were that popular." I asked her for a cappuccino with an added shot, and she went to work on the espresso machine.

While I waited for my drink, I sensed a presence behind me and noticed a tall man wearing a baseball cap and looking at the T-shirt collection. Louise popped a lid on the cup and handed me the drink as I paid for it.

As I turned to go, out of the corner of my eye I noticed the man in the baseball cap starting to follow me. He caught up with me as I went through the doorway into the main room of the Lodge.

"I wonder if I could talk to you," he said. Before I could answer, he continued, "Nobody will tell me anything, and I thought that since you seem to be in charge of that yarn retreat . . ." He let his voice trail off and sighed deeply. "What happened to Edie Spaghazzi?"

I led him into a quiet corner of the room and looked at him intently. "And you are?" I said.

"Just an acquaintance of hers. My name is Michael." His face was hidden by the shadow of the hat, but it seemed that his eyes were darting around as if he didn't want to be overheard.

"You only have one name?" I said.

"There's no need for last names. Like I said, I was just a passing friend. We met in the dining hall last night. I didn't see her in the morning and then I was gone all day. I heard some rumors." He didn't finish the thought and looked at me. He seemed nervous and took off the baseball cap and ran his arm along his forehead. I got a better look at him now that there was no shadow. He had a rather stubborn-looking jaw, but there was worry in his dark eyes. Mostly I noticed the white lock of hair hanging over his forehead.

I didn't believe his relationship with Edie was quite as casual as he was making out. He seemed much too concerned to have just had a conversation about cypress trees or something the night before. I didn't want the responsibility of telling him the truth, so I offered him Lieutenant Borgnine's card.

Michael pushed the card away and shook his head vehemently. He quickly replaced the hat, clearly wanting the safety of the shadow to hide in, then backed away a few steps before he turned and took off.

I was left wondering if I'd handled it wrong. I considered going after him but realized I wouldn't know what to say if I caught him.

Somewhere in the midst of our conversation the dinner bell had rung. When I looked around the large lobbylike room, I noticed it had already cleared out. I walked toward the door.

The dining hall was already busy when I got there. Though I'd never said anything about it, the group had automatically continued going to the same table. I saw that Kris was already seated next to Olivia. Melissa and Sissy were a few steps ahead of me and were pulling out chairs by the time I got to the table.

I wanted to sit next to Lucinda, hoping we would get a chance to talk. I recognized her Prada bag and grabbed the chair next to it. A moment later, I saw her coming from the serving area, carrying a basket of rolls.

"These should be much better," she said, setting them on the lazy Susan in the middle of the table. She leaned toward me as she took her seat. "Kevin St. John should stop hassling you and attend to his kitchen. Those rolls were stale." Lucinda spun the centerpiece so the rolls were near Melissa and Sissy. Ever the restaurant person, Lucinda explained that she had gotten the kitchen staff to split open the rolls, spread them with garlic butter and then toast them a moment.

"Well?" she said expectantly as Melissa took two of the rolls and pushed one on her daughter.

Sissy seemed exasperated with her mother, but then that was pretty much a constant. I think she would have liked to toss the roll back in the basket and make some haughty comment to her mother. Let's just say, been there, done that with my mother. But Sissy glanced at Lucinda's face and must have decided it was better to be considerate than to fuss with her mother. She took a bite, and her eyes said it all. Lucinda had scored a hit.

"What did Tag want this time?" I said when Lucinda had finished watching everyone taste the rolls. She turned to me and chuckled.

"I'm so glad to be here. I love that man, but he makes me crazy." She rocked her head from side to side and rolled her eyes in amused exasperation. "Okay. Here it is. He's upset because the menu says to check out our daily homemade desserts. Since there aren't any of your desserts this weekend, he's serving ice cream sundaes. He says it's false representation because neither the ice cream nor the sauce is homemade. The fact that the whipped cream is whipped at the restaurant wasn't enough for him."

"But that's my fault," I said, suddenly feeling guilty for

not at least baking some things in advance. Lucinda was in the process of telling me that was nonsense when we were interrupted as Bree rushed up to the table. Her brows were knit, and she seemed like a rubber band that had been pulled too tight. Even her blond curls looked tense. "I have to talk to that police officer. I can't stay here for the rest of the weekend. My boys need me. I just talked to them and my husband took them out for chili dogs and then to a carnival in a church parking lot and let them go on a roller coaster. I'm sure he didn't bring their little jackets or hand sanitizer." Her lips began to tremble, and a big tear rolled down her cheek. Just then her phone chirped, letting her know it was a walkie-talkie call. She put it to her ear and tried to swallow back her tears. "Oh no," she said, rolling her head hopelessly. "That was my youngest. He just threw up. I knew the combination of the chili dogs and the roller coaster was a disaster." She laid the phone down on the table and sank into a chair. "This is all so traumatic for me," she said between sobs. "Being away from home alone, leaving my boys for the first time and then Edie getting killed." She seemed about to cry again but swallowed it back. "You don't think that police officer really thinks I'm a suspect?"

The whole table tried to calm her down. Even Scott looked over from his usual spot at the table behind us. She finally seemed on an even keel and not like she was going to split any second, but I was still concerned.

I realized it was up to me to do something. Distraction was always good. It was another lesson I'd learned during my substitute teaching days. "Melissa and Sissy, we don't really know much about you," I said, hoping to change the subject. "How did you happen to sign up for this retreat? How did you even hear about it?" I asked. I instantly regretted lumping the mother-daughter team together when I saw that Sissy looked like smoke was going to come out of her ears.

Sissy rolled her eyes upward and stuck her arm toward her mother. "It was all her idea."

The two women strongly resembled each other. Both were the same height with long, rambunctiously curly hair, but clearly in a effort to look different, Sissy had separated hers into braids while Melissa wore hers loose. I'd call the beige slacks and red and white pin-striped shirt that Melissa wore classic casual. Sissy had on jeans that purposely looked ragged, paired with a black-and-white striped low-cut tee that seemed to be constantly slipping off one of her shoulders, exposing the top of a tattooed rose.

"I don't know if all of you know that we come from Fresno," Melissa said. She waved her arm in the direction away from the water to indication its location. "I handle customer service for an online company." Sissy was making faces.

"What she means is, she answers the phone in our kitchen and listens to people complain."

Melissa gave her daughter a forced smile. "Whatever. But it is because of my job that I found out about this retreat." Melissa explained that since most of the people who worked for the online company worked out of their houses, they'd never met. "The owners put together a meeting here last year so we could see each other face to face and do some brainstorming. Our family vacations have always been to Yosemite, which, don't get me wrong, is great. But I'm a sea person, and I took one look at this place and fell in love with it.

"I was in the gift shop looking over their selection of

yarn, and I saw your aunt. Well, I recognized her as the former Tidy Soft toilet paper lady, and when she saw me holding the yarn we got talking and she told me about this retreat. Edie came in, and Joan introduced us. There was something weird going on. Edie was nothing like she was yesterday. She was subdued and seemed to want to get away from us. I saw her winking at a man in the corner of the gift shop."

"Really?" I said. "Did you notice anything special about him?"

Melissa shrugged. "He had on a baseball cap, and I wasn't really paying that much attention to him. I figured he was probably her husband." Melissa seemed perturbed as she continued. "You know, last night at the wine toast, I tried to remind Edie that we'd already met, but she claimed not to remember."

A guy in a baseball cap? Could it be Michael, the man I'd just met, who claimed to be barely an acquaintance of Edie's?

I tried pursuing the subject, asking Melissa what else she remembered, but Kris stepped in and pointed at her watch. "You better get your food before they stop serving."

Once everyone had their dinner, the conversation turned to the events of the evening. There was to be a short concert in the auditorium put on by a jazz chamber music group who were guests of the hotel and conference center. The schedule my aunt had made up showed there was a Nite Owl Knit-Together after that.

Kris explained what it meant. "Your aunt always liked the group to do some communal project that could be donated." I must have had that deer in the headlights look, because Kris said not to worry; even though it was beyond her duties as project designer and instructor, she'd handle it.

I held on to Lucinda's arm as the rest of the table pushed back their chairs. "I need to talk to you," I said in a low voice.

Out of habit, my friend began to put the dishes onto a tray behind us. "You're off duty," I said and got her to sit down.

"You're right. Tag's obsession with things is rubbing off." The rest of the dining hall cleared out, and soon it was just us and the kitchen staff cleaning up.

"Okay, shoot. What's on your mind?" she said. "Is it about Edie?"

I nodded vehemently. "You have no idea what you've missed." Lucinda listened intently as I told her about my call to Frank and his many suggestions. Her eyes got wide when I told her about the missing double-point knitting needles. "Do you think those are the ones . . . ?" She didn't have to finish. I knew what she meant and nodded that I thought they were.

"And you didn't tell Lieutenant Borgnine?" she said.

"I know I didn't kill Edie, so why would I tell him something that might incriminate me? I might as well just hold out my hands and say, 'Arrest me.' My plan is to find who did it and hand them over to Lieutenant Borgnine, and then where the needles came from won't matter." I surprised myself by saying that, because up until that moment I hadn't realized I even had a plan.

Lucinda sat up and seemed very animated. "I love the idea of us playing detective." She pulled out a piece of paper. "We should make a list of suspects."

"I'm more concerned about what we don't know. How

can we figure out who did it when we don't even know for sure how Edie died."

I noticed Lucinda was looking out the window at the crowd of people on the path. "They must be going to that concert," I said, and Lucinda nodded longingly.

"You really want to go, don't you? Jazz chamber music?" I said, making a face.

"Tag and I never get to go anywhere. Owning a restaurant is twenty-four-seven, particularly when one of the owners is Tag. An occasional movie would be nice. So, yes, even jazz chamber music sounds appealing."

"Why don't you go? We can talk about this later. Besides, I have an idea, and it's something I have to do alone."

13

WHAT WAS MY IDEA? IT WAS WHAT MY FORMER boss Frank had suggested—flirt with a cop. But what did I know about flirting? I'd be the first to admit that I didn't have a clue how to pull off that hair-twirling, false-eyelash-batting girly stuff.

I left the Vista Del Mar grounds and went to my place. I looked down the street and saw that Dane's red truck was parked in his driveway, so I knew he was home.

Since I wasn't sure about pulling off the flirting thing, I armed myself with something I was sure of—freshly baked butter cookies. I always made a point to keep a couple rolls of dough in the refrigerator for just such an emergency. It only took a few minutes to preheat the oven and a few more to bake the cookies. Presentation counts, so I arranged them on a plate with a doily, grabbed an empty measuring cup and headed for the door.

As I started down the street, I noted with relief that there weren't a bunch of cars parked around my cop neighbor's house or music blaring. Maybe Mr. Party Guy was taking the night off.

As I walked up his driveway, I was suddenly enveloped in the most delicious garlicky scent, which made my stomach gurgle and reminded me that I'd been too busy dealing with my group to get my dinner. All I'd eaten was half of one of Lucinda's doctored rolls. Trying to think of something clever to say, I knocked on the door.

I almost backed out and took off, but before I could take a step back, the door opened and Dane Mangano stood in the doorway.

"I thought I'd take you up on the offer of a cup of sugar," I said, holding up the empty glass measuring cup. "And I brought cookies." I held them out and waved them under his nose.

I didn't have to worry about my flirting lack, because Dane took up the slack. His lips curved into a teasing smile as he gestured for me to come in.

"Finally I get the chance to show you what a good neighbor I am." He stepped aside and let me pass, taking the measuring cup out of my hands. "You can have all the sugar you want." Inside, the garlic smell was even more intense. I glanced at his living room as we passed through. The feeling was very masculine—leather furniture and a big-screen TV—but the red Indian print blanket hanging on the arm of the sofa and basket of pine cones sitting on the old wood coffee table softened the look. The fireplace appeared to be used often, and a stack of wood sat next to it. A tall bookcase sat against one wall, and along with books, it had framed photographs and some kind of awards.

He had me follow him to the kitchen, where I found the source of the wonderful fragrance. A big pot of tomato sauce was simmering on the stove. I noticed an oval platter of cooked spaghetti noodles sitting on the counter. Obviously I'd gotten there before the party started. *At least he feeds them*, I thought. And, well, I was salivating at the delicious smell. As I'd said, I was a master at dessert but a dud at the day-to-day kind of cooking. He put the measuring cup on the counter and took the plate of cookies from me, snagging one before he put them down. I could see how good they tasted by his expression.

"Hang on a second," he said, picking up a bottle of olive oil and drizzling some over the cooked spaghetti before tossing the noodles to mix it. "It keeps the spaghetti from sticking together," he said, noticing that I was watching him.

The kitchen reminded me of my aunt's. These weren't tract houses, but they had been built at the same time by the same builder, so it made sense that they were similar. The big difference was my aunt had taken the freestanding garage and turned it into a guesthouse. I was pretty sure Dane had turned his into a party room, since his red truck was always parked in the driveway and the music always seemed to blare from his garage.

He seemed less imposing now that he was out of uniform. The cargo pants hung low on his hips and did a nice job of showing off—was I going to say his butt? I moved my eyes up to the gray T-shirt he wore on top and found myself noticing the bulge of his biceps and his well-developed chest. I bet there was a six-pack hiding under there.

I chastised myself for my thoughts, reminding myself of his too many nights a week of entertaining. But it was impossible not to notice that he was very attractive, even if he seemed a little cocky. I suppose his height was considered average, but it just made him seem more compact and like he could spring into action. I'd seen him jogging by my place at night sometimes, and he could definitely move.

In my worry about flirting, I'd forgotten to look at my page of notes. What did I want to ask him? Here was my chance, and I was blowing it. I searched for anything. If I couldn't ask about Edie, maybe I could find out the details of what had happened to Amanda Proctor. "Do you know anything about a woman who fell off the bluff near the lighthouse?" I asked.

He finished with the noodles and gave the sauce a stir. "I don't recall her name offhand, but she was here for one of these retreats. The medical examiner ruled it an accident."

I noticed there was a question in his voice. "But you don't think it was?"

He shrugged. "I just thought it seemed weird that she'd be sitting on a bench, knitting, and then stand so close to the edge that she'd fall off." He shrugged again. "The ME thought a gust of wind might have knocked her off-balance." He glanced downward. "I was the first responder. She'd been there for a few days when somebody climbing on the rocks saw her and called it in." He shook his head. "I won't go into the gory details, but she was still holding a handful of yarn.

"Sorry for the delay," he said, wiping his hands on a cloth dish towel and turning to face me. "So which is it, brown or white?"

"Huh?" I said.

"Brown or white," he said for the second time.

I gave him a blank look and he winked. "The sugar you wanted, remember?" he said with a teasing smile as he picked up the measuring cup off the counter. "C'mon, sweet-cakes, we're neighbors. You don't need an excuse to stop over. I saw you drooling over the spaghetti. Sit down and I'll get you a plate."

"Sweetcakes?" I said, wrinkling my nose.

"That's what you do, isn't it? Make sweet cakes," he said. His dark eyes were dancing in a friendly way as he pulled out a large white plate and used a funny-looking tool to grab a bunch of noodles.

"Muffin would be more accurate, but let's not get into nicknames." I was practically drunk from the smell of the spaghetti sauce, and my stomach was making all kinds of begging noises. Still, I tried to say no, but he said it was too late as he ladled on some sauce and added a shake of ground cheese.

"Mind if I wash my hands?" I said.

"Be my guest." He pointed down the hall to the bathroom.

Just like my aunt's guest bathroom, this one had a door to the outside. How convenient for his party crowd. I didn't intend to snoop, but after I'd finished with the soap and water there wasn't a towel. I was just going to check the cabinet in the corner of the bathroom for something to dry my hands with. As soon as I opened the door on it, a stack of women's clothes fell out. I put most of them back without looking, but I couldn't help checking out the sweat suit on top. It was pink and one of those designer things that had words across the butt. This one said *HOT.* I quickly refolded it and put it back.

The towels were on the next shelf, and as I pulled one out, I almost dropped it. Directly next to the stack of fresh towels at eye level were several industrial-size boxes of condoms. I shut the door fast, stifling an embarrassed laugh. I suppose you could at least give him credit for being prepared.

His parties must be even wilder than I'd imagined. I had a hard time looking him in the eye when I came back into the kitchen. He'd put out a place mat, silverware and a napkin, with a plate loaded with spaghetti in the middle.

He took another cookie and gave me a thumbs-up as I dug into the spaghetti. He pulled out a chair and sat across from me. I barely stopped eating long enough to give him a thumbs-up in return. Let's say I more or less inhaled the whole plate. I was scraping up the last of the noodles and felt like licking the plate.

"Look, I know you didn't really come for the sugar, and you aren't just dropping by to say hi. Don't get me wrong, I'm glad you came by, but you want to level with me and tell me what's going on?" While I was still considering what to say he continued. "I know you're worried after what happened to that woman in your group. If you're looking for reassurance, I'm here to give it."

"What do know about Edie Spaghazzi's death?" I said, suddenly remembering what I wanted to know. "Like how exactly did she die? When exactly did she die? Did Lieutenant Borgnine notify her family? And did they dust those knitting needles for fingerprints?"

He did a double take. "Aren't you direct?" He started to give me the reassurance speech, but then he grinned. "Don't tell me you're doing the Nancy Drew thing."

"I'll have you know I'm experienced," I said. "I worked for a private investigator in Chicago, and he's advising me." When he continued to grin, I went on explaining that I felt responsible for the group and felt like I had to make sure whoever was responsible got caught before everyone went their separate ways. I started to talk about the group and how they were all panicky because they felt like they were both suspects and possible targets. "I can't let them down. I have an issue with not finishing things," I said. Then I rolled my eyes. "Why am I telling you?" I thanked him for the food and started to get up. I needed to get back and get out of there before his bevy of guests started to arrive.

"Hey," he said, following me to the door. "We're on the case. True we don't have a lot of murders in Cadbury, but we'll get the guy. Don't worry, even if it's kind of weird. By the way, those silver needles weren't the cause of death."

"What?" I said, stopping. I thought back to finding Edie and the rancid smell. "Of course, the red stuff wasn't blood. It was throw up, wasn't it?" I said. "There was no blood. She was dead when somebody stuck them in her."

"Very good that you figured that out," Dane said before continuing. "After hearing from a number of people that the victim appeared very drunk after drinking only one glass of wine, and after finding a phenobarbital pill wrapped in a tissue in her purse, the medical examiner did some tests." Dane stopped as if considering how to proceed. "I don't know how to put this delicately, but the preliminary findings were that her vomit contained wine and phenobarbital. Alcohol and sleeping pills can be a deadly combination."

"So that's what killed her?"

"The sleeping pill in her purse wasn't in a prescription bottle," he said, ignoring my question. "Any idea where she got the pills?"

I just shrugged and said I didn't know much about her or

131

for that matter anyone in the group except Lucinda. I didn't want to mention Olivia's sleeping pills and put any more heat on her unless I was sure she was the killer.

"So are you going to tell me the cause of death or what?" I said.

He cracked a smile. "Persistent, aren't you? I like that trait, maybe because I have it, too. The medical examiner said the wine and medication might have killed her if she hadn't thrown up. Actually, he said he thinks the cause of death was suffocation. At first, he thought she choked when she threw up, but then he noticed there were some markings on the pillow that matched the residue on her face.

"So somebody used the pillow to smother her," I said, and he nodded.

"Here's the weird part," Dane began. "If it hadn't been for those needles sticking in her chest, the medical examiner said he might have just considered it an accidental death from the drugs and alcohol. He probably wouldn't have even considered the markings on the pillow. But those knitting needles changed everything. She couldn't have stuck them into her chest herself. You better believe we're looking at any prints on them. Any of your group missing needles like those?" he asked, trying to sound casual.

Appear nonchalant, I told myself. There's no way he could know the fingerprints were mine. I tried to cover by saying I was new at knitting and didn't really know much about needles or who had what kind. I didn't do well in the nonchalant part, and he gave me a pointed look.

"I just shared with you. It's only fair that you share whatever you know with me," he said, clearly not buying my play at ignorance.

I heard a car pull up in front and the sound of voices as some people got out. Instinctively I glanced toward the sound and at the same time started to get up. "Sounds like you've got company," I said.

"You don't have to rush off. They'll let themselves into the studio," he said, gesturing with his head toward the garage. Studio, huh? Is that what he called it? What, was that a polite way of saying orgy room?

"I have to get back to my group," I said, grabbing my empty measuring cup. He followed me to the door and rushed ahead to open it for me.

"Too bad you can't stay. You could learn a few things," he said.

I'll just bet I could.

133

14

"THERE YOU ARE," KRIS SAID WHEN I CAME INTO the living room area of Sand and Sea. "I'm glad you made it." Was there a little reproach in her voice or was that my imagination? But then she had made a point that it wasn't part of her duties to handle this evening knit-together event. At first I had referred to her as the retreat leader, but then she'd made it clear she wasn't. After that I wasn't sure what to call her. Knitting teacher didn't seem to cover it. So, I just used her name.

When I'd gotten outside at Dane's, his guests had already gone into the garage, so I never got a look at them. I just heard the instant boom of pulsating music. I'd hurried back to my place and picked up another batch of the butter cookies to share with the group.

A fire crackled in the fireplace, and the soft lighting made the living room like area of the two story building feel cozy and inviting. Lucinda looked up from one of the easy chairs with a question in her eye and I tried to communicate that I'd talk to her later. I wasn't sure I wanted to tell the group about my trip to Dane's.

"I thought you understood what the knit-together was," Kris said. "The idea is that everyone makes a predetermined-sized square and then they are given to a charity who puts them together into blankets before they are donated to a local shelter." She looked at me, waiting for some kind of recognition. "Your aunt provided the yarn."

"Oh," I said, glancing around at the group and noticing that some of them were knitting.

"I had some sample skeins from the yarn company who is behind Retreat in a Box. But there wasn't enough for everyone." Kris watched as I set the plate of cookies down on the coffee table. "I was glad to help out, but . . ." She didn't have to finish. I got it. It was really my responsibility. But what was I supposed to do?

I asked about the concert as a stall. It seemed only Lucinda had stayed through the whole thing, and there wasn't much to say other than you certainly couldn't sing along.

"It makes me glad I never made it," Kris said. "Kevin St. John stopped me and wanted to talk to me about working with him on more retreats. He was trying to get me to commit to being the head knitting instructor. I had to explain to him that this is my last. I'm going to be too busy promoting Retreat in a Box, traveling around and doing demos at all kinds of yarn events."

I looked around to see what everyone was doing. Scott must have gotten some of Kris's yarn and had positioned himself in a shadowy corner. His eyes kept darting toward the door, and he seemed ready to ditch his needles if anyone came in. Lucinda was holding a selection of needles but had no yarn. Bree said she'd had the ball of pale pink yarn and the white plastic needles in the backpack she used as a purse. I'm sure the whole group was glad she'd left her phone and tablet packed away for once.

"I love that we're all going to make the same thing," she said. I noted that Bree had already completed several rows. Melissa and Sissy both had yarn, though not the same kind, and were sitting side by side, knitting in unison. Melissa stopped abruptly and looked at her daughter's work.

"I don't know why you you're using that red bouclé yarn. It's so hard to see the stitches." Melissa pulled out the other end of the royal blue yarn she was using and offered it to her daughter. "The skein is big enough to make two squares. We can knit from either end of it." Sissy looked at her mother with such horror I almost laughed. Been there, done that. It sure looked different viewing it from the outside. Melissa was just trying to be helpful to her daughter. I leaned closer and saw that the red yarn was covered with bumps, while the royal blue yarn was smooth.

"Maybe you can't see the stitches in my yarn, but I can see them perfectly," Sissy said, before making an irritated sound as she looked at her work. She turned away so her mother couldn't see what she was doing, but even to a novice like me, it was obvious she'd found some kind of mistake.

Olivia had chosen an overstuffed chair in the far corner of the room near a window that looked out over the dark slope in front of the building. She wasn't knitting and didn't seem to mind that her hands were idle.

"You know enough to make a square," Kris said to me.

It hadn't even occurred to me that I was supposed to actually take part in this activity, and I started to hem and haw, but Kris continued on and said that I could use any size needles or type of yarn and she'd help me make the adjustments so the square turned out the right size. I felt like I was being backed into a corner.

Lucinda suggested we go to the gift shop and pick up some yarn.

"Why don't you get some of your aunt's stash?" Melissa said. "There are probably needles, too."

The comment surprised me, and I perked up. "How did you know my aunt had a lot of yarn and needles?" I thought of the needles that had disappeared. Obviously for them to have been taken, someone had to know they were there.

The group laughed at my question. "Everyone who does anything with yarn usually has a closet full of it and needles coming out the kazoo," Bree said. "You should see what the other Ewes have."

I slumped, disappointed that Melissa knowing my aunt had needles wasn't a clue. It also became obvious they weren't going to let me off the hook from joining them.

"I'll get some yarn for me, Lucinda and Olivia and be back," I said, getting up. I had been through the Vista Del Mar grounds enough times in the past two days that I easily found my way to the driveway in the dark. As I crossed the street, I glanced toward Dane's. There were cars parked on both sides of the narrow street and light coming from the garage. Obviously, the party was in full swing.

Just as I was about to go into my aunt's through the kitchen door, Lucinda joined me. "I thought you might need some help. Not that I'm an expert."

"Compared to me you are, and thank you, I'm glad for any help I can get. Besides, now I can tell you what I did while you were snapping your fingers to the jazz chamber music." Lucinda chuckled and rolled her eyes.

"I must be desperate for entertainment to have sat through that. You have no idea. It was all plink, plunk."

As we rummaged through my aunt's closet, I told her what Dane had said, and maybe I also mentioned what I'd found in his bathroom.

"I guess even Cadbury cops need some kind of release," she said with a grin. "So the knitting needles didn't kill Edie. Suffocated? Did he say how?" Lucinda said. Before I could answer, she remembered seeing the pillow on the floor.

I told her about the contents of the throw up. "Barbiturates and wine? I guess that explains why she could barely stand up." Lucinda poked through a bag of yarn. "Edie seemed so upbeat. It's hard to think she'd do something like that. It seems pretty hard-core."

"Maybe she didn't know she was mixing a sleeping pill with alcohol. Maybe somebody spiked her wine."

"But you said they found a loose sleeping pill in her purse," Lucinda said.

"Right," I said, realizing that put in hole in the "spiked her wine" theory. "Besides, I'm sure she would have noticed if someone dropped something in her glass. It just seems kind of convenient that she was so loopy when someone put a pillow over her face."

We talked about who had access to the glasses and who also had control of who got which glass, and one name jumped out: Kevin St. John. "He was the one pouring and handing out the wine," I said. "And Edie did know him from before. He looked pretty uncomfortable when she was first talking to him. Maybe she had some information on him he wanted to bury," I said. "But we can't figure that out now. And we better get back. I am supposed to be in charge." That's when I got it. The title *retreat leader* belonged to me.

Lucinda found several skeins of light gray wool. There was enough for both of us and Olivia with some left over. "This ought to be easy to use." She explained that certain kinds of yarn presented few problems. "Worsted-weight in a light color is the easiest to work with." Lucinda chuckled at her own comment. "Don't I just sound like an expert? Actually, I just heard that from Melissa."

We looked through the needles next and picked out a pair of large ones. "This way I can make my square faster," I said. We grabbed several other sets to bring along so Olivia could have her choice. While I snagged a tote bag from my aunt's collection and packed up the supplies, Lucinda fixed her hair and put on fresh lipstick. I didn't even think to glance in the mirror.

When we came outside, I saw something dark and small moving through the plants in the backyard. I shined my flashlight on it and saw that it was the black cat. Instead of taking off, it sat down near us.

"There's that cat again," Lucinda said. "He seems to like you."

"Him?" I said. "How can you tell?"

"I'm not a cat expert, but something about the face makes me think it's a male."

"He must belong to somebody around here," I said.

"Maybe, maybe not," my friend said as the cat walked

away with a flick of its tall before we headed back across the street. In our absence, everyone but Olivia had continued to work on their squares. I was touched when everyone wanted to help me start mine. Only Kris acted as a taskmaster and said I needed to learn how to do it myself. The whole thing about learning how to fish instead of being handed one, again. Personally, I would have taken the help. I doubted I'd be knitting when the weekend was done. Actually, I was wondering if I'd even keep it up all weekend.

But for now, I didn't want to make any waves. Olivia reluctantly accepted a skein of yarn and picked from the needles I'd brought. Lucinda was able to start her square on her own, but I had already forgotten how to cast on. Kris did a demo and told me how many stitches I needed so my square would turn out about the right size. Once I had the stitches on my needle, I began knitting and was surprised when my fingers seemed to know what to do on their own.

"See, your fingers already remember," Kris said, nodding with approval as I went through the first row. Then she picked up her own work. I was shocked to see that her square was already almost complete. I think she was very happy to blend into the background.

Bree held up her work and tried to compare it with everyone else's. "Oh no," she wailed. "I thought were supposed to make it in the garter stitch."

"There's no wrong way, Bree," Sissy said. "Kris said the only requirement was that they're about the same size."

Bree apologized. "I'm just so used to being with a group that is all working on exactly the same thing."

"And you worry about getting it wrong and somebody

coming down on you," Sissy said, giving a side glare at her mother.

"Among other things. Have you ever noticed how loud silence is?" Bree said. She pulled her gray hooded sweatshirt closer around herself. "I mean when you're used to being with your kids like all the time and your husband has the TV on tuned to some basketball game with all those bouncing balls and squeaky shoes and then suddenly you're in a room by yourself without any noise. Well, maybe a bird singing or the sound of the ocean coming from outside. But the silence inside just seems so spooky. And being by yourself starts to feel really weird. Like the thoughts in your head start blaring out at you."

"Give it some time. You'll get used to it," Olivia said. She had been staying on the outskirts of the group, but when she began on her square, she had pulled her chair in closer to get better light. I was beginning to get used to her distracted look and took it as normal for her. I had also accepted that she didn't seem to want to be here and was clearly disturbed about something. She had taken the yarn I'd offered along with the needles and without looking down had cast on her stitches and begun to knit as if the needles were on autopilot. I think we were all surprised when Olivia spoke. But as soon as the words were out of her mouth, she looked away and stared at the crackling fire.

"Does that mean you live alone?" Bree said to Olivia. "You haven't told us much about yourself."

"There's nothing I want to tell," Olivia said. I was glad she looked at the group when she spoke. It was too creepy having her stare at the fire while she talked to us.

"We can all see there's something on your mind," Melissa said. "You'll probably feel better if you talk about it."

Olivia shook her head with such vehemence, the reddish hair that framed her almond-shaped face flapped back and forth. "I know when people get together and start knitting, it turns into a therapy session. And I'm sure you all mean really well, but I don't want to talk about anything." And that was the end of it. She went back to staring at the fire as her needles kept clacking.

Sissy was sitting, hanging her legs over the arm of the wing chair and looked toward Bree. "It sounds like you really need some time to yourself. That you've lost track of who you are," Sissy said. "I know what that's like."

"Now, Sissy, don't start airing our dirty laundry," her mother said with a warning in her voice. Melissa spoke to the group. "It's just mother and daughter stuff."

I listened to their wrangling and thought of my dealings with my mother. Is that what we sounded like? I groaned to myself and made a mental note never to fuss with my mother again—at least not in public. I was sure they'd been arguing like that since Sissy had learned to talk. I knew we had.

I noticed Kris yawning and knew that she'd gone beyond the job she'd been hired for, and I appreciated it no end and told her. Then I mentioned I'd seen her being interviewed by the Channel 3 TV news reporter.

"Oh, that," she said. "While you were all out on your walk, I needed to stretch my legs. The reporter was hanging just outside the gate and snagged me." Kris smiled. "Just like Kevin St. John requested, I was discreet. When she asked about Edie, I just brought up the Retreat in a Box launch instead. You have no idea how important that is to me. And as for helping out tonight, this is the last time I'll be doing a retreat like this, so I don't mind doing something extra," she said, sounding a little nostalgic. Her gaze moved over the group. "Between Joan not being here and with Edie's death . . ." Her voice trailed off as she swallowed a few times.

"Edie was certainly the spark in the group," Lucinda said. "She was a spark wherever she went. After she mentioned that she'd eaten at the Blue Door, I thought about it and it all came back to me. She made quite an impression. Well, most customers don't ask to speak to the cook so they can suggest he try their Osso Buco recipe." My friend reminded us of how Edie had brought up her meal at the restaurant when we first heard about Amanda. Lucinda held her knitting in mid-stitch. "She must have seen Amanda leaving for her walk just before she came to the restaurant." Lucinda swallowed hard. "While Edie was raving about her Osso Buco, Amanda had probably already fallen and was lying helpless amidst the rocks."

I asked if Edie was alone at the restaurant, and Lucinda had to think. "She had such a presence I almost forgot about her dining partner. She was with a man, but he seemed to be trying to hide in the corner."

After the scene Lucinda had described, who could blame him?

"It was probably her husband," Sissy said, but Kris shook her head.

"I don't think so. Edie told me that these retreats were her chance to get away from home and all that went with it."

"You don't happen to remember what the guy looked like, do you?" I said. Lucinda stopped knitting and concentrated.

"No, I don't. There was something that stood out about him, but I can't remember what it was."

"I wonder if that's the same man I saw Edie with when I first met your aunt Joan. He kept kind of a low profile, so I didn't get much of a look at him," Melissa said.

"Do you think you both would recognize the man if you saw him again?" I asked. Neither seemed certain. "I think his name is Michael," I said. "And he's here at Vista Del Mar now." The whole group seemed to suck in their breath. I told them about meeting him and his questions about Edie.

"Maybe you should talk to Lieutenant Borgnine and tell him about this Michael person. He sounds kind of suspicious to me," Kris said. "Maybe he was just playing dumb when he asked all those questions about Edie."

"So in case you'd seen them together, you wouldn't think he was a suspect," Lucinda said to me.

"Good thinking. Tell Lieutenant Borgnine about him," Scott said. "Anything to get the heat off of us."

I noticed he'd been staying out of the conversation. He had never moved from his position in the corner, so anyone passing through the area wouldn't necessarily think the man in the preppy khakis and blue oxford cloth shirt was part of our group.

He was working on a square but was using two short needles with a cable between them. By now I knew enough to get that they were called circular needles. Kris had explained that they were used when knitting in the round, hence the name. They were also quite discreet compared to a long pair of metal needles, and could be slipped into the briefcase Scott used as a tote.

Something had been on my mind since I had talked to Dane. I decided to put it to the group. "Do any of you know anything about Edie taking sleeping pills?" They waited, expecting me to say more. I made a quick decision to spare them all the gory details. So I said nothing about the residue on the pillow and the fact that the knitting needles weren't the cause of death. I just mentioned I'd heard the medical examiner thought she had taken sleeping pills.

"Edie take sleeping pills?" Bree said, starting to shake her head. "I can't believe she did that." Bree suddenly looked uncomfortable and stopped herself.

"You were going to say something," I said. Bree fidgeted with her hoodie and looked down at her square, poking at the yarn.

"It's just Edie was telling me what she thought of Olivia's sleeping pills. Edie called them a crutch and said she would never take them, and well, she said we ought to make sure that Olivia didn't take too many because she seemed so upset about something, she might . . ."

Olivia snapped out of her usual oblivion and her eyes flashed. "Commit suicide? No way. I would never . . ." She threw the young mother an annoyed stare. "I just brought the sleeping pills to get through this weekend."

"Maybe she gave Edie the sleeping pills," Melissa said to the rest of us.

"Don't be ridiculous," Olivia said, her voice rising in emotion. She rummaged around in her purse. "I didn't give one to Edie or anyone else. I took one myself, and there were ten in the bottle." She held up the bottle for them to examine it and then went to put it back in her purse. I noted that the prescription was for phenobarbital.

"Not so fast," Melissa said. "Let's see how many there are now."

"You can't be serious," Olivia said. Her face was flushed with anger.

"I think you better let us see how many pills there are," Kris said. "Just to end the discussion."

Shaking her head with annoyance, Olivia poured out the contents on a piece of paper. Everyone stood up and gathered around, beginning to count.

A gasp went through the group as they all came up with the same number.

"That can't be," Olivia said. "I know I brought ten pills and I took one. How can there be only five?"

"Have we figured out who was the last one to see Edie alive?" Kris said. Suddenly Olivia pushed back her chair so hard it fell backward before she rushed off to her room.

15

FOR A MOMENT THERE WAS JUST SILENCE IN THE wake of Olivia's abrupt departure. Then Sissy looked around the group. "It was Olivia, wasn't it?" Sissy said with a hush in her voice.

"That's right," Melissa said. "I didn't even think about that when I told Lieutenant Borgnine that she had walked Edie back to her room because she seemed so wobbly."

"I don't know if you noticed, but Olivia never touched her wine. Maybe she was trying to keep a clear head for a reason," Kris said. "And doesn't it seem odd that someone so indifferent to the group would have suddenly been so concerned that she offered to take Edie to her room?"

"So, nobody saw Edie after that?" Scott called from his corner.

There was an uncomfortable silence, and then a log in

the fireplace made a popping sound and dropped with a soft thud, which made the whole group jump.

"You all stopped knitting," I said. "We should continue on with our squares." I tried to get them over the rough spot, but there was no going back to the cozy atmosphere of the knit-together.

"I'm going to call it a night," Kris said, putting her things back in her tote bag. I had to remind myself that she had gone above and beyond her duties to help me with the knit-together and there was no reason she had to stay. Everyone else followed her lead and put away their knitting. Though it was ten o'clock, no one seemed to be thinking of going to bed. Melissa and Sissy said they were heading to the Lodge for a game of table tennis. I was glad I didn't have to referee that.

Scott just waved as he walked outside, giving no indication of his plans. Bree grabbed her backpack with her tablet sticking out and said something about Wi-Fi being available only in the Lodge. I wondered if she was going to have her husband wake up the kids so she could read them a bedtime story.

Lucinda and I were the only ones left. "What do I do with the information about Olivia?" I said.

"You could pass it on to Lieutenant Borgnine," Lucinda offered.

I shook my head with a decided motion. "Not unless I have proof she killed Edie. Otherwise it feels disloyal. And I thought of a reason why Olivia might not have touched her wine. She knew she was going to take a sleeping pill and she knew they didn't mix." I thought over what I had just said, but it didn't make me feel much better.

"I suggest we let it rest and adjourn to my room." Lucinda got up and stretched. I grabbed my bag and we went down the first-floor hall toward her room. I avoided looking at the housekeeping carts blocking Edie's room.

Lucinda flipped on the lights and collapsed on the narrow twin bed under the window. Once again when I looked around the sparse room I thought of an old dormitory room or maybe something from a camp. Certainly not a hotel room. No soft mattress cover or mound of pillows or any hint of luxury. And yet it was the perfect room for someone going on a retreat. Weren't you supposed to be stepping away from the world to a simpler place?

My friend motioned for me to sit, and I took the other twin bed. All of a sudden Lucinda leaned back and started waving her feet in the air until her Cole Haan sneakers went flying off her feet and landed in different corners of the room.

"I've wanted to do that for a long time," she said with a giggle. "Tag would have a fit and probably be scrambling to put the shoes in a perfect parallel position under the bed. I know I should be upset about Edie, but I have to say I am really enjoying this weekend. Kris is brilliant the way she came up with an individual project for each of us. It's just a little more than the first day and already I can purl." Lucinda pulled out the square she'd started and waved it in front of me. "Look, I'm doing the stockinette stitch."

She reached into my bag and took out the little bit I'd done on my square and pointed out the difference between the two.

"Now I get it," I said, noting that mine was the same on both sides, with rows of ridges and rows of smooth, but with hers, each side was completely different. One side was all smooth and one was all ridges.

Lucinda leaned against the wall and stretched out her legs on the bed before starting the next row. She seemed to enjoy messing up the bedspread with her stocking feet and knitting with abandon. "You don't know what it's like living in such precise order. If I did this at home, Tag would be straightening the bedspread as fast as I mussed it."

"All I can say is thank heavens my aunt hired Kris for this weekend. Too bad she won't be doing the retreats anymore. But then I guess it isn't my concern anyway, since this is my first, last and only retreat."

"These Petit Retreats must have been a lot of work for her. You have to remember, it's a job to her. It sounds like the Retreat in a Box thing is definitely a step up. What a great idea," Lucinda said. She repeated what Kris had said about being able to go into a yarn or hobby store and by filling out a questionnaire, have a project custom designed for you. "Aren't computers amazing?" Lucinda said. "I'll probably be one of her first customers."

I didn't say anything, but if Kris was depending on my business for her Retreat in a Box, she was going to be in trouble. I would work on the project she gave me, but then I planned to hang up my needles.

Eventually we ended up talking about Olivia again and whether she was really a suspect. "I think so," Lucinda said. "We know she has something on her mind. We know that Edie said one of her stick-her-foot-in-her-mouth comments to her. Maybe Olivia was like a rubber band pulled too tight and Edie's comment made her snap."

"And somehow she got the sleeping pills in Edie's wine, so when she got Edie back to her room she could smother her with ease." I finished saying it and realized what I'd said. "Eeww, what an awful thought."

But I needed to know more about Olivia to figure out if

that scenario could be true. Then I thought of my aunt's papers for the retreat. I had been carrying her purple file like it was some kind of shield, and only recently had I tucked it into the recycled plastic tote bag I'd found for the yarn and needles. I pulled it out and opened it, thumbing through the pages until I found the one marked *Olivia Golden*.

I had read through the sheets before the retreat and again as I was greeting people, but it was different now that I'd gotten to know everyone. I found Olivia's sheet, hoping for some kind of clue, but it was as empty as I remembered it. Just bare-bones information, and it said the trip was a gift, but not from who.

"Maybe if we find out who gave the trip to her, it might help," I said. I put the sheet back in and thumbed through the rest of the pages before closing the file. At the back, I found two pages had gotten stuck together. The top one was Bree's information, but I hadn't seen the other piece of paper before. It was filled with my aunt's distinctive handwriting and seemed to be notes of a sort. She had listed the group and written strings of words that must have made sense to her but seemed cryptic to me. Like after Scott's, it said, *BBB*.

"Look, here's your name," I said. I pointed it out, and next to it was *#344*. When I took it back, I swallowed hard when I saw my name was on the list, too.

I read over what it said. *S&SS*. "What does that mean, and why is my name on the list?"

Lucinda sighed. "Your aunt talked me into the retreat. I bet she planned to do the same with you. Whatever S&SS means, I'm sure it was something nice. You know she loved you."

I am not a crybaby, I repeated in my head as I felt my eyes beginning to well up. I tried to will the water back, but it kept coming. In an effort to hold back the dam, I avoided looking at my name on the list and checked what she'd written next to Edie's. *2 at 1*. What did that mean? Olivia's listing just had *lux*.

"I don't know what any of it means," I said to Lucinda, feeling full of regret. "Who am I kidding? I can't take my aunt's place even for this weekend." I put the sheet back in the file, which dislodged a page at the back. I scooped it up and shook my head. "Here are the notes I took from my call with Frank," I said, shaking my head in annoyance at myself. "If I'd had them when I saw Officer Party Hardy, I might have been able to ask him some intelligent questions."

I guess it was the stress, but my eyes got watery again, and before I could push them back, tears started to roll down my cheeks. Embarrassed, I got up to leave, but Lucinda stood next to me and put her arm around my shoulders, which was a little bit of a reach since I was taller than she was. But it didn't matter; the support felt good. She just let me cry, and then when I was done, handed me a tissue.

"Feel better?" she said.

I forced a smile and nodded. It was like after a storm when the ground is still wet but the air is all clear.

I put the sheets back in the file and shut it, noticing that Lucinda was trying to hide a yawn. I realized that while I was a night owl and normally would have just started to bake around now, Lucinda wasn't. I packed up my stuff and wished her a good night.

When I left her room, I instinctively looked down the hall toward the blockade in front of Edie's room. I was surprised to see that the door to her room was open and two men were standing in the doorway. The walls of the hall were dark wood, and the lighting wasn't the brightest, so it was easy for me to disappear into the shadows and ease my way down the hall until I was close enough to hear them.

Even from the back I recognized Kevin St. John. Not only was he the only person wearing a suit in the casual atmosphere of the hotel and conference center, but there was something about his posture. He always stood very tall, and the way he held his head made it seem like he was looking down on all the little people. The man next to him was a little shorter, and there was something rumpled about his appearance.

"I'm sure you'll want to pack up her things," Kevin said, but the man kept staring in the room.

"The cops said she was alone," the man said, "but did you see her with anybody?" Kevin started to explain the retreat, but the man stopped him. "I was thinking about something different. A man," he said.

As much as I would have liked to hear more, I didn't want Kevin St. John to catch me skulking in the hall. I slipped away without making a sound and then crossed into the living room area where we'd been knitting a short time earlier. The fire was down to embers, and all the chairs were empty.

Outside the air was cold and damp, and I zipped up my fleece jacket. There was a constant roar from the ocean just a short distance away. I followed the path back toward the heart of the conference center. I was about to turn onto the driveway that led to the street, when I glanced toward the Lodge. Light was pouring out of the windows, illuminating the area around them. It seemed like a beacon in the quiet darkness of the rest of the place. I was curious to see if anything was going on there and, like a moth, followed the light. I stopped at the first window and looked into the large room that served as a social hall. The table tennis and pool tables were both quiet. In fact, it seemed like the whole room was quiet except for the person manning the registration desk. Then I saw Bree. She was hunched into the corner of a couch in the sitting area. She had her arms wrapped around herself as if she were trying to hold herself together. Her tablet was sitting on the coffee table in front of her, but the screen was dark.

I wasn't sure where my responsibility for the group ended, but after what happened with Edie, it seemed better to err on the side of overdoing it. I went inside and walked up to her.

"What's wrong? Did your kids claim your husband is making them sleep in the doghouse?" I said, trying to lighten the moment. It didn't work, and her eyes got big and round as she looked around the empty room.

"I'm afraid to go to my room. I'm afraid to stay in there all alone. What if I'm next?" She looked like she might start to sob at any second. I wanted to tell her there wasn't some mad murderer on the loose and that it was personal to Edie, but the truth was, I didn't know for sure. She repeated the whole story of how she'd never gone anyplace alone before, never stayed in a hotel room alone, that she was supposed to come with another of the Ewes, but she'd canceled.

"I didn't sleep a wink last night and that was before . . ." Her voice trailed off.

"C'mon," I said, reaching out my hand. "I'll walk you to your room and make sure everything is okay." I watched her shoulders relax as she put her tablet in her bag and prepared to leave.

She hung on to my arm as we walked back to the Sand and Sea building. When we got to the hall, the housekeeping carts were still on duty, but the door at the end of the hall was shut and the whole area was silent.

I walked Bree to her room and pointed out that she had people from the retreat as neighbors. But it did no good. She hung on to me even when we were inside her room. It was only when I offered to stay until she fell asleep that she finally let go. I sat on the other twin bed while she changed into her sleepwear.

"All this is easy for you," she said. "You're used to living alone. You don't have to worry about your kids forgetting who you are when your husband starts acting like Peter Pan and they all have too much fun."

I let out a little laugh. "It really isn't easy for me," I began. Why not tell her the truth. "You have your life together. You have a family and a group of people you knit with. I bet you have no trouble finishing things you begin."

Bree seemed surprised by what I said. "Of course I finish things. You have to with kids. And all the Ewes finish the projects we start."

Then I told her my whole story. How I had trouble sticking with anything. "Even this weekend. This is outside of my comfort zone, but I am doing it because of my aunt." Bree hugged me and thanked me for sharing. She said she'd thought I had everything so together. Ha, that was a laugh and a half. It seemed to make her feel better, and then I did something that surprised even me. I suggested we work on our squares together.

She sat next to me, and we took out our knitting. It was quiet except for the soft clicking of our needles. The repetitive motion and the silence melded together, and I felt the tension of the day leave as my eyes started to grow heavy and finally closed.

16

I AWOKE WITH A START, CONFUSED ABOUT MY surroundings and the fact that I was sitting up. It took a moment for the mental fog to clear, and when I saw Bree's blond frizz of curls against my shoulder, it all came back to me. I checked the window and saw that it was just getting light. I got up carefully and then laid her down and covered her with the blanket from the other bed. She was in such a deep sleep, she didn't even stir.

Outside, misty fog was floating in, blurring the edges of the dark wood buildings. The street was empty, but still I looked both ways, thinking of my aunt. She had been hit just about this time of day. As I dashed across the street, I glanced toward Dane's. No cars this time. Party over.

Thinking of my bed and catching a little more sleep, I started up my driveway. The silence was broken by the rhythm of footsteps.

"Morning, neighbor," Dane said. I turned toward the voice. He came up the driveway behind me and started running in place. His pace began to slow, and he said something about cooling down. He wore black shorts, a gray T-shirt stained with sweat and sneakers. The bare arms and legs made me shiver, but he seemed fine despite the chilly outside temperature.

How could he party all night and then be off jogging at dawn and look so good? Did I really say that even in my head? Okay, there was no denying that he was hot looking. But it was more than looks. There was something about the vibe he gave off. I stopped my thoughts before they could go further. This was Mr. Party Hardy, I reminded myself.

"All quiet on the retreat front?" He gave me a once-over and mentioned I was still wearing the same clothes. I instinctively patted my hair, and it felt like it might be sticking up all over my head.

"You're just who I wanted to see," I said, remembering the sheet of notes from my conversation with my old boss. I would seize the moment. Of course he misunderstood my comment and turned on the flirty charm.

"Really?" he said with a big grin.

"I wanted to ask you some things about the investigation of Edie Spaghazzi's death." I watched as his cocky smile deflated, a little. "I realized that the door to her room was locked when we got there, so I wondered how somebody got in. And was there a sign of a struggle?"

His grin ramped up again. "This is for your Nancy Drew business, huh?" He seemed to be considering what to say for a moment before he continued. "You really don't need to worry about the case. Lieutenant Borgnine was a big-city investigator before he came here. I'm sure he has all the bases covered." I thought he was going to end it there and not give me any info, but he shrugged to himself and talked on. "But I suppose there's no reason you can't know." He glanced up and down the street and seemed concerned. "It's kind of confidential, though. I'm not sure we should be discussing this out in the street." He nodded toward my place with a question in his eye.

I wanted the information, so I guessed I was going to have to play his game. He followed me up the driveway and into the guesthouse. As soon as he closed the door behind him, he unabashedly began checking out the place. The way he looked around, you'd think it was a crime scene. He caught me staring at him. "Sorry for being so nosy, but I was curious to see what your aunt did with the space, since my garage is similar."

"No mirrors on the ceiling here," I said, trying to keep the sarcasm out of my voice. But since he'd offered me spaghetti at his place, it seemed rude not to offer him something, particularly since I wanted to pick his brain. "So how about some coffee or something?" I said as he moved his snooping to what went for a kitchen.

"I see Joan put in an all-in-one unit."

"Is that what it's called?" I said, watching as he opened every door on what I called my kitchen. It was very compact but had all the essentials and according to him was actually all connected. There was a counter with a refrigerator below it, a small stove on one end, a sink in the middle, two cabinets above and a microwave mounted over the counter area. I had brought in a three-level cart to hold my baking equipment, which seemed an odd mix with the stripped-down kitchen.

"For someone who does all that cooking, you don't have much in the way of supplies," he said as he opened the cabinets.

"Baking. I do baking. And I don't do most of it here," I said.

He opened the refrigerator, saying he was curious how much it held. When he opened the freezer compartment, he pulled out a frozen entrée. "You eat frozen dinners?"

"I don't have the way with tomato sauce you do," I said, taking the ziti entrée out of his hand and putting it back in before shutting the door.

"Would you like some coffee and oatmeal?" I said, finally. I opened the cabinet and took out a box of instant oatmeal, and he wrinkled his nose.

"Cooking the real stuff only takes a few minutes longer," he said. He grabbed my hand and led me back toward the door. "I'll answer any questions you want, but over a decent breakfast."

Was I really letting him take me back to his place? Anything to get the necessary information.

We went in through his kitchen. Whatever had gone on the night before, he'd cleared up the evidence. Not a dirty dish in the sink or a soaking pot on the stove. It was surprising how homey his kitchen was for a guy, and a party hardy guy at that. He refused my offer of help and told me to sit at the table.

Within a few minutes, he'd made oatmeal from scratch, coffee and fresh-squeezed orange juice. He set a bowl of the steamy cereal in front of me. I was surprised to see it dotted with butter and sprinkled with walnuts and raisins. He picked up a bottle on the table and drizzled a little maple syrup over the top, announcing as he did that it was the real kind that came from trees.

"How'd you become such an accomplished cook and homemaker?" I asked, gesturing toward his well-appointed kitchen.

"Is that the question you wanted to ask me?" he said in a teasing voice as he slid into the seat next to me.

I rocked my head with frustration. Why was he making this so hard? I rolled my eyes at him, and he laughed and urged me to eat while the oatmeal was hot. It was delicious, so delicious I was tempted to swoon as I ate it, but I didn't, sure that he would take that as some kind of response to his company.

"So, what's the information you want?" he said as I scraped the last of the oatmeal from the bowl.

I debated whether I should tell him about the list of things to consider Frank had given me but decided to leave it out. Why tell him any more than I had to? I'd already spent too much time. Now it was just get the information and get out of there. Even if the coffee was delicious and the strong brew just what my brain needed.

"I noticed that the door to Edie's room was locked when I got there . . ."

"And you want to know how we think the killer got in," he said. I noticed that he'd begun to say *we*, even if the real investigator was Lieutenant Borgnine. "There was no sign of forced entry, so it looks like Ms. Spaghazzi let the person in."

"Do you know if Lieutenant Borgnine thinks she struggled with the assailant?" I was pretty impressed with my word choice. It made me sound almost professional. Dane reacted with a grin on his angular face.

"You're getting the terms down, huh? No, it doesn't seem like she struggled. The only thing we found under her fingernails was yarn fibers from her knitting." He paused as though he was thinking about saying more.

"And . . . ?" I encouraged.

"And it's kind of odd, because the natural tendency when someone puts a pillow over your face is to fight."

"How about this? She was so out of it from the wine and sleeping pills, she didn't know what was happening to her?"

Dane seemed a little perturbed. "A possibility. You might be getting carried away with this Nancy Drew stuff."

"What about the knitting needles?" I tried to sound very casual. "Any idea where they came from?"

"Nancy, you're falling down on the job. The woman was there for your knitting retreat. There was a cloth bag in her room with yarn and several sets of needles." He waited a beat for emphasis. "Ta-da, I think it seems like a safe deduction they were hers and the killer just helped themselves."

So, he didn't know that Lieutenant Borgnine wasn't so sure that the needles had belonged to Edie. Or was it part of some setup? "Don't you cops have some kind of gut reaction that points you to who did it?" I said. It was an attempt to see if they had Olivia in their sights. He pushed his empty bowl away and picked up his mug.

"I'm not sure I should disclose that," he said.

I tried all the hair twirling and eyelash batting I could muster, but he didn't budge, and I was running out of time. I started to take my bowl and juice glass to the sink, but he told me he'd take care of it, and I thanked him for the breakfast.

Realizing he'd never answered my question about how he'd learned his homemaking skills, I brought it up again. But he just changed the subject.

"You showed me yours," he said, vaguely gesturing in the direction of my place. "I'd be glad to show you mine." His garage studio was clearly visible through the window over the sink. "I have mirrors all over the place, and the whole floor is soft and cushy."

Eewww!

17

AFTER LEAVING DANE'S I'D GRABBED A SHORT NAP
and a fast shower. When I came outside, I looked around for
the black cat, but there was no sign of it. Even so, I set down
a dish with some yogurt just in case it came by. As I sprinted
across the street, I saw the van from Channel 3 pulling up
outside the gate to Vista Del Mar. The same reporter I'd seen
on TV the night before jumped out and stepped in front of
me as I tried to pass. Her cameraman got out of the other
side with his camera loaded on his shoulder.

"Could I have a word?" she said. She was doing a good
job of blocking my path, and I didn't have much of a choice.
The wheels in my head were whirring with everything I
shouldn't say. When she asked me my name, I almost said,
"No comment."

"Everybody is being very close-lipped about the investigation," the reporter said after she'd gotten my name. "Can

you tell us what the mood is like inside Vista Del Mar? Are the guests worried there is a killer on the loose?"

I turned on a smile and said that in general murders were committed by people who knew the victim, so most of the guests didn't seem concerned. I started to walk away, but she walked with me.

"I understand some double-pointed knitting needles are a key clue to the case. Do you have anything to say about that?"

"No comment," I said, moving away. She tried to follow me and ask me more questions, but as I entered the driveway and the Vista Del Mar grounds, it was as if she'd hit an invisible door and stopped.

As I kept walking, I replayed my conversion with Dane from earlier in the morning and realized much of the information was like an arrow pointing right at Olivia. There was no forced entry, because Olivia could have walked right into the room with Edie. And no struggle because Olivia could have just waited until Edie passed out to do her work with the pillow. The fact that Olivia was missing sleeping pills looked even more suspicious.

As I reached the center of Vista Del Mar, I passed a group following a man in a khaki camp shirt. From the tidbit of his spiel I heard, I figured it was some kind of nature walk. Another group, all in yellow T-shirts that said *Alpine Esoteric Society*, headed up the path toward a meeting room. Two kids carrying pails ran ahead of their parents in search of the boardwalk that led to the beach.

To all of them, this was a normal Saturday morning, and murder wasn't on their minds. I must admit, Kevin St. John had done a good job of handling things about Edie discreetly.

I was sure there were probably some guests who knew someone had died, but no one seemed concerned, let alone panicky. Well, except for my group.

"There you are," Lucinda said as I walked to the group's
table in the dining hall just as they were finishing breakfast.
"I tried your cell phone, the landline and sent you an email."
She got up and hugged me. "I'm so glad to see you. When
I couldn't reach you, I was afraid . . ." She didn't have to say
the rest. I got what she meant. She thought I'd been victim
number two.

I hugged her back and apologized. "I'll explain in a minute," I said, noting that she was perfectly coordinated as
usual. The black slacks and loose teal blue silk top were
elegantly casual. I felt my lips to see if I'd remembered to
put some lip balm on as I noted her subtle but complete
makeup job. Not a surprise—in my haste I'd forgotten.

I'd turned my phone to silent when I was sitting next to
Bree as she was falling asleep. I hadn't been home to answer
the landline and had been in too much of a hurry to check
emails.

Bree was out of her chair a moment later. She hugged me
like a long-lost friend. "Thank you for sitting with me last
night."

Melissa's head shot up. "What is she talking about? Is it
something about Edie?" I wondered if I should say anything.
Would Bree be embarrassed? Apparently not, because she
stepped in and told the group about what I'd done. Kris put
down her coffee cup and looked at me with an approving
smile.

"And you were worried about being in charge," Lucinda
said, stepping close and dropping her voice.

"What a nice thing to do," Sissy said from across the table. I had a feeling it had been her idea to sit across the table from her mother. The moment was interrupted as Bree dropped her cell phone on the table with a thud.

"Hanging on to it and staring isn't going to make it ring," Olivia said, pushing the phone toward Bree.

Olivia had a plate of untouched food in front of her. After the phone episode, she went back to eavesdropping on a family sitting at the next table. Olivia was leaning so far back in her chair, I was afraid she might go over backward. Whatever was going on didn't seem to be pleasing Olivia. Her mouth was pursed, which made her brows furrow. The odd part was, the family seemed to be having a good time.

And even though Scott was sitting at another table, he actually lifted his hand in a greeting to me. Maybe he was making progress. Though I doubted his table companions would have guessed that the man in the lime green polo shirt had a bunch of knitting stuff in the briefcase at his feet. I looked around for the elusive Michael so I could point him out to Melissa and Lucinda, but he wasn't there.

I wanted to tell Lucinda about my breakfast with Dane, but not in front of the others. Instead I grabbed the thermal pot and poured myself a cup of coffee before taking one of the empty chairs.

"There's something we need to talk about," Melissa said. Her tone of voice made it sound like some kind of problem, and I felt myself girding for it. "Because of Edie's . . ." Melissa started, but she caught herself before she said *death*. "Because of everything with her, we missed out on the morning workshop and none of us were really functioning that well for the afternoon one. I know I shouldn't be thinking about things like our workshop when she's lying on a slab somewhere, but still." She let it hang in the air.

It hadn't occurred to me that the missed time would be a problem. But now that she mentioned it, I saw how it was. Between going with us to find Edie and then being questioned by the police, Kris had been gone for just about the whole session. And she was the workshop. The whole point was that she was supposed to be there to help them.

"I'm sorry," Kris said with a shrug. "It wasn't by choice. I would have much preferred to be with you in the meeting room." It seemed like her attitude was that it was over with and, given the circumstances, the group should just accept they'd lost that time with her.

Melissa didn't say anything, but her expression did. She wasn't happy with what Kris had said.

"There must be something I can do to make it up," I said. I was thinking off the top of my head. "What if I talk to Kevin St. John and see if instead of having our last workshop Sunday morning, we can have the room for Sunday afternoon as well?" I looked toward Kris. At first I didn't think she liked the idea. The way things stood now, she would be finished after the morning workshop and could head home to Santa Cruz while the group was having their last lunch. Maybe it was the pressure of having everyone staring at her with hopeful expressions, but she finally smiled and nodded.

"Certainly, if you can get the room, I'll stay," she said.

Someone pointed out that Kevin St. John had just come into the dining room. "And look who he's with," Olivia said with a groan.

Kevin St. John was standing just inside of the door of the dining hall with Lieutenant Borgnine and the rumpled-looking man I'd seen the night before. All three of them were staring at me, and then they turned and went outside. As always, the manager was wearing an impeccable dark suit, and the almost no-neck police lieutenant had the same jacket I'd seen him in before.

I was pretty sure the rumpled man was Edie's husband. I rushed after the trio, caught up with them outside and heard the tail end of their conversation.

"I realize this is very hard for you," Kevin St. John said in a solicitous manner. "As I told you last night when you arrived, we'll do anything we can to make this time easier for you. I'm so sorry about the room. I thought it had been taken care of." The three men all turned toward me as I stopped next to them. I was going to introduce myself, but Kevin St. John beat me to it.

"This is Casey Feldstein," Kevin St. John said to the rumpled man. "She's the one in charge of your late wife's retreat now." Let's just say that the manager's tone was full of reproach.

I put out my hands and took one of his in both of mine. "I'm so sorry for your loss. Edie was a special woman." I was close enough to get a good look at him. He was on the tall side and had longish black hair. I'd call his looks ordinary, the kind of guy you would have a hard time picking out of a crowd. The clothes didn't help. He wore a plaid shirt over black cotton pants and a beige bomber-style jacket that looked like he'd sat on it.

The man seemed a little surprised by my gesture. "Lou Spaghazzi," he said in a gravelly voice. "So you're the one in charge. How could you have let something happen to my Edie?" Behind him I could see Kevin nodding his head and giving me a disparaging look.

"I'm so sorry," I said. "We're trying to find out what happened and who is responsible," I said. Kevin's eyes bugged out at my comment, and he gave me a disparaging shake of his head this time.

"Don't worry, the investigation isn't up to some amateur sleuth," Lieutenant Borgnine interjected. "The Cadbury police are on top of the situation, and I am sure we will have the guilty party identified before the weekend's end."

"That's tomorrow," Lou said with a disbelieving tone. He looked at me. "I know Edie loved these knitting things, but I think there was something more. Maybe you know something. Did you see her with a man?" he asked.

What was I going to say? I had seen her talking to a man who I was pretty sure was Michael. He'd claimed they had some kind of vague acquaintanceship. He might or might not have been Edie's dinner companion at the Blue Door, and he may or may not have been the man Melissa had seen her talking to. Personally, I thought what Michael had said about their relationship was bogus and that he'd been the man with Edie on all those occasions, but I wasn't sure. And why upset Lou Spaghazzi any further?

Finally, I said that as far as I knew all she came to Cadbury for was the knitting. Lieutenant Borgnine seemed to be listening to my comment, then he turned to Edie's husband.

"If you can think of anything else, let me know." The two men shook hands, and the lieutenant left us. Kevin St. John said Lou was going to pack up Edie's things.

"I'm going to accompany him. A man shouldn't have to

do something like that alone." There was more reproach in Kevin St. John's voice aimed toward me. "Someone truly in charge knows things like that and handles them accordingly." I got it. Not only was he making it sound like it was my fault Edie was dead, but I was handling everything poorly.

Thank heavens it was already Saturday. Just one more day of dealing with him. I paused, thinking of the business about asking for the meeting room for the afternoon. It didn't seem the best time to bring it up.

I could practically hear my aunt's voice telling me to step in and help Lou with the packing up. "It's so nice of you to have handled this so far," I said to Kevin St. John in such a sickeningly sweet voice it was making me nauseous. "But I will take over from here."

No surprise, the hotel manager wasn't happy with my comment and reluctantly backed away.

I didn't think Lou cared if anyone accompanied him, and we walked in silence to the Sand and Sea building. As we went inside, I said we should have gotten a key.

He held up the key in his hand. "Mr. St. John gave me Edie's key." He started to walk ahead of me. "I can handle this myself."

"I'm sure you can, but it will be easier if you're not alone. Do you know what happened to the other key?" I said, remembering the point she'd made when she registered that she wanted two keys.

Lou turned back to look at me. "He just gave me one."

I dreaded seeing the room again, remembering my first view the day before and, well, the smell, which by now I figured would have only gotten worse. He opened the door and walked in ahead of me. The first thing I noticed was that it now smelled like bleach and cleaner. The bed had been stripped, and the pillow was gone. Evidence, maybe. A cleaning crew must have come in once the cops released it, because there wasn't even a hint of the red puddle that had been on the floor. Frankly, I was relieved.

I tried to make conversation as he went through the room picking up Edie's things. But he was acting almost as if I weren't there. He seemed to be looking for something as he ruffled through the items on the dresser. I tried not to be too obvious that I was watching him. Finally, he picked up her cell phone but made some disparaging sound as he tried to turn it on. It looked to me like it had been stepped on. He threw it in the suitcase with the rest of her things.

"I guess that's it," he said, looking around the room. I walked him back outside through the grounds to a small parking lot near the Lodge. He put the suitcase in the trunk.

He looked down at the ground. "Thank you for coming with me," he said. "Having someone there did make it easier." I felt for the man. He seemed to be struggling. Or was it just an act?

I asked him if he was driving back to L.A., but he shook his head. "I'm not leaving until Edie's killer is caught," he said. He got into his blue Ford Focus and pulled out of the parking spot in a hurry. He was already down the driveway before I'd walked away. I noticed a card on the ground that must have fallen out when he got in. When I examined it, I realized it was one of those folders hotels use to hold plastic key cards. It was empty, but when I turned it over I saw the logo of the Lighthouse Inn.

Why wasn't he staying at Vista Del Mar?

18

I STOPPED IN THE LODGE BEFORE I WENT TO MEET up with the group. Kevin St. John was holding court with some guests, telling them the history of the place and how it was truly a step back into a more peaceful time. He didn't appear happy to see me, but that seemed to have become a given. I waited until the group headed outside before approaching him.

I had two things to ask him and didn't think he'd want to answer either of them, but there was no choice.

"Everything went fine with Lou Spaghazzi," I began, trying to smooth the way.

Kevin St. John nodded and repeated that he could have handled it. "The only reason we brought him in the dining hall was that he wanted to meet the person his wife had talked so much about." The manager flicked a bit of lint off his sleeve. "I didn't realize until too late that he meant your aunt."

Now it was a time for my questions. I couldn't stall, because he'd merely walk away. "I noticed that you gave Lou only one key, but didn't Edie have two?"

Kevin St. John looked perturbed. "Not that it is any of your business, but I gave Mr. Spaghazzi the key the cops found in her room and gave back to me."

I sputtered and said I was sure that Edie had asked for two.

"Really?" Kevin St. John said. "In the interest of settling this quickly . . ." He waved for me to follow him behind the counter. He motioned to the hooks that went with the rooms in Sand and Sea and pointed to 103, which had been Edie's room. A key was hanging from the hook. "Mr. Spaghazzi has the other one for the rest of the weekend since the room is paid for."

What? I knew I wasn't crazy. I'd heard Edie ask for two keys. Well, I now knew how the murderer could have gotten into her room. They must have lifted one of her keys—not a problem since I saw her put it in her sweater pocket and she tended to drape it over the back of the chair in the dining hall. Then whoever had done so just brought it back here. And who had the easiest access but the man glaring at me? I realized it was useless information on its own. No one would believe me, anyway.

"Was there something else, Casey?" Kevin St. John said when I didn't walk away. I brought up extending the retreat through Sunday afternoon and explained why.

He took his time thinking about it. Then he surprised me by saying yes. He picked up on my surprise. "I'm doing it for the reputation of retreats at Vista Del Mar," he said curtly, then turned his back, making it clear our moment was over.

I'd already missed the beginning of the workshop, but at least I was bringing good news.

They all looked up when I came in, and I told them right away about the extra workshop. They surprised me by giving me a mini round of applause.

I was glad to see that they were all working on their projects. I'd decided the correct title for Kris was workshop leader. A pair of knitting needles and something royal blue was on the table in front of her. When she wasn't helping anyone with their project, she spent the time on her own project. She'd explained at the beginning of the weekend that she was making a cardigan sweater for her daughter.

She had barely talked about her family at all, or her personal life. Just a passing remark about being a single parent with two teenagers. I couldn't imagine what that was like. I found it hard enough to just take care of me.

Kris pointed to my seat and urged me to get going, reminding me that there was no workshop in the afternoon. When I looked puzzled, her face lit up in a perky smile. "You didn't forget the yarn tasting, did you?" They all laughed when they saw my stricken response.

"Don't worry, your aunt made all the arrangements, down to the van driving us into town," Kris said.

I picked up the tiny bit of scarf I'd made so far. It looked pathetic when compared to the progress the rest of them had made. I felt even worse when I saw the stack of finished squares everyone had turned in. Mine was a lost cause. There was no way I would have it finished in time to give it to Kris. I would stick with the scarf. I began to work my needles.

Melissa was standing next to Kris, and they were poring over the black-and-white scarf Melissa was making. It was pretty impressive to see the houndstooth pattern come out of the combination of the two yarns, though apparently there was a mistake somewhere.

"Did you make that?" Melissa said, touching the heathery gray sweater Kris had on over a pair of tan cargo pants. I suppose I shouldn't have been surprised when Kris nodded. Melissa watched as Kris expertly unknitted until she reached the problem. As Melissa took back her project, she asked for the pattern of the shawl the workshop leader had worn the first night, saying it looked like just the thing to work on when she was watching television. I looked at my strip of scarf again and thought about how out of their league I was.

Scott was the only one of the group who didn't seem to need any help, but then his mountain to climb had nothing to do with cables or two-color knitting, but was just about outing himself. I envied the bliss on his face as his needles clicked away.

Melissa sat down and turned to her daughter. "You don't have to bother Kris if you have trouble with your cables. I can help you." Sissy rolled her eyes so far up in her head, I thought they were going to disappear.

Olivia had really taken off with the cashmere yarn, and the sparkly purple shawl was coming along nicely. I couldn't believe how fast they all knitted. I seemed to be moving at a snail's pace.

Lucinda went up to Kris after Melissa had finished. My friend seemed to be having trouble figuring out whether she was supposed to start a row with a knit or a purl stitch.

I was surprised when Scott joined the two women. "I think I can help," he said. He demonstrated on his work. His yarn was so big and the stitches so obvious it was easy to see the bumps and smooth spots. Lucinda got it right away, and he seemed pleased.

"I wish I could teach my own daughter how to knit," he said, and his shoulders slumped. "But if I did, well, then everybody would know."

"What's so bad about that?" Melissa said. Scott hung his head.

"I know what Kris said about sailors knitting, but I don't think my wife would buy that. And you don't understand. I'm a regional manager of the Sandwich King chain. If the people under me knew, they'd . . ." He shook his head. "I don't think they'd respect me. They'd think I was some kind of goofball. And as for my boss. Ha," he said. "If he knew, I could just kiss that promotion good-bye." He looked at all of us. "C'mon, you have to see what I mean." He picked up his needles and started a row. "I look weird, right?"

I was surprised when Olivia was the one to speak. "Not weird. Just surprising. I don't get why it's anybody's business that you knit. Your wife, well, yes, but why do the people under you and your boss have to know about it?"

"You're saying that because you think it really is weird that I knit," he said. "Edie thought it was weird that I wouldn't tell anybody. Every time I went to her house, she worked on me to be up front about it. The thing about Edie is that sometimes she pushed things too hard."

Melissa joined in. "It's not the usual thing men do. You could look at it as being special. What do you think, Bree? What if your boys wanted to learn how to knit?" All eyes turned to her. She'd been looking at the table, staring at her work. When she looked up, tears were rolling down her cheeks. "My boys," she said in a warbly voice. "I called and

176

they didn't want to talk to me. They were in a hurry to go out on some adventure my husband cooked up for them." She stopped. "If they don't need me, then who am I?" She did her best to swallow back her tears. "Sure I'd teach them to knit if they even remember who I am when I come home."

It was a relief that when the workshop ended, they could all go to their rooms and have a little free time before lunch. Lucinda hung back and we found a bench on the boardwalk that gave us some privacy.

"Tell me everything," she said.

I did an information dump on her, and by the end her mouth was hanging open. Of all the things she could have commented on, she brought up Dane.

"I knew he liked you," she said with a devilish smile.

"He likes everybody. I'm not interested in being one of a crowd. I can only imagine what kind of stuff goes on in his *studio*." I turned the subject back to Edie's murder. I asked Lucinda if she remembered Edie asking for two keys, and then I told her why I was asking.

"To be honest, I don't remember. And even if she did, it's not that hard to get behind the counter in the Lodge. Anybody could have slipped back there and hung up the key."

"Gee, thanks, just when I thought I had something to show that Kevin St. John killed Edie."

"Don't you just wish," Lucinda said. "What about Edie's husband?"

"I don't know what the story is about him. I'm not sure if he's the grieving husband or he's just trying to make it look that way." As I said that, I took out my cell phone and called the Lighthouse Inn. "I have a hunch."

I used what I'd learned from working for Frank. The first

thing to do was make friends with the person you wanted the information from. It was easy with the woman who answered for the Inn because she was bored and happy to talk to somebody. I fudged a little bit and said that I worked at the Blue Door and that I was in charge of reservations and thought I'd made a mistake. "We have a reservation for a Lou Spaghazzi. He gave the Inn as a contact number. The trouble is I'm new and I got things mixed up and I can't tell if it was really an old reservation for Thursday night or if it's for tonight."

I got a little nervous when she offered to ring his room. "If you don't mind, I'd rather he didn't know I was so inefficient. If he said something to my boss, it could be my job," I said in a confidential manner. "You know how it is. You make one little mistake and you're out the door. In this case, the blue one," I said, trying to make a joke.

Lucinda was watching it all incredulously.

She was very sympathetic and asked me what she could do to help. "Could you tell me when he checked in?" I said, trying to sound casual. "If he didn't check in until Friday, he wouldn't have had a reservation for dinner on Thursday, now would he?"

"That's nothing. Hang on," she said. A moment later, she came back on the line. "The reservation must be for tonight because I see he checked in on Friday," she said. She stopped abruptly, and I heard her saying, "Hmm," as she seemed to be checking something. "This is kind of odd. Someone checked in on Thursday for one night and listed the same license plate number." I asked her what the name was. "Lance Sloan," she answered. "Maybe whoever checked them in got the plate number wrong." She said, "Hmm," again and then mentioned that Lance had paid cash.

"Thanks, you're a lifesaver," I said. When I clicked off the phone, Lucinda acted mock-indignant.

"I had no idea I was such a tough boss," she said with a laugh in her tone. Her smile changed to openmouthed stunned when I repeated the conversation. "Lance Sloan," I said, with a knowing nod. "People tend to keep the same initials when they give fake names. It's obvious he checked in for one night as Lance and then after he'd gotten the call from Lieutenant Borgnine checked in as himself so it would look like he just got there," I said. "Well, it's official. Lou Spaghazzi is a suspect. As for motive, he seemed crazed that Edie was meeting someone up here."

"But she kind of was," Lucinda said. "There was the guy I saw her having dinner with and the man Melissa saw her with when she met Joan."

I remembered the picture on her cell phone from the first night and told Lucinda about the man in the baseball cap with the sunset in the background. "What if Edie's husband saw that photo and got suspicious? He could have followed her up here and seen her talking to the guy and gone into a jealous rage," Lucinda said.

"Who would have thought that Edie was juggling men and managed to stir up so many people," I said. "She seemed like such an ordinary woman."

"Looks can deceive," Lucinda replied.

In the distance the lunch bell began to ring. Lucinda stood up. "It's such a treat to let somebody else worry about getting all the food out. Are you coming?"

I shook my head. "I need to take care of some stuff at my place. Will you oversee lunch for me?"

Of course, Lucinda said yes. You can take the woman out of the restaurant, but you can't take the restaurant out of the woman.

I had gotten halfway across the grounds when I crossed paths with Kris. She looked upset about something as she stopped me.

"I'm not sure what to do with this information," she said. "Edie told me that if Scott didn't come clean to his wife by the end of the weekend, she was going to do it for him. I know she meant it in the best of ways, but if he found out, well . . ." She let her voice trail off as I got her drift. "Do you think I should tell Lieutenant Borgnine?"

19

AS LUNCH WAS ENDING, I WAS STANDING OUTSIDE the Lodge with the doors of the white Vista Del Mar van open, waiting for my crew. Though I didn't quite get what a yarn tasting was, I was glad we were all getting out of Vista Del Mar for a while.

The something I had to do while they were eating was to change. I'd dressed in such a hurry in the morning, I hardly looked appropriate to accompany the group on the yarn tasting. I was beginning to understand that as the person in charge, I was supposed to dress like it. I replaced the jeans, T-shirt and fleece jacket with a pair of gray slacks and a black turtleneck. I redid my hair so that it hung smoothly to my shoulders and added a burnt orange cowl I found at my aunt's.

While I was waiting, Lou Spaghazzi went by. He seemed to note the change in my appearance and that I seemed surprised to see him back there. "I'm keeping my eyes on things," he said, gazing around the grounds. "I don't get why Edie wanted to come to this place. The accommodations are about as fancy as a prison cell. With all the dark wood and gloomy weather, this place seems creepy. Like anything could happen here." He stopped to use a toothpick to get something out of his teeth. "I didn't realize that woman Joan was your aunt. Too bad about her accident. I heard some other woman who came to these retreats tripped over the cliff by the water. That's three people dead all within the last six months. It makes you wonder."

The information I'd just gotten certainly did make me wonder about him, and I almost called him Lance to see how he would react, but he was too quick for me and had gone up the path before I could put my thoughts together.

I heard a burst of conversation as Melissa and Sissy arrived with Lucinda. My friend gave me an appraising look and then a thumbs-up. The rest of the group trickled in, including Scott, and everyone climbed in the Vista Del Mar van and we headed for town. I thought back on what Lou had said. To me, Vista Del Mar had always seemed just a little moody, but looking out at it now, I could see his point. There was definitely something slightly sinister about the dark buildings, the grounds left wild and untamed and the waves crashing into the rocky shore.

The van left us off in downtown Cadbury. Being Saturday afternoon, the area was busy with locals and tourists who came from all over. Who could blame them? The Monterey Peninsula was definitely one of the most beautiful spots in the world. And Cadbury by the Sea was a genuinely appealing small town. The main street was called Grand Avenue and lived up to its name. It was wide with a strip of park down the center dividing the two lanes of traffic. It wasn't a beach town, but rather a seaside town, and the water was visible from everywhere. Gulls flew overhead, and now that the clouds had cleared, the light had a special iridescence from the sun mixing with all the salt spray in the air.

I looked at the row of stores in front of me. They were appealing without being cloyingly cute. No "Ye Olde" anything here. It was a tourist destination, but the locals pretended not to notice.

Lucinda stood next to me and looked up the street toward her restaurant. The former house looked inviting with its white siding and blue trim. Window boxes hung at every window with perfectly color-coordinated pansies, thanks to Tag and his fanaticism.

It had only been two nights since I'd done my usual baking, but I missed it. When I went to work, the rest of Cadbury was usually in bed. I liked looking out over the quiet streets as I pulled out the ingredients for the restaurant's desserts. And I capped off the evening with all the batches of muffins. It was my own little world of wonderful smells and delicious outcomes.

Lucinda was looking at the converted house with other things on her mind. "Do you think I should stop in and maybe check on things?" she said. She had scrunched up her face in concern. I grabbed her arm and shook my head.

I led the group around the corner to a side street that sloped down toward the water. The houses were small here. The colorful authentic Victorians were mostly on the other side of Grand Avenue. With their pastel colors, turrets and fish-scale siding they were a treat for the eyes. I was particularly fond of a large one painted buttercup yellow that was a bed-and-breakfast. The Delacorte sisters lived in one of the grandest Victorians at the very top of the slope the town was built on. I'd never been inside, but it was painted a lavender gray and had a lovely private porch on the third level that was supposed to have a view over the top of town down to the water. I'd heard you could sometimes see whales from there as they stopped to feed in Monterey Bay.

Cadbury Yarn was in a converted bungalow. It had an inviting porch with a wicker rocker, along with a rainbow-colored wind sock that blew in the constant breeze. A happy-sounding bell tinkled as the door opened and we filed inside.

All my aunt had said on the schedule was "yarn tasting," and I still didn't know what that meant. I'd only been in the store once, to confirm they had everything ready for the retreat. All I did know was that Gwen and Crystal, the mother-daughter team that owned the yarn store, would handle it and I could just be an observer.

Gwen grabbed Kris in a hug and was effusive about the sweater the master teacher was wearing, but she also seemed to be asking something about a shawl and why she wasn't wearing it. Kris ended the topic with a wave of her hand toward an empty spot off to the side of the room.

"That would be perfect for the kiosk," Kris said before thanking Gwen for being the first store in the area to carry Retreat in a Box.

"It's such a lovely idea," Gwen said. "People come in all the time wanting to make something but with no idea what."

The rest of the group moved from the entranceway into what was probably once the living room of the house. I caught up with them as Crystal was talking to them. I wondered how she got along with her mother since they worked together.

They certainly weren't a matched set. Gwen was old-school Cadbury. Plain, sensible clothes and shoes, minimal jewelry and no makeup. On the other hand, the woman standing before me was wearing jeans with layers of different-colored shirts on top, and two scarves wound around her neck. I laughed when I noticed the unmatched earrings. Why not? One ear had a small hoop and the other a large one. When I looked down at her feet, I saw that she was wearing mismatched colorful socks, too. Her eyes were outlined in black, and her lips were a glossy pink. And she had the hair I'd always wished for. Hers was a puff of short black curls, that looked like tiny Slinkys.

I'd only seen her a few times, but I immediately liked her. Lucinda had filled me in on her story. Crystal had run off with a musician named Ricx Smith. They'd gotten married and moved up to San Francisco. The marriage had lasted long enough for her to have two kids before he took off on some personal journey to find himself, with the help of a young blond. Crystal had moved back to Cadbury and in with her mother and had to deal with endless I-told-you-sos, because of course, her mother, Gwen, had seen the writing on the wall as far as Ricx was concerned from day one.

Ricx? I was guessing that his real name was Rick and the *k* was changed into an *x* to make him sound more like a rock god.

"I was just explaining the yarn tasting," Crystal said, addressing me. "You know how you can taste wine before you buy it? This works the same." She had held up a skein of pretty blue and purple yarn as she spoke. "You can't tell by looking at this what it will look like when you knit with it. Will the colors be stripes or more of a heathery tone or

185

will it be downright awful looking? And what will the yarn be like to work with?" She pulled off a length of it and held up a pair of knitting needles. "So you try it out and find out."

She took the group past the cubbies filled with yarn arranged by color to a room at the back, no doubt once a dining room. A long wood table was surrounded by captain's chairs.

She gestured with her arm—the way Vanna White pointed out letters on *Wheel of Fortune*—to the baskets of yarn available to try and pointed out the selection of needles in old mason jars on the table. "Let the tasting begin," she said, holding up her shears.

I was the only one who held back. The rest were like kids in a candy store.

Scott found a dark blue yarn flecked with bits of white and silver. "I bet my wife would love a scarf made out of this."

"Beautiful, isn't it?" Crystal said, giving her mother a sidelong glance. "I told you these specialty yarns would be a hit." I listened and nodded to myself with understanding, imagining what it would be like if my mother and I had a business together. Crystal undid some of the skein to show him how the yarn changed textures and thicknesses. "If my mother had her way, the whole store would just be plain yarns," Crystal said as she snipped off a long piece for him.

The rest of the group found yarns that pleased them, and Crystal and Gwen cut off lengths for them to try. I was just relieved not to be concerned with everyone's well-being for a few moments. I hung back, never thinking of trying any of the yarn myself. I had enough on my plate with the kit Kris had given me.

Then I caught a glimpse of one of the yarns in the basket and couldn't resist the urge to pick it up. "Dr. Blue's Wild Ride," I said, admiring the unusual yarn I'd first noticed when they'd brought it to the Vista Del Mar gift shop.

"Pretty, isn't it?" Crystal said. "You want to try some?" My first impulse was to say no, but I couldn't seem to put the yarn down. I'd always thought of yarn as being one color, but this kept changing as the strand went on. First it was a fuzzy blue, then it was mixed with some strands of purple metallic and farther up there were sparkles.

"I wouldn't know how to try it," I said, explaining my novice standing.

"I'll show you," Crystal said. She cut off a strand and grabbed a pair of plastic needles out of the jar on the table. Her fingers were almost too quick to follow as she cast on some stitches and began to knit. "You could just do all garter stitch," she said as she zoomed through a row. After a few rows, she handed it to me. "Here, you give it a go," she said. I have to admit that it was pretty cool when I saw how the changing yarn looked when knitted.

"I'm not trying to sell you or anything, but if you buy it and have trouble, you can always come in here and I'll help you."

I brightened at the idea. Maybe it was the fuss with her mother, but I felt like we were kindred spirits.

"Sold," I said when I'd finished with the strand and made a tiny swatch. I followed her as she went to the bin.

"You might be able to get by with three skeins for a scarf, but it's probably better to get four."

I looked at the price on the yarn and suggested I get three now and come back for a fourth if I needed it.

"I'm not trying to push yarn on you, but you want to make sure you have all the same dye lot."

My look gave me away again, and she grabbed a couple of skeins of worsted-weight gray yarn. She showed me the label, and both were called pearl grey, but when she held them next to each other, they were different. One was definitely darker than the other. "Same color but different dye lot. You want all the yarn to have the same number, particularly in any of the hand-dyed yarns we have." She pulled out two more skeins to show how different they were even though they were both lavender sunset.

"Got it," I said, pulling out another skein of Dr. Blue's Wild Ride.

Crystal showed me the right size needles to use. "I might already have this size," I said. "My aunt left me all her knitting supplies."

"If you want I'd be glad to help you figure out what size the needles you have are."

I nodded, appreciative of the offer, and said when the retreat was over, I'd get in touch with her. She scribbled her number on the receipt she'd written up for the yarn.

"How's the retreat going after what happened to Edie?" Crystal said in a low voice. She glanced in the direction of her mother. "Mom thought it was best we didn't say anything about anything, just put on the tasting like nothing happened. I went along with it, but it seems kind of odd. Edie was a force of nature," she said. "You know what she said about my earrings?" Crystal gestured toward the unmatched pair. "She said it was dangerous to throw off symmetry. Dangerous?" She put up her hands at the absurdity of the comment and then began to talk about what she'd heard on Channel 3 News.

"Supposedly Cadbury PD is on the case and are close to naming a suspect."

"Really?" I said and explained I'd been cut off from everything.

"Vista Del Mar will do that to you," she said with a smile. "The supposed charm of the place is that it's like the old days and you can step back from the modern world."

I asked if they'd given any hint to who the suspect was, but she shrugged. "I'm not so sure how on top of things they are. They never found the driver in your aunt's accident, and the whole thing with Amanda Proctor is just weird."

I asked her why. "She came to the yarn tasting your aunt put on, and I talked to her. She was a smart woman. Too smart to be standing on the edge of cliff, knitting. I think either it was suicide or someone pushed her."

Kris grabbed Crystal's arm. "Sorry to interrupt, but some of the others are waiting to get their yarn cut."

I don't know why I felt so annoyed at Kris for interrupting. All she was doing was trying to handle things. The very thing I'd wanted her to do. Did that mean that I wanted the position of leader? I was shocked to realize that I thought I did. I cared that Bree was afraid to be alone. I truly wished Olivia would tell me why she seemed so unhappy. I wanted to help Scott admit to his wife he was a knitter, so he'd be free to follow his passion. And as for Melissa and Sissy, well, I didn't really think there was much I could do besides separating them. I watched them as they tried out the different yarns, fussing the whole time. Finally, Gwen and Crystal went to the old-fashioned glass case that served as the checkout as we formed a line, holding our skeins and supplies.

"Hmm, a lot of you are buying the serendipity yarns," the older woman said.

Crystal gave her mother a knowing nod. What Gwen did next surprised me. She patted her daughter on the shoulder. "You were right. This store needs your touch."

"I hope you'll come back when the kiosk is up," Gwen said to Kris as she rang up her yarn. "I can't wait to see it. Just imagine, it's going to say *Kris Garland's Retreat in a Box*."

Kris blushed, but it was easy to see that she was very pleased at what Gwen had said. "The yarn company is doing a whole promotion with me, but even if they didn't, I'd be sure to come back here."

"Tell us how it works again," Bree said.

"Let's say Casey came in here looking for something to make," Kris began. "She'd go up to the touch screen and answer some questions, and the software would not only figure out the perfect project for her, but generate a pattern and a supply list for the store." Kris gestured toward Gwen. "The store personnel will put together the yarn, needles and other tools, along with instructional DVDs. All of it will be placed in a tote bag like the one you all got." Kris smiled at the finish.

"So it will be just like our workshop," Bree said.

"Not exactly. It's going to be a little more standardized than your projects are."

Lucinda put several skeins of a heathery dark gray wool on the counter so Gwen could ring them up. "I think this would make a great scarf for Tag. He's always saying he's cold." She handed over her credit card and rolled her eyes. "Am I nuts? You know he'll find some mistake I made in the knitting and never let me forget it." She looked at Kris. "What would your computer come up with in a situation like that?"

"A woven scarf from the Pendleton shop," Kris said with a sly laugh.

"I think I'm making the scarf for me," Lucinda said.

When we'd all paid for our purchases and were heading for the door, Gwen came up to me. "I'm sorry Joan isn't here. This was her idea, you know." She patted my shoulder in a reassuring way. "She'd be so happy that you were continuing the tradition." I wanted to tell her this was just a one-time thing, but she seemed so pleased that I'd stepped into my aunt's shoes, I didn't have the heart to tell her.

Afterward, Lucinda led us down the street to the Blue Door restaurant. Tag was busy supervising the setup for dinner, but Lucinda brought the group in anyway. She had everyone sit down and then waltzed in the kitchen and sweet-talked the cook until he made us afternoon tea. Tag looked like he was going to bust a gasket.

20

WHEN THE VAN LET US OFF BACK AT VISTA DEL
Mar, there was free time until dinner. The group all went
their own ways, anxious to try out the yarn they'd just bought.
I wanted to talk to Lucinda about solving Edie's murder, but
she started jumping and trying to click her heels while saying, "Free again. I'm free again." I didn't want to ruin her
buzz and didn't stop her from going back to Sand and Sea
with the others.

I went across to my place to think. Was Crystal right?
Was Cadbury PD going to name a suspect? Who was it?
Kris's question about what to do with the information about
Scott had ended up being rhetorical. She'd walked away
before I had answered. And what did naming a suspect mean
anyway? If anything it seemed like it would tip someone
off it was a good time for them to take a trip to Brazil.

What did I have? It all seemed like a mishmash, and here

it was almost Saturday night. The only thing I could think of was calling my old boss.

"Okay, Feldstein, what is it now?" Frank said. "You do know it's Saturday and two hours later here. You might not have realized it, but I do have a social life."

"Sorry to get in the way of your evening," I said. He was right. I'd never thought of him having a social life, or a life outside the agency. When I'd come into the office and left it, he'd always been reclining in his office chair. I guess I thought he lived there.

I apologized again for the call and started telling him about running out of time and the yarn retreat ending and how I didn't know what to do next. I was just getting to being worried about the night's activities when Frank cut in.

"Okay, Feldstein, I got it. Let's cut to the chase. Give me your list of suspects."

"Well, there's Kevin St. John," I said, and Frank made a groaning noise.

"Feldstein, the names mean nothing to me. You have to tell me who they are. How does this St. John guy fit into the big picture? Is he the husband? Remember, I told you that's always where the cops start—and usually finish."

I started to explain who Kevin St. John was, but Frank stopped me again. "What's his motive, Feldstein?"

"I'm not sure what she said to him, but the dead woman managed to say the wrong thing to just about everybody. But there's something else." I told Frank how Kevin wanted all of my aunt's paperwork about the retreats and that he wanted to put on the future retreats himself. "I've kind of been stalling about handing it over, and he might be worried that I'm going to keep putting on the retreats. What if he killed Edie, I mean the victim, to make me look bad as a retreat leader?"

"I see where you're going, Feldstein. And he stuck those needles in her to make it look like it was one of your knit people. Could be."

"About those needles," I said, feeling uneasy. I told Frank that I was pretty sure the needles stuck in her had been taken from my aunt's. "And there's something else. They probably have my fingerprints on them."

Frank chuckled. "Don't sweat it, Feldstein. You're not in the system. I know because I did a background check on you when you came to work for me. Just don't do anything stupid like agree to give the cops your prints." He paused before continuing. "And don't give them a chance to lift your prints off of something." He went on about how tricky cops could be, picking things out of the trash or grabbing a coffee cup in a restaurant.

I started to say I'd only talked to Lieutenant Borgnine the one time so far and I didn't think there was anything he could take with my prints on it. Then a black thought crossed my mind. "Remember you suggested I flirt with a cop to get information?" I said. I told him how Dane had invited me over for breakfast.

"And probably some nookie, too," Frank said.

"He doesn't need any nookie from me. He turned his garage into an orgy room."

"And . . ." Frank coaxed.

"I offered to put my bowl and juice glass in the sink, but he insisted I leave everything, that he'd clean up."

"And you left your glass on the table, didn't you? Not

good, Feldstein. They're probably matching those prints up as we speak."

"Don't say that, Frank. Dane, the cop, had today off. Maybe he hasn't taken the glass in yet."

"I'd sharpen up those flirting skills and make a quick trip back there. Just a hint, but if you see the glass, I recommend an accident. No prints on a smashed glass."

I sat hugging the phone after we'd hung up. What if the suspect they were going to name was me? Not if I could help it.

I went outside and started down the street toward Dane's. His red Ford 150 truck wasn't in the driveway, and there was just a lone Honda parked at the curb. When I got to his driveway I walked up it with the idea of looking in the window. I had my fingers crossed that I'd see the glass in a plastic bag waiting to be taken in. I had stand on my tiptoes, and the light was low inside, so I pressed my face against the window, trying to see in.

Suddenly the light came on and a woman walked in the kitchen. The first thing I noticed was that she was wearing the pink sweat suit I'd seen the first time I'd been there.

She jumped a little when she saw me but wasn't nearly as startled as I would have expected. She came to the back door and opened it.

"If you're looking for Dane, he isn't here," she said in a nonchalant tone. I tried not to be too obvious as I looked her over. She had red hair. I mean, really red hair. Cherry red, which didn't go well with the pink sweat suit. The heavy makeup didn't go, either. When she turned I saw *HOT* in big white letters across her butt. So maybe sweat suit was the wrong term for it. What difference did it make, anyway? She was obviously part of his party crew or maybe his girlfriend. I guessed her name was Chloe because it was written in glitter across the front of her white knit shirt that barely covered her midriff.

"You must be new. The group isn't here yet. If you want you can go ahead into the studio and get started on your own. I heard there are some new toys."

Eww. I wanted to make it clear I wasn't part of the party hardy crowd, but that really wasn't the point now. I had to think fast. And maybe I wasn't thinking as clearly as I should have. Frank had made me crazy about the orange juice glass, and all I could think of was finding it and breaking it.

"No thanks on the studio," I said. "I think I left something here this morning. Maybe I could look for it?"

The woman looked me up and down. "You were here this morning?" she said with interest. "As in from last night?"

Uh-oh, I didn't want to get caught up in some kind of jealous rage thing with her. "No, no. Nothing like that." I didn't wait for her permission and started looking around the kitchen. The table was clear and so was the sink. She was walking right behind me, firing questions that I didn't want to answer. How well did I know Dane? Where did we meet? How come she'd never seen me before? I kept answering with shrugs, as I moved faster around the room toward the dishwasher. I didn't dare look at her as I pulled it open and then pulled out the top rack. There were still some flecks of orange stuck to the two small glasses.

"What are you doing?" she said as I stared at them. I had no time to think. All I could remember was what Frank said about no prints on a broken glass as I grabbed both of them out of the dishwasher and threw them on the floor. I might have stamped on them before I ran for the door.

I ran all the way home and didn't look back. Once I was inside I slumped in my one chair and began to laugh hysterically, thinking of the look on the woman's face.

I almost jumped out of my skin when I heard a loud knock at my door.

21

I THOUGHT I'D MADE A CLEAN GETAWAY, BUT THE woman with Kool-Aid-colored hair must have followed me. Why? What was she, the official custodian of Dane's dishes? Maybe if I didn't answer the door, she'd give up and go away. There was another knock on the door, only now it sounded more like she'd pounded on it. Geez, all I did was break a couple of glasses. Frank had just gotten me so nuts about destroying the evidence, I wasn't thinking straight. Right, it was Frank's fault. There was another loud pound on the door. Okay, it wasn't Frank's fault. I had to take responsibility for my own actions.

At the third pounding, I figured she wasn't giving up and went to the door. "Look, I'm sorry about the glasses. I'll be glad to replace them," I said through the closed door.

"Glasses? What are you talking about? Casey, open up."

"Lucinda?" I said with surprise and relief as I pulled the door open wide.

"What's going on?" she said, gazing at me with concern. "Is something wrong?"

"Not exactly," I said before spilling the whole story about the fingerprints and my effort to get rid of them. By the end of the story, she was laughing.

"I wish I could have seen her face when you smashed the glasses. So, the cop has a girlfriend. I'm not surprised. He's pretty hot."

"I think she's just one of a group. She thought I was a new recruit for the orgy. She said I could go on into the studio and play with some of the toys." We both said, "Ewww" together.

"I almost forgot what I came for," my friend said. "Your parents are across the street."

"What? But they're in Chicago," I said, wondering if I'd heard her right. What could my parents possibly be doing there? I'd broken down and told them I was hosting the Petit Retreat, but why would they just show up? Lucinda had met them at Joan's funeral and knew all about my relationship with my mother.

"And there's a guy with them. Kind of tall and always smiling. Oh, and he kept making it look like a coin was coming out of Kevin St. John's ear as your parents talked to him."

"They were talking to Kevin St. John?" I said with a sinking feeling.

"The lord and manager of Vista Del Mar didn't seem amused by the coin trick. The guy had short dark hair that reminded me of something."

"The sugar on a gumdrop, maybe?"

"Yes, that's it exactly," she said. "He has that short hair that sort of sticks out all over."

"It's really a long crew cut," I said.

Betty Hechtman

"So then you know who he is," Lucinda said.

"Yes, I know who he is. How about Dr. Sammy Glickner, my former boyfriend. The person my mother found for me and expected me to marry." I gave Lucinda the short version of our relationship. Dr. Sammy, as he was called, was a urologist, but his real love was magic. The trouble was there just wasn't any sizzle in our relationship. He was goofy and pretty funny most of the time, but what was that saying—all very nice, but not really good? He deserved somebody who would appreciate him. I had really done him a favor by breaking up with him. So why was he here?

"What are you going to do?" Lucinda said, noting that I seemed to be frozen in position.

"I'd like to just stay here and turn out the lights and pretend I'm not home," I said, looking around at the interior of the guesthouse. "If I thought dealing with the woman with the cherry red hair was bad, it was nothing compared with dealing with my parents and Sammy." I stopped and took a deep breath. "Whatever they're here for, it can't be good."

"What do you want me to tell them?" Lucinda said, apparently thinking I was serious about hiding out.

"Nothing," I said, rocking my head in capitulation. "I'm a big girl and can deal with this."

Lucinda offered to be my support, but I said I had to deal with them myself. I was grateful when she offered to go on ahead and meet up with the retreat group in the dining hall.

We walked across the street together and into the grounds and went our separate ways. Lucinda looked back and gave me a thumbs-up for encouragement.

"Here she is, Babs," I heard my father say as I walked into the Lodge building. The three of them were in the small sitting area but got up when I approached. Sammy walked around my parents and got to me first. He had his hands behind his back, but when he reached out to hug me, he was holding a bouquet of roses. Real roses—not the fake flowers he used in his illusion.

"Good trick," I said as he pressed the bouquet on me.

"The trick is, it's not really a trick," he said with a happy laugh. There was something teddy bearish about his build, and when he hugged me, he towered over the top of my head. I recognized the familiar scent of Pierre Cardin cologne he always wore.

Didn't he get that we'd broken up? He seemed so happy to see me, it made me want to cry. Lots of women would be thrilled to have him after them. He was a good catch. Good job, not the kind of guy who would cheat. I had no doubt he would be a good father. He was funny, too. How many times had I been feeling lost about my life, only to have him start telling me funny stories until I forgot all about it? But even with all that, I didn't want him. Could it possibly be because my mother had pushed so hard for him?

I refused to believe I was that childish. I was sure there was something else that kept me from falling into his arms.

"Mr. St. John said one of the people on your aunt Joan's retreat died. Actually, he said she was murdered," my mother said with a heavy sigh. "Casey, I don't know why you went through with the retreat in the first place. You should have just canceled the whole thing to begin with. You could have told them about Joan's death. You know, if you had just asked your father and me, we would have given you the money so you could have given them all refunds. What do you know about putting on a retreat?" My mother stepped closer to me and dropped her voice. "So, you think it was someone in your group who did it?"

"Mother," I said in the hopeless tone I'd heard both Sissy and Crystal use to their mothers. Nobody knew how to find your sensitive spot better than your mother. "I have it under control," I said. "What are you doing here?"

The three of them looked at one another, and my father was chosen as the spokesperson. "Honey, your mother was worried that you were going off on a tangent again. We thought it best that we talk in person." My father at least was dressed casually in a pair of khaki slacks and a polo shirt with a sports jacket. He reached in his pocket, took out a cherry lollipop and pressed it in my hand. Even with all the talk about sugar being evil, my pediatrician father had always carried a pocketful of lollipops to give to his patients and me, ever since I'd been a kid. About the sugar thing, he thought moderation was the watchword. It was impossible for my mother to go casual.

You had to understand that shopping and clothes weren't of interest to her. She had a personal shopper who would have an array of pantsuits ready when my mother came in. There were work pantsuits, dressy pantsuits, and maybe the tan one she was wearing was supposed to be a sporty pantsuit. She kept her dark brown hair short in a style that required little attention. The only personal touch to her appearance were dangle earrings. She chose them to reflect her mood. Today's were little lightning bolts, which reminded me of a piece of jewelry connected to Elvis Presley. He'd said it meant taking care of business, which was exactly what my mother had in mind.

I was glad I hadn't changed out of the gray slacks and black turtleneck. At least I looked kind of businesslike.

"Oh, Ned, we don't have a lot of time. Let's get to the point," my mother said. I didn't really want them to get to the point, at least not that quickly. I was still recovering from the fact they were there. I offered them dinner in the dining hall.

"I suppose we could have dinner here if that's what you want," my mother said, looking around at the rustic surroundings. "We're staying at one of the resorts in Pebble Beach. We thought we would take you to dinner there." Of course they were staying there. Pebble Beach was all fancy resorts with gourmet restaurants and world-famous golf courses.

"I can't just leave my people," I said, suddenly feeling very protective of Vista Del Mar and its more primitive setting. As I said it, Bree walked through the large room that functioned as a lobby for the hotel and conference center. She had her cell phone stuck to her ear, but when she saw me, she got off her call.

"My boys called me," she said in an excited voice. "And thank you again for last night. I know I was being silly, but if you hadn't sat with me, I never would have fallen asleep."

I watched the effect Bree's comments had on my mother. She looked surprised and a little worried. As soon as Bree went on to the dining hall, my mother shook her head. "Tell me you're not going to try to take on your aunt's retreat business. You told us it was just this one. Mr. St. John said he would be only too happy to carry on Joan's tradition and put on future yarn-related retreats himself. He said he needed some papers from you."

"So this is some kind of intervention?" I said.

"We can discuss it over dinner," my mother said. "In this dining hall place, if that's what you want."

I wanted to stay on my turf, and led the way out of the Lodge to Sea Foam. I was glad the line had already moved inside the dining hall. Kevin St. John must have thought my parents were allies in his quest to get all the paperwork, because he insisted on comping their meals. I waved to the group at our usual table and by their sympathetic looks figured that Lucinda had told them who I was with.

We chose a table far from the crowd in a quiet corner. Just as I was going to sit down, I noticed that Michael had come in and was surveying the tables. It was the perfect chance to ask Lucinda and Melissa if he was the man they'd seen with Edie. I started to get up from the table.

"I have to take care of something," I said. My mother eyed me with that all-too-knowing look. The unspoken message was she knew I was trying to run away. I could only imagine her reaction if I said I was investigating Edie's death.

"I'm sure it can wait," she said, and I sat back in my seat.

Sammy sensed an awkward moment and went off to get his food, though it seemed like mostly what he did was entertain everyone with silly tricks and his friendly manner.

My mother watched him. "As soon as Sammy heard we were coming to talk to you, he asked to come along. I hope you realize how much he cares about you." I answered with a dismissive wave of my hand. My mother didn't understand. Everything I'd said about things being all very nice, but not very good with Sammy was only part of it. I was really doing Sammy a favor. I had trouble sticking with things . . . and maybe people, too.

"Let's just get to why you're here, so we can get it over with," I said.

Some discussion went on between my parents as to who should tell me "the plan." My mother must have said five times, "Ned, you talk to her. She'll listen if it's coming from you."

Did they think I was six? Like I couldn't hear them arguing. Finally, I just stepped in and ordered my mother to tell me whatever it was.

"Your father and I talked it over. Since you seem to have such an interest in baking, we thought you should become a real professional. So, we're here to offer you cooking school in Paris." She took a folder out of her bag and pushed it across the table. I let it sit there a moment, then my curiosity got the better of me and I opened it.

There was a booklet about the cooking school and enrollment papers, which I noted were filled out. "Everything is done, even a place to stay lined up. The classes start next week. All you have to do is hit the accept button," my mother said. "Sammy thinks it's a great idea. And when you finish you can come back to Chicago and who knows . . ." My mother looked me in the eye. "Where are you going to find someone better than Sammy?"

During my mother's deliberate moment of silence when everything she said was supposed to sink in, Dane marched into the dining hall. He roared through the room like a ball of energy. I was stunned when he made his way directly to our table and me.

"What's with coming over and breaking my dishes?" he said.

"It was a mistake. I'm sorry. I'll get you some new glasses."

"So why did you do it?" He was standing his ground, and I got the impression he wasn't going to leave until I gave him some kind of explanation. What possible excuse could I come up with on such short notice? All I could do was tell the truth.

"I thought you were trying to get my fingerprints off the glass."

Dane shook his head in confusion. "Why would I want to do that? Besides, if I was trying to get your fingerprints, why would I put the glass in the dishwasher?"

He definitely had a point. But when I smashed the glasses, I wasn't exactly thinking things through. Dane was still staring at me, as was everyone else. I certainly didn't want to go into my call with Frank and my frantic thinking.

"I'm sorry, it was a mistake," I said in a low voice, hoping he would drop it and leave.

At last, Dane threw up his hands and left, just as Sammy came back to the table carrying a plate of food. He joined my parents in watching Dane go out the door.

"Who's he?" Sammy said.

"That's a good question," my mother said. "And why are you concerned about your fingerprints?"

"Just a misunderstanding," I said, avoiding my mother's gaze and very glad that Dane hadn't been in uniform. "Why don't I go and get dinner for you two?" I said, getting ready to push back my chair, but my mother put her hand on my arm.

"In a minute," my mother said. "Mr. St. John offered to take over this weekend retreat. You could leave with us right now." She leveled her gaze at me. "What difference will it make to your group? It's not as though you're a knitter. In fact, the idea of you running a knitting retreat is kind of absurd."

Yarn to Go

"Your mother has a point," my father said. "My sister started knitting when she was a kid. I remember when she dragged the family to some sheep-shearing competition and wanted to get a spinning wheel. She was always teaching someone how to knit. She thought it was some kind of cure-all to whatever your problem was." My mother looked underimpressed as he spoke, which changed to eye rolling when he mentioned that my aunt had tried to teach my mother to knit. "Joan thought your mother making a scarf would keep her grounded."

I wish I'd been a fly on the wall for that one.

He gave me a sympathetic nod. "Joan would have appreciated that you wanted to handle this final retreat, but there's no reason for you to stay now. Particularly with the murder."

"Walk away now, honey," my mother said.

Uh-oh, my mother had pulled out the big guns; she'd called me *honey*. So far Sammy had been staying out of the conversation, but now he jumped in.

"Case, your parents are right. You don't belong here." He waved his hand in the direction of the dining hall, and I expected something to magically appear, but this time it was just a gesture. It made me laugh that he called me Case. How was one letter really shortening my name?

"I found a French cooking school in Chicago," Sammy interjected.

My father noticed me glancing in the direction of my aunt's house. "We can get people to take care of liquidating Joan's house and the contents. Mr. St. John already offered to help handle it. You can just go pack up a few things and come with us to Pebble Beach and we can all fly home together on Monday."

"Think about it, Casey. After cooking school, no more of this baking in the middle of the night. You'd be wearing one of those white coats with your name embroidered on it." My mother didn't say it, but I knew she was thinking I'd be a professional something.

Finally they stopped, and both my parents looked at me, waiting for some kind of response. "Did I hear you right? This time you are trying to get me to quit something?" I was incredulous. "All the flak I got for leaving law school, and giving up teaching and now you want me to walk out in the middle of this retreat and my job as a dessert chef and muffin provider?"

My mother looked a little uncomfortable but then nodded. "Sometimes quitting something is the right thing to do."

I was stunned by their offer. Cooking school in Paris? Wow. It would be a game changer. I agreed to think about the cooking school offer, but told them there was no way I was walking out on the retreat.

"Now let me get you dinner," I said. I went off to the cafeteria line and came back with two plates of steaming food. My parents were gone, and only Sammy was still at the table.

22

"WHERE'D MY PARENTS GO?" I SAID, SETTING THE plates on the table.

Sammy pulled out the chair next to him. "They went to the gift shop to look for postcards," he said. "You know that your mother took your answer about the cooking school as a yes."

"You're kidding," I said, wishing she were still there so I could set her straight. I slid into the chair and put one of the plates of fried chicken and mashed potatoes in front of me, though I didn't feel much like eating. "How'd they hook you into coming?"

"They said you were in trouble." He shrugged sheepishly. "I know we're supposed to be broken up, but I thought I might be able to help."

Did he have to be such a nice guy? The truth was I was

kind of glad to see him. I knew he really, really liked me, and he was comfortable to be around.

"What's with the guy with the broken dishes?" he said. His smile had faded into almost a pout. I knew what he was asking. He wanted to know if there was something going on between me and Dane. Ha! Not likely with the crowd of women around him and his orgy studio. I touched Sammy's arm and thanked him for coming before explaining that Dane was a neighbor and a cop. "And not anything to me besides that," I said. I heard Sammy let his breath out in relief.

"I've missed you," he said. The truth was I'd missed him, too, but since I couldn't give him what he wanted, the kindest thing to do was say nothing and leave him free to hopefully meet some nice woman. I stopped my train of thought. Was I really that noble? No. Probably not.

"So you're not the least bit worried staying here with some murderer on the loose?" Sammy said. He looked out into the darkness through the tall windows. "This place looks pretty creepy to me."

I wouldn't tell my parents about looking into Edie's murder, but Sammy was different. "I'm not worried. In fact I'm kind of looking into it myself." I reminded him that I'd worked at the detective agency.

"Case, that was for a few weeks, and didn't they mostly handle cheating spouses and insurance fraud?"

"Maybe they did, but I learned a few tricks while I was there, and my former boss is kind of advising me. Frank said I had a way of getting people to talk." As I was talking to Sammy, I noticed that Michael was sitting at a table alone. "See that guy over there," I said, discreetly gesturing toward

Michael. "I'd really like to use my skills on him." I shrugged dejectedly. "The trouble is, he already knows there's a connection between me and the victim, so there's no way he's going to open up to me now."

"Do you think he killed her?" Sammy was gazing at him intently now, though Michael was facing away from us.

"Here are the facts. Edie, that's the victim's name, was married but might have been seeing a man when she came to the yarn retreats. But the cops don't know anything about him. I don't think they've even questioned him."

"So what do you want to know?" Sammy asked, keeping his eye on the guy.

"Well, what I'd really like to know is if he killed her, but I doubt he'd admit that. So, I guess I want to know if he saw her that night and what exactly was going on between them."

Sammy's face lit up in an enthusiastic smile. "Maybe I could talk to him. He would just think I was a stranger. Another lone guy staying here." I was going to protest, but Sammy talked on. "People talk to me, too," he said. "All those guys coming in for prescriptions for the little blue pill are always nervous and talk their heads off to me. Let me have a go."

Why not? I watched as Sammy went to the man's table and pulled out the chair next to him. Most of the diners had finished and were leaving. The retreat table had cleared out except for Lucinda. When she saw me sitting alone, she came over and joined me. The first thing I did was point out Michael and ask if he was the one she'd seen Edie eating with.

My friend shrugged. "Maybe. Probably. I wish I'd paid more attention." But what she really wanted to know was what was going on with Sammy and my parents. I told her about their offer.

"Are you taking them up on it?"

I played with the mashed potatoes on my untouched plate. "My first thought was to absolutely say no, but it was a knee-jerk reaction because they were offering it. But then I started to think about it. Paris, cooking school, learning how to make croissants so it's so second nature I could do it with my eyes closed." I let out a sigh. "I'd be a professional chef," I said.

Lucinda leaned over and hugged me. "I don't know what I'd do without you. Or what the restaurant would do without you. Our dessert business would die without your fabulous baking. You do know that people come in and order their dessert before they order their meal because we run out all the time. I could talk to Tag and see if we could up what we're paying you."

"I didn't say yes, yet," I said, interrupting my friend. "I'm just thinking about it."

"Tag has been punting all weekend, telling customers that your desserts will be back after the weekend. I told you how upset he was having to serve only ice cream."

"I suppose I could go by tonight when everyone is in bed here and make some pound cakes for tomorrow." I didn't say it, but I was thinking they might be my farewell desserts.

"I'll call Tag and tell him," she said, hugging me quickly before pulling out her cell phone and heading somewhere quiet.

As soon as she left, my cell phone began to vibrate, and

I saw a text message from Sammy. "Mission accomplished. Meet me outside."

It was cold and dark, and I wished I'd grabbed a fleece jacket. The damp air went right through the turtleneck. Sammy stepped out of the blackness into a pool of light coming from the window of the dining hall. I didn't mean to, but I jumped, and Sammy steadied my arm.

"You sure you're really up for investigating a murder?"

"I'm fine. Nerves of steel and all," I said. "So what did you find out?"

"His name is Michael and he's a CPA. It was easy to get him talking. The guy was nervous and felt guilty and wanted to spill he guts to somebody who wasn't a cop."

"He confessed?" I said.

I couldn't see Sammy's face that well in the darkness, but I think he was rolling his eyes. "Now you're making me feel like a failure," Sammy said. "He didn't say he killed her; he just gave me a motive."

Sammy knew he had my full attention and was enjoying the moment. "It's kind of nice having something you want," he teased. I nudged him to get him to continue. "Okay, here it is. He comes here every couple of months to see a client he has in Monterey. Like you thought, he was meeting that woman but said he was going to end it. The guy is married. It seems she called his house and he was feeling guilty about it anyway. He said he was going to tell her it was over."

"I don't suppose he told you where he was the night she died."

"And I thought I'd done so well," Sammy teased. "You want me to go back?"

I took his arm and hugged it. "You've already done more than I could. How exactly did you get him to open up?"

Sammy chuckled and stood a little taller. "Saying you're a doctor of urology works like magic. Guys figure you're an expert on the equipment. He seemed to think a guilty conscience was affecting his and maybe coming clean to someone would be a cure."

"Oh," I said, thinking it was more information than I really needed. Sammy looked toward the boardwalk that led to the beach and suggested we take a walk.

"You better go now," I said. "My parents are probably waiting for you." It was better to push him to go, like ripping a Band-Aid off quickly.

"I can just call them and tell them I'll be a while. I could take a cab later."

"No," I said, shaking my head for emphasis. "I still have activities with the group. But thank you for coming and talking to Michael." He didn't make a move to go. "Well . . ."

I wasn't sure what the etiquette was with someone who used to be your boyfriend, and we stood there awkwardly for a moment before I finally went ahead and hugged him. He immediately took the opportunity to wrap his arms around me.

"Are you so sure it's over between us?" he said, leaning close to my ear. When I looked up to speak, he kissed me. Here was the problem with that. There had just never been that sizzle between us, at least for me. I had never said anything, but Sammy had figured it out. He'd even offered to take an Internet kissing class. Kissing school? Really? He stepped back and our gazes met in the darkness.

"Well?" he said, hopefully. My nonanswer was an answer,

and he seemed deflated. I didn't have the heart to tell him it wasn't about technique or something you could learn from on online class. I had never mentioned it, but I thought a lot of it might have had to do with the fact that my parents were so anxious to push us together.

You would think after that kind of shutdown, Sammy would have been in a rush to leave, but no, he still stood there and reached toward my hair. "Look, a star must have fallen from the sky," he said as he seemed to pull a metal disk out of my hair. It was blue with twinkling lights.

"You have done that a million times and I still don't know how you do it," I said.

He grinned at me. "That's because I'm a master magician."

I asked him to do it again, but he shook his head. "Magic is all based on misdirection and surprise. Figuring it out is all about knowing where to look, and I make sure you're always looking in the wrong place." He sighed and stepped back. "I know what the problem is. Your parents like me too much, and I have the fatal affliction of being a nice guy. If only I could wave my magic wand and turn into a bad-boy, heartbreaker jerk, you'd be all over me."

I was afraid he might be right.

23

I NEEDED A COFFEE TO FORTIFY MYSELF FOR THE evening ahead. The encounter with my parents had left me feeling drained, and seeing Sammy had left me confused. And as for my investigating, here it was Saturday night already, and all I had was a bunch of suspects. What were the chances I could wrap this up by the next day? I hadn't even thought about what I would do if I actually got the goods on whoever had killed Edie.

Who would have figured that Edie was juggling men? I would never have guessed it by looking at the men she was juggling, either. But then I guess all the people having romantic entanglements don't necessarily look like soap opera stars.

And as for the rest of my suspects . . . I had to wonder what Edie's real relationship with Scott had been. He had mentioned coming to her house to knit, but maybe there was more. Was Edie really keeping three balls in the air? Then

I remembered what Kris had said about Edie outing him if he wouldn't do it himself. That sounded like a motive to me.

Kevin St. John certainly had a place on the list. Edie had said something to ruffle his feathers that first afternoon. And there was something creepy about him. What was hiding behind that placid moon-shaped face of his? He wanted complete control of Vista Del Mar. Maybe Edie knew something that could topple his world.

It was hard to imagine Bree would have been off the phone or tablet long enough to figure out how to kill Edie. Melissa and Sissy were always together, so unless they'd worked as a team, it seemed unlikely. I supposed I should include Kris, but Edie seemed to be so fond of her. What about Lucinda? No, that was too ridiculous.

And then there was Olivia. She was a big mystery. Who had given her the trip and why? She had a bottle of sleeping pills. Maybe she was totally lying when she claimed to be surprised to find some missing. Did Edie take them on her own or, more likely, take them without knowing? I looked at my watch and realized the evening workshop was starting soon. If she took them without knowing it, they had to have been in the wine. But how did the sleeping pills get there? Maybe Kevin St. John had gotten hold of them. But how could he have dropped all those crushed pills into Edie's glass just before he handed it to her? I wished I'd asked Sammy about how to get a pill into a wineglass without being seen. It seemed like a magician sort of thing.

My head was spinning as I walked through the Lodge thinking about it all. I was relieved to see that my parents and Sammy weren't in the gift shop and glad that the coffee cart was still dispensing drinks. I ordered a cappuccino with an extra shot of espresso and took the white foam–capped drink back into the great room. The seating area was full, and there was a soft din of conversation. I stopped next to the registration counter. As I glanced around, my gaze stopped on the wall of photographs.

Some of them were quite old. You could tell by the hairstyles and clothes. I glanced at one of a group of birders. Their utility vests and binoculars around their necks were timeless, but the longish stylized hair was all the 1980s. A group of cheerleaders with their ponytails and pageboys from the sixties were caught in mid-cheer on the grassy area across from the Lodge, and the group of very serious-looking writers gathered in the sitting area with their pens poised had the look of the fifties.

Even though I'd seen the picture before, the one with Joan and the retreat group still came as a jolt. Seeing my aunt dressed in that rosy pink sweater she loved so much, looking so happy surrounded by her retreat group, seemed so strange, but at least now I understood why she was holding a burgundy knitted square. Edie had made two and held one in each hand. The other women showed off their squares as well. Kris and someone I didn't recognize held a partially done blanket made from the squares.

I sensed someone standing next to me and almost jumped when I turned and saw Kevin St. John. How did that man keep showing up without making a sound?

"I hear you're leaving us," he said with his usual placid expression. "How lucky for you to have a family who cares so much about your well-being that they were willing to fly halfway across the country just to talk to you. And what a fantastic offer to send you to cooking school in Paris." He gave me a benevolent smile. "I told them I would be glad to take over the retreat immediately and take care of the liquidation of the house and its contents. You can just walk away now. I will oversee the workshop tonight and tomorrow. I already have someone in mind to empty the house, and then we'll put it on the market. A house and guesthouse like that in this area should sell fast."

Before I could tell him to hold off on his plans, he'd put his hand on my shoulder and was trying to steer me toward the door. I looked back just in time to see Olivia Golden coming out of the office area. There was no mistaking her reddish hair as she walked with her head down closely followed by Lieutenant Borgnine. Instinctively I looked at her hands and saw that there were no handcuffs.

"You don't even have to worry about giving me your aunt's records. I'll just help myself after you drop off the keys. So, you can leave now," Kevin said, seemingly oblivious to the pair leaving his inner sanctum. As if there was any way he didn't know. Olivia went directly to the door without looking up and was gone before I could react.

Lieutenant Borgnine's head jerked up, and the stubby-shaped man stepped in front of me. "Leaving? I thought I'd told, I mean *asked*, everyone in your group to stay put for the weekend."

I put up my hands in capitulation to Kevin, who seemed to be trying to hide his consternation as his plan was thwarted. Then I looked at Lieutenant Borgnine. "What's going on with Olivia Golden?"

The policeman answered by saying good night and walking away.

The group was already gathered in the meeting room

when I rushed in. "Where's Olivia?" I said in a breathless voice, seeing that her spot was empty. They'd already started working on their individual projects, and I blew in like a cold wind, shattering their relaxed mode. The workshop leader looked up from helping Sissy with the cables on her light blue scarf and glanced around the table.

"She must be running late," Kris said, keeping her eye on Sissy's work. The large meeting room had a different vibe at night. The fire in the fireplace added some warmth, but the curtainless windows looking out into the darkness made it feel exposed.

Lucinda noted my frantic mode and set down the off-white scarf she was working on. "Casey, is something wrong?"

Melissa made a tsk sound. "Is something wrong? Are you kidding? Something has been wrong since Edie got killed." The mother turned to me and seemed concerned. "You think something happened to Olivia now?" Still holding her needles with the black-and-white patterned scarf hanging off of them, the woman with the unruly hair stirred the group up, and they all started up again on being stuck there and the idea that one by one they were going to be murdered.

The door opened with a woosh, and I caught sight of Olivia's almond-shaped face and black velour jacket as she came in. I let out a big sigh of relief, and a titter of nervous laughter went through the group as they started talking amongst themselves about it being ridiculous to think they were all going to die.

Olivia didn't look distracted now. Her gaze was very focused as it moved from face to face around the table. "Okay, who did it?" she demanded.

Their moment of lightness ended as they picked up on her distraught expression, and there was a flurry of "Did what?"

My friend popped out of her seat and began to treat Olivia like a dissatisfied customer at the restaurant. She pulled out a chair for her and offered to get a cup of tea. Lucinda went so far as to pick up a chamomile tea bag and show it to Olivia. Not that it did any good. Olivia was fixated on staring at each person around the table.

"You know what you did." Olivia's dark eyes were narrow, and her mouth was set in an angry straight line. As much as I'd been concerned about the faraway look she'd had most of the weekend, I preferred it to this.

When no one spoke up, Olivia turned to me with her hand on her hip. "An anonymous someone called the cops and told them about the sleeping pills missing from my bottle and said they'd seen me holding Edie's wineglass and that must have been when I put the sleeping pills in it so she'd act all dopey and I could walk her back to her room and suffocate her with a pillow. The caller said I'd insisted on walking her back to her room. That cop in the wrinkled sports jacket hunted me down and took me into some office and said it would be so much easier if I just told him the truth. In other words," she said, "he wanted me to confess."

A gasp went through the group. "But I thought she was stabbed with the knitting needles," Melissa said. She looked around at the others, and Scott nodded in agreement.

"That's what I thought, too," Sissy said.

Kris looked at me directly. "Casey, what about you? Do you have more information?"

I hadn't brought up all the details before. I suppose it was an effort to protect them and to try to get their minds off of what had happened. But after Olivia's outburst, and now that they were asking me directly, I told them what I had heard about how Edie had died. They listened with rapt attention as I explained that the medical examiner thought the cause of death was suffocation from a pillow being put over her face. I mentioned she'd thrown up and that they'd found a sleeping pill in Edie's purse. "As for the knitting needles," I said, "I think they were for effect and to plant somebody else's fingerprints at the scene." I didn't mention the fingerprints were mine.

All eyes turned back on Olivia as she began to protest. "I just walked Edie back to her room. She had trouble with the key so I used it for her and then gave it back to her. She went inside and closed the door. That's it." Olivia surveyed all of us to see if we believed her. "And I know how the sleeping pills disappeared from my bottle," she continued. "You remember the first night at dinner, my purse disappeared?" She looked over the group for some sign of acknowledgment. I tried to think back, all the while wondering if what she was saying was true or if she was trying to get us to go along with some alibi she'd given Lieutenant Borgnine.

I had been so wrapped up with myself that first night, worried about dealing with the group and worried I'd fall apart before the weekend ended. Then it came back to me. I did remember her purse had gone missing at dinner. She'd insisted that she'd put it on the back of her chair and it wasn't there. Everyone had looked around and it had finally turned up under the table.

Olivia stopped talking and glared at each person again

while they all stammered their innocence in the purse caper. Her gaze stopped at me, and I put up my hands.

"I didn't do it," I said.

"It could have been someone else completely—someone who wasn't part of our group," Melissa said. For once both she and her daughter were in agreement, and they nodded.

"Someone could have walked behind Olivia's chair and pulled the purse off the back," Sissy said. "Then when they were done, they could have shoved it under the table from anywhere."

"We wouldn't have noticed because we weren't expecting it," I said, thinking of what my old boyfriend Sammy had told me about how he did the trick with the star in my hair.

"That has to be it," Bree said. "It can't be one of us."

"It had to be someone who knew about the sleeping pills," Scott said.

"And somebody who was planning to murder Edie," Lucinda added.

Olivia still seemed distraught. "Don't you see? Somebody is trying to frame me!"

"Did Lieutenant Borgnine say how he thought you put the drugs in Edie's wine without her noticing?" Melissa asked.

The young woman put her head in her hands in a hopeless gesture. "Mother," Sissy groaned as Olivia's eyes flashed anger.

"I'm just asking because I think that's a pretty major point." Melissa looked around at the rest of the group, and they nodded, seeing her reasoning. That is, everyone except Olivia, who was staring out the window mumbling to herself.

"Why did I ever accept this trip? I didn't want to come. I wouldn't have come if he hadn't forced me."

Kris asked who she was talking about, but Olivia ignored the question and turned back to the group. "It wasn't even my idea to walk Edie back to her room. Somebody told me to do it."

"That would have been me. Though *told you* is a bit strong. I think it was more of a suggestion when I saw you leaving," I said, feeling my knees grow a little wobbly. "Someone had nudged me and pointed out that Edie seemed to be having trouble standing up." I glanced around the group hoping whoever it was would come forward.

The silence was deafening. Kris finally spoke up. "We all noticed that Edie seemed drunk."

"What if the killer's plan hadn't been to smother Edie with the pillow?" Scott said and hung his head. "I had a problem with pills before I turned to knitting, and I can tell you that if the sleeping pills missing from Olivia's bottle were in Edie's wine, it would have been enough to send her off into the big sleep if she hadn't thrown up."

"It's funny that you should mention that," I said. "I heard that if it hadn't been for the knitting needles stuck in Edie's chest, the medical examiner might have ruled it an accident from the sleeping pill and wine mixture and never noticed that the residue on the pillow matched up with residue on Edie's face." I didn't say what the residue was, but I think they all got that it was throw up.

"And it would have been case closed," Olivia said. I am sure she was thinking that then she never would have been a suspect. She looked worn-out.

"Maybe that's what happened. Whoever put the drugs in

Edie's drink expected them to kill her," Lucinda said. "They could have come to check to make sure she was gone and when she wasn't, finished the job with the pillow." My friend moved on to talking about tablecloths in the restaurant and food stains. "I wonder if Lieutenant Borgnine realizes that whoever smothered her probably got some of the throw up on their clothes." A ripple of "yuck"s went through the group, but Lucinda continued. "Somebody ought to tell Lieutenant Borgnine. I bet there's a way to match it up."

No one volunteered.

The conversation went back to who could have taken the sleeping pills from Edie's purse. They talked about dinner the first night, the crowded dining room and that it was true that lots of people had walked past the table.

"That creepy manager in his black suit came by a bunch of times," Sissy said. "Don't you remember, he kept asking if everything was okay?"

24

I THOUGHT THE GROUP WAS GOING TO SWALLOW their tongues when the door opened and Kevin St. John walked in. They all just stared at him, while he didn't seem to notice their reaction.

"I just wanted you to know that I am here for all of you. For this weekend and for all the future yarn retreats. I'm putting together a brochure for all the different kinds of retreats Vista Del Mar will be hosting. There will be bird-watching, writers' workshops, quilting, and the ones you would be interested in I'm calling Yarn by the Sea." He had a forced smile as he moved his gaze around the room, making sure he made eye contact with everyone. It seemed like something he must have learned in a speech class. In other words, it felt kind of fake.

"And I promise you, our retreats will run seamlessly." He didn't exactly mention Edie, but it was clear he was saying there wouldn't be any murders during his retreats. He was still acting as if it was my fault. I let him do his spiel without interruption. He ended by reminding the group about the family-friendly Jerry Lewis movie in Hummingbird Hall and added that there was a popcorn cart offering complimentary popcorn.

I caught up with him as he headed toward the door. I know it was childish, but I couldn't help it. I told him that even if Lieutenant Borgnine hadn't said anything about me having to stay, I wouldn't have left my group before the end of the weekend. "And about the rest of it. I know my parents probably made it sound like a sure thing, but I haven't decided whether to take their offer or not."

Kevin didn't miss a beat. "But you will still give me all of your aunt's papers regarding the retreats, no matter what, right?"

I didn't answer. I know I'd said I would give him all the paperwork, and he did seem to be making plans to continue on with the yarn retreats, but the more he kept asking for them, the more I didn't want to give them up.

The workshop never went back to normal. Olivia's accusations had been like a bucket of cold water on the group. The whole sense of us working together on our knitting was gone. Was there any way I could get that feeling of camaraderie back?

When the group broke up, most of them headed toward Hummingbird Hall. I caught up with Bree just outside the meeting room.

"I am going to be gone for a while. If you need company again . . ." I left it hanging, but Bree surprised me by her response.

"Thank you for last night, but after hearing about the

challenges you're dealing with, I realized I can stay by myself. It may feel a little uncomfortable, but I want to conquer my fear." For once we weren't interrupted by her phone or the boys beeping her on their walkie-talkie app. I realized I hadn't seen her on her tablet, either. I mentioned it and asked if she was okay about it, remembering how upset she'd been at their silence before.

"We had a nice conversation earlier. They were going to play with their friends, and then the dads were taking them out for pizza and miniature golf."

She seemed confused and relieved at the same time. "I guess they don't need me as much as I thought. And my friend who was supposed to come called to ask how it was going. She thought it was great that I was finally making something that was just my project." Bree leaned over and hugged me. "I am getting used to being on my own. I think I like it—at least for a little while."

Lucinda had stayed behind and was clearing the paper cups off the table and wiping up around the coffee and tea service. She stopped in the doorway, and when Bree left, Lucinda joined me. "I overheard. It seems like she's gotten more than knitting out of this weekend." Lucinda looked around her warily. "I was afraid Kevin might pop out of the bushes." When it seemed clear we were alone, Lucinda continued. "Who do you think told on Olivia?"

I dropped my voice. "So then you think Olivia really did kill Edie?"

Lucinda shrugged. "The pieces fit. The sleeping pills were missing from her bottle. She did walk Edie back to her room. She could have engineered all the stuff with her purse."

"How about this? Suppose the person who really killed

Edie told Lieutenant Borgnine the stuff about Olivia just to throw him off their track?" I said.

"Interesting thought. Do you have any idea who that could be?" Lucinda said.

"No, and I don't think I'm going to be able to work this out by tomorrow. Who am I kidding? Like I could really solve a murder based on a few weeks spent working at a detective agency. I must be nuts." I hung my head. "I'm afraid it will turn out like everything else in my life—left hanging. The idea of cooking school in Paris is looking more and more appealing. If I could finish that I would be a real chef."

Lucinda furrowed her brow with concern. "You know the saying, it's always darkest before the dawn. Don't make any decisions now."

"You're right about not making a decision. At least I know I am staying until the end of the retreat."

"Come to the movie," Lucinda said, taking a step in the direction of Hummingbird Hall. "A few laughs would do you good."

"No. I need to go home and pick up some things, and then I'm going to the restaurant to bake some desserts."

"I'm sorry I told you what my finicky husband said. He can serve ice cream sundaes for one more day." She stopped and looked at me. Neither of us said anything, but I knew we were thinking the same thing. If I took my parents' offer there were going to be a lot more days that Tag would have to serve those sundaes.

"There's no discussion. I'm doing it," I said. Lucinda offered to come with and help, but I urged her to go on to the movie. This was her weekend off. Reluctantly, she went down the path, and I headed in the other direction toward the driveway that led to the street.

When I got back to my place, I checked the plate of yogurt I'd left for the cat. It was licked clean, but there was no sign of him, and I hoped he was okay. I went into the guesthouse and turned on the lights. I had been so busy with the retreat, I hadn't checked my emails. I sorted through them and chucked all the junk mail. It was a little eerie when I saw that there was a message from Edie.

When I opened it, I realized she'd sent it from her smartphone just after the opening workshop. It said how much she appreciated me doing the workshop for my aunt. She had attached a photo of the group. I don't think Edie meant it to sound like a reproach, but she mentioned I wasn't taking photographs the way my aunt had and so she was taking it upon herself to take photos for me.

The email went on to say how much she had liked Joan. She thought the cops had been remiss with their investigation. How was it possible that they didn't find the car since it had to have been damaged?

Leave it to Edie; from beyond the grave she had managed to say the wrong thing. Even though the cops has assured me that they checked all the mechanics and body shops in the area for a car with the kind of damage consistent with the accident and come up empty, I always felt I should have done something more. Edie's comment opened that feeling up all over again. But what could I do now?

My leg brushed the red print fabric–covered box that held all of my aunt's papers regarding the retreats, and I remembered why else I'd stopped in. Kevin St. John was so persistent about wanting Joan's files, I wondered if there was something I'd missed in them. I flipped through the file marked *Petit Retreat*. I had taken the sheets that pertained to the group out before the retreat began. I looked through the pages left. There were a bunch of notes about knitting, something that looked like an essay.

What could Kevin St. John want with those papers? The flash drive I'd looked at before had gotten caught in the bottom of the file, and I left it there. I thumbed through the rest of the materials in the box. The only file that seemed to have anything Kevin St. John would want was the one with the mailing list, vendor list and capsule descriptions of possible yarn retreats. It seemed he was just being annoying. I packed everything back in the box and gladly put the lid on it.

I got up to go, but then I hesitated, still thinking about Edie's email. The same question came back to me. Was there anything I could do now? I looked at my watch and calculated the time in Chicago. *Frank always claimed to be a night owl*, I thought as I punched in his number. I barely got out *hello* before he figured out who it was.

"Feldstein, what is it? I don't even get a good-bye from you when you leave town and now it's like every five minutes I'm hearing from you."

"Sorry, Frank. I just wanted to run something by your super detective mind." I heard him laugh.

"Feldstein, if you're trying to flatter me, you need some lessons. So, let's forget all this chitchat. What do you wanna know?"

I told him about the hit-and-run and how no damaged car had shown up. "I feel like I should have done something more. Is there anything I can do now?" I said.

Frank's tone softened. "No reason for you to feel guilty,

Feldstein. It was the cops that flubbed up." He paused a moment, and I heard canned laughter coming from his television. "I had a case once . . ." He stopped and chided himself. "No reason to give all the boring details. Here's the meat of the matter. The creep that hit your aunt could have conveniently gotten into another accident that would cover up the damage. That could be why the cops came up empty."

"Frank, you're a genius," I said. I heard him laugh.

"Still trying with the flattery stuff, huh? That time it sounded a little more like you meant it. Feldstein, do you know what to do?" he asked.

"Yes, thank you," I said.

"Good, Feldstein. So, then this is the last call of the night?" He sounded gruff, but I was pretty sure it was all an act. I promised that it was, and just before he hung up, he told me to let him know how things turned out.

I rebooted the computer and went to the site of the newspaper that covered the whole Monterey Bay area. I did a search for the news stories on the day of my aunt's accident and the day after. I avoided the story about Joan. I knew it by heart anyway. She'd been out walking in the early morning and had been struck on the street in front of the cemetery. There was just the cemetery, a golf driving range and some empty land before the ocean, so there was no one who'd seen what had happened. I went ahead and skimmed all the news stories for that day and found nothing, but when I went to the next day's articles—bingo!—I found what I was looking for. It was an amusing small article about a car trying to turn a Sandwich King into a drive-through. The gist of the story was that someone identified only as *a driver* had stepped on the gas instead of the brake and driven up on the curb and into a post protecting the wall of a Sandwich King. There were no injuries except to the car and the post outside the fast-food joint. Sandwich King? Why did that stir a memory?

Could that have been the car that hit my aunt and then the driver tried to cover up the damage with new damage? But even if it was true, how could I prove it now? I shut down my computer and went back to the matter at hand. If this was going to be my last night of baking in Cadbury, I wanted to do the whole thing.

I packed up the ingredients for muffins and went looking through the cabinet for some doilies. There wasn't going to be time to frost the cakes I was going to bake. But I didn't want to leave them plain, either. The alternative was to shift powdered sugar over them using a doily as a template. There was one left, but it ripped when I tried to take it out. Rather than trying to cobble it together, I went across to my aunt's, thinking there might be some there.

I was relieved to find the door locked just as I'd left it. When I turned on the kitchen light and everything looked fine, I felt even better. I found a package of doilies and took out several. I got ready to go, but when I glanced around the familiar room I felt an emotional tug. What would happen to all of Joan's things if I took my parents up on their offer and let Kevin liquidate the house and the contents?

The shopping bag with my aunt's things was still sitting where I'd left it when I had first brought it home from the hospital. It had been too painful to deal with them, and I had avoided looking at the contents closely, but knowing this might be one of my last chances, I finally looked inside. How odd, the pink sweater she'd worn on the last morning of her life was the same one I'd seen in the photograph on the wall in the Lodge. But then it was her favorite sweater. I took it out and hugged it to my chest; the familiar scent of her perfume still clung to it. There was a sudden clatter, and I jumped until I realized I was holding the sweater upside down and Joan's keys had fallen out of the pockets. I scooped them up along with some tissues and put them back, before dropping the sweater in the bag.

I did a brief tour of the house and noted all the things my aunt had made. For the first time I got the point of her handicraft. It was a connection to her that lived on even though she was gone. I picked up the throw on the end of the couch. Kevin St. John would probably just put it in a garage sale and somebody would buy it and have no idea she had put all those loving hours into making it.

Still, the concept of Paris and cooking school was tantalizing. Maybe I could pack up the things of hers I most wanted. And do what with them? I sighed as I looked around the room. All this had become quite a responsibility. Not my strong suit. Maybe Kevin St. John's offer was a blessing in disguise.

I loaded the baking stuff into my yellow Mini Cooper and drove the short distance to the main drag. It was a relief to have nothing to worry about for a while but getting the eggs to room temperature.

The Blue Door had just closed, and the last stragglers were paying their checks and leaving. Tag brightened when he saw me and I explained my mission. To look at his perfectly combed brown hair and shirt without a wrinkle, no one would guess he'd just put in a full day handling the restaurant. But that was Tag, meticulous about everything. The only thing that stood out about him was that he had almost too much hair for a man his age and there wasn't a hint of gray.

"There will be some of Casey's fabulous desserts for tomorrow night," he said to a couple heading toward the door. They stopped and gave me an appreciative nod.

I sat down at one of the tables while the waitstaff finished clearing and setting up for the next day. The cook and his assistant were finishing up. Shortly afterward they grabbed their backpacks and said good night before leaving. I looked out the window over the street. There was a light drizzle falling, and the pavement had a sheen. The movie theater had just let out, and people were heading to their cars. No one had an umbrella. It had to be a real downpour for Cadburians to pull one out.

I watched the *open* sign go off on the café across the street. Cadbury by the Sea was an early town, even on Saturday night.

I didn't think Lucinda had told Tag I might be leaving. He seemed too calm. Tag didn't deal well with change. He had taken a while to adjust to my baking at night and would probably take just as long to get used to me not being there. The only thing I said to him when he left was good night.

Finally, I had the place to myself and turned on the radio to a moody jazz station. I began to lay out the ingredients for the pound cakes and then got lost in baking. The rhythm of the stand mixer was soothing as it turned the ingredients into batter. Every now and then I glanced out at the street, which was empty except for an occasional car. I was ready to pour the batter into the tube pans when I heard the glass on the front door rattle. I turned down the radio and listened. Someone was jiggling the door knob.

The door was locked, right? I remembered with a queasy stomach that Tag had said to lock up after him, and now I realized that I hadn't.

25

I GRABBED MY PHONE AND PUNCHED IN 911 WHILE I tried to peek out of the kitchen to see what was going on without being seen. The porch was dark, but I could make out something moving. There was definitely somebody out there, though they seemed shrouded in something dark, like a hoodie. I saw the door handle turning and had the sinking feeling that even if I hit the call button on my phone now, the cops wouldn't get there in time.

I was on my own.

I looked around the kitchen with the idea of arming myself. Tag's favorite perfectly seasoned cast-iron skillet was sitting on the stove. It was certainly heavy enough to do some damage, but it was also heavy to hold. Even so, I grabbed it with both hands.

I lifted it high and stepped into the dining room, ready to defend the restaurant. At the same moment, the door flew open and I saw the hooded figure had a gun. I made a move to strike and he yelled something, but I didn't hear it. The adrenaline was pumping, and I was like a crazed warrior.

The frying pan came down with a whoosh and knocked the gun out of the assailant's hands. Now what? Should I make a grab for the gun and then hold it on him while I called the cops? I didn't know anything about guns, but I certainly could figure out which end to point at him. All this thinking happened in a split second, and I dove for the gun, but he was faster and grabbed my hand and pulled it back, while he retrieved the weapon.

I tried to make a move with the skillet, but he kicked it out of my hand. He dragged me back to standing as he straightened and then flipped off the hood.

Dane?

"What are you doing here?" he demanded. His voice sounded strained, and I realized adrenaline had been pumping for him, too. And I thought cops were so cool that nothing fazed them. "And what's with the frying pan? You could have made the gun go off." He picked up the heavy utensil and laid it on the counter by the cash register.

"The real question is, what are you doing here waving a gun around? I work here, remember?" I said.

"I wasn't waving my gun around, at least not until you went crazy with the frying pan. And you weren't supposed to be working this weekend."

We both stopped and took a few deep breaths and let the adrenaline level drop for both of us.

"I know because the whole town has been grumbling about being muffinless for the past few days," he said, finally cracking a smile on his angular face.

"Tag Thornkill was upset about serving store-bought ice cream, and I came in as sort of an emergency cake situation." I looked toward the kitchen and thought of the half-filled tube pan. "Aren't you off duty?" I gestured toward the jeans, black T-shirt and black hoodie. I didn't mean to notice, but he could sure wear a pair of jeans, and when he took off the sweat jacket, the sleeves of the T-shirt strained against his arm muscles. I know it wasn't fair, but I compared his body with Dr. Sammy's. Sammy had him on height by a few inches, but let's just say the sleeves on Sammy's polo shirts (he never wore T-shirts unless you counted the white under-shirts he often wore) never had any problem getting around his biceps.

"I'm never off duty, completely. I was going by in the truck and I saw something moving up here and figured someone was robbing the place." Dane had assumed a cocky sort of stance. I had the feeling a quarter would bounce off his abs. Any money dropped on Sammy's midsection was likely to disappear. But there was a certain cuddly quality in Sammy's panda bear build.

While I was busy sizing up his outfit and body, he went on to explain that he'd been on his way out of town, making a grocery run to the twenty-four-hour market in Monterey.

"I thought you were tied up with your people in the studio." I blushed when I realized what I'd said. Did they really do stuff like that? Tie each other up and make interesting uses of his handcuffs? Ewww.

Dane seemed unconcerned with my comment. "We broke up early tonight. Though I think some of them were going to continue on their own. All the action made everyone hungry, and they cleaned out my place before they left. I don't know what it is with those people and chocolate syrup—"

"What about Chloe?" I said. I didn't really want to hear the rest of the chocolate syrup story.

"She left a long time ago. She's not into group stuff."

"I don't really need all the details," I said quickly. It was hard for me to keep my "ewww" silent. "Now that everything is straightened out," I said, looking toward the kitchen, "I need to finish." I expected him to put the hoodie back on and leave, but instead he dropped the sweat jacket on a chair and followed me.

"Mind if I watch?" He looked to me for an okay. I wasn't used to having an audience, but then again I might get some information on how the investigation was going. And I wanted to ask him about something.

Before we were even in the kitchen, he brought up the broken glasses. "I'll replace them," I said. "I'll get you a whole new set." He asked again why I was concerned about my fingerprints being collected, and I gave him a helpless shrug as an answer. I don't think he was happy with my response, but he seemed to understand that was as much of an answer as he was going to get.

I finished pouring the rest of the batter in the tube pans, while he replaced the cast-iron skillet on the stove.

"There really isn't much to watch," I said. I checked the oven thermometer and then slid the pans in. He grabbed the timer, and when I told him how long, set it.

"What about muffins?" he asked.

"The ingredients are in there," I said, pointing to the reusable grocery bag on the counter. Before I could make a move, he was unloading everything.

He looked at the cocoa and chocolate chips and licked his lips. "Are you making Heal the World with Chocolate? My favorite." By now the baking pound cakes filled the air with their sweet buttery fragrance, and Dane took a deep breath and sighed with pleasure. "What a great smell."

As I began to mix the ingredients for the muffins, I brought up the other car accident I'd read about in the newspaper article, the one that happened the same day as my aunt's hit-and-run. "What do you think? Could that have been how you missed finding the car that hit her?" I said.

He appeared a little stunned by the abrupt transition but then clicked into cop mode and seemed uncomfortable. "Uh, this is awkward," he said. "We should have checked for any other accidents." He apologized and said he'd make sure they tracked down the car from that accident at the Sandwich King. He caught my gaze. "I know you're still upset about your aunt's accident, but you need to let go."

"But what if it wasn't an accident?" I said.

Dane seemed doubtful. "Who could possibly have wanted to kill your aunt?" There was a moment of uneasy silence before he changed the subject and asked what I was doing.

I poured the liquid ingredients into the dry ones and explained that with muffins you stirred just enough to barely blend them. When I glanced up at Dane, he was watching me with interest. I suppose his square-jawed face might look stubborn, but his dark eyes seemed to connect, and he had a nice mouth. Why was I looking at his mouth, anyway? This was Mr. Party Hardy. Off-limits, not interested. Maybe his mouth wasn't so special after all. Maybe it was just a regulation set of lips.

Dane helped by lining the muffin pan with paper inserts.

I spooned the batter in all the cups and put them into an oven separate from the one baking the cakes.

Dane offered to help me with the cleanup.

"Really?" I said.

"Really. You've had kind of a tough weekend. It's the neighborly thing to do." I filled a sink with hot soapy water, and he rounded up the bowls and utensils. "So then were those people your parents?" he asked as I began to wash and he handled the rinsing and setting on the counter.

"I bet it took a lot of cop skills to figure that out."

"Yeah, lots of investigation. Your mother looks just like you."

"But that's where the resemblance ends." I told him both my parents were doctors and were less than thrilled with my careers choices.

"Why? What else have you done?" he asked. Why hide anything? Besides, I was leaving. I gave him the whole rundown of my assorted professions.

He blinked a few times as I went through the list. "It sounds like you have certainly sown your wild oats in the career department."

"Maybe it's not in the past tense," I said.

"What does that mean?" Dane took the soapy spatula from my hand and ran it under the water.

I told him about my parents' offer.

"It must be nice to have parents who care like that," he said. When I asked about his family, he just shrugged it off. "So then this is just another thing you're dropping and moving on from?"

"I'm not dropping anything. I'd be going to school to become a professional."

"Really?" he said. "I thought the definition for professional was that you got paid for it." He gestured toward the ovens. "Unless I'm mistaken, the dessert and muffin money is how you're supporting yourself."

"Maybe you're right. I am sort of already a professional. But why stay? My aunt had friends here and she had built up the retreat business. I just put on this one because I couldn't refund everyone's money. And there was a murder in the middle of it. What kind of retreat leader am I? I barely know how to knit." I could feel him watching me, and my eyes started to flash. "I know what you're thinking. Go on and say it. I don't finish things."

"We finished washing up the dishes," he said, trying to lighten the moment. I paused to see if he was going to leave, but he made no move to go.

"So, that guy. Is he your boyfriend?" Dane pulled out a drawer and replaced the clean utensils.

"Yes, no. He was, but he isn't anymore," I said, feeling uncomfortable talking about Sammy. I didn't want to talk about my personal life anymore. It was much easier to talk about the murder investigation. "Do you think that Lieutenant Borgnine will have it wrapped up by tomorrow?" I asked.

"You do know about the tip he got," Dane said.

I nodded and then asked who it had come from. When he said an anonymous source, I asked if it was a man or woman. "All Lieutenant Borgnine said was that it was an anonymous source."

"Lieutenant Borgnine isn't really going to arrest Olivia Golden?"

Dane looked away. "I can't really say. All I can tell you

is that the lieutenant isn't doing anything until he has some hard evidence that ties her to the murder."

"Like maybe when she smothered Edie, she got some throw up on her clothes?" I offered. He nodded in a noncommittal manner. "Maybe you should have a look at some other people's clothes. You know that Kevin St. John wasn't exactly a fan of Edie's. He seemed perturbed when she asked about his social life. I bet he knew about Olivia's sleeping pills. I don't think anything gets past him. You do know that he served the wine that night?"

Dane put his hand up to stop me. "Kevin St. John a murderer? I don't think so."

"Wait, there's more." I told him how the hotel manager wanted to make sure he got to handle the retreat business in the future. I had even figured out why. The Delacorte sisters had made a very favorable deal with my aunt on the price of the rooms and the meeting space, so she could keep the cost of the retreats reasonable. "If Kevin St. John takes over the retreats, he can jack up the prices."

Dane nodded and said something like "interesting." I thought he was just humoring me.

"You ought to tell Lieutenant Borgnine to question someone named Michael who is staying at Vista Del Mar. He had something going on with the victim."

"Seriously?" Dane said. "I don't think the lieutenant would take the suggestion well." The timer for the cakes went off and Dane helped me pull out the tube pans and set them on racks to cool.

"Remember how you asked who would want to kill my aunt? Maybe it was all about a way for Kevin St. John to get the retreats back. And then when I showed up, he started to

Betty Hechtman

worry I was going to take over her business. Having a murder during my first weekend wouldn't earn me a gold star with the Delacorte sisters. I'm sure he wasted no time in telling them about it and made it look like it was my fault, hoping they would cancel the deal they made with my aunt."

Dane seemed unconvinced. "Everyone in town knows he thinks of himself as the lord of Vista Del Mar, and he is certainly protective of the place. But murdering somebody to make you look bad? I think you might just be a little paranoid." He watched as I took the muffin tins out and set them on racks to cool. "But I will mention it to Lieutenant Borgnine," he said.

By now I was able to take the pound cakes out of their pans. I did some final cleanup until the cakes were cool enough to decorate.

Dane watched as I laid the doily on one of the cakes and used a sifter to sprinkle powdered sugar over the top. When I lifted the doily, there was a lovely lacy white pattern. I finished with the other cakes and then packed up the muffins to go. I thanked Dane for his help and handed him his own bag of muffins.

He waited until I locked up the restaurant, and we paused for a moment on the sidewalk in front of it. The main street was deserted, and the stop light flashed red for no one. By now the drizzle had lightened into mist. I wondered if Dane had paid much attention to my comments about Kevin St. John or merely attributed them to me being overwrought and tired.

"Well, I guess this is good night. Thanks for the muffins," he said. He'd dropped the cocky stance, and his smile was more genuine than teasing. The tiny droplets of water had

244

settled on his wavy dark hair, reflecting back the streetlights. He hesitated for a moment before he gave my shoulder a friendly squeeze.

"Thanks." He held up the packet of muffins. "Are you really going to walk out on Cadbury tomorrow—I mean today?" he said, after glancing at his watch. "A lot of coffee drinkers are going to be lost without one of your morning muffins."

I started to soften at his flattery, but then he went and ruined it. "I was hoping you'd stay around long enough to join the group in the studio at least once. It's fully equipped— everything for your safety and comfort."

Right, I thought flashing on the box of condoms and stack of women's clothes. Before I could comment, he got into his red truck and drove toward Monterey and the all-night market.

Ewwww.

26

I FINALLY WENT HOME AND FELL INTO AN
exhausted heap on my bed, still fully dressed. But I'd left
three golden pound cakes in the clear-covered pedestals. They
looked simple but elegant with the lacy powdered sugar
design. And at least part of Cadbury was no longer totally
muffinless. I'd left a basket of freshly baked Heal the World
with Chocolate muffins outside the door to the gift shop and
kept a basket of them for my group. The powers that be might
nix the cute names, but that would still be their name to me,
and apparently to Dane as well.

I awoke to my phone ringing.

"Casey, are you okay?" Lucinda sounded concerned. I sat
up quickly and took in my surroundings and the fact I was still
wearing my Saturday night outfit of gray slacks and a black
turtleneck, with a residue of powdered sugar. Lucinda continued talking as I stretched and tried to acclimate myself.

When I got a look at my watch, I understood the call and her tone of voice. It was after nine and the breakfast bell at Vista Del Mar had long since rung.

"I'm doing my best to handle the group, but everyone got a little nervous when you didn't show up."

As we spoke, I was already moving across the room, pulling out a fresh set of clothes before heading toward the shower.

"It's all my fault. I should have never told you that Tag was upset about the dessert situation. That man is so literal. Did anyone even object that the ice cream sundaes were made with ingredients from the Cadbury market?"

I cut in and told her about the cakes. "Casey, you are the best. I knew we were making the right decision when we hired you as our dessert chef." She paused a moment and then her voice dropped. "I understand the lure of Paris and cooking school, but I don't know what the restaurant is going to do without you. Or what I'm going to do without you. You're the only one I can be honest with about everything."

I felt a little choked up by her comments. Even though I'd claimed not to have made a decision about going, it seemed like everyone else knew I was. It had always been so easy to move on before. I ended the call by telling her I'd be there before the end of breakfast.

I was out the door in barely ten minutes. I rushed across the street into Vista Del Mar. No surprise, the sky was white and the light flat. The feeling was different as I went toward the dining hall. I noticed that people were already packing up their cars. Well, I'd almost made it through the retreat. Just a few more hours and it would be done. As for solving Edie's murder—maybe I was going to have to face it that I was full of hot air. Just my usual MO of leaving unfinished business.

I passed Kris's SUV and saw she hadn't packed it yet. I knew she was anxious to leave, which made me extra grateful that she had agreed to stay for an additional workshop after lunch. I was convinced that Kevin St. John had only agreed to let everybody check out late and had given us the meeting room for the afternoon to try to generate goodwill for his future retreats. One thing I knew for sure: Any event he managed would never have any heart in it. What would Kevin St. John do if he got a retreater like Bree? Was there even the slightest chance that he would help her over a rough spot?

When I passed another cluster of parked cars, I saw the lanky figure wearing the baseball cap whom I recognized as Edie's "friend" Michael with no last name. He was loading a suitcase and briefcase into the back of his black Prius. He closed the back and was heading toward the driver's door. Was he leaving?

It seemed wrong to let him go without some shot at talking to him. Thanks to Dr. Sammy I already knew the basics and that Michael had a motive to kill Edie.

I caught up with him and made some lame comment about the weather. He nodded in a noncommittal fashion, but at least he stopped. Now to stall until I figured a way to get him to give away his secrets.

"So, you're not even staying for lunch?" I said, gesturing toward his car. I was about to make a comment about the menu when the rumpled figure of Lou Spaghazzi charged into the scene.

"Sneaking out like the rat you are," Edie's husband said. He was standing only inches from Michael now.

Michael seemed confused by the comment and put up his hands. "Sneaking out of here? I don't think so."

"I've been looking all over for you. You know who I am, don't you?" Lou said, trying unsuccessfully to get in the other man's face.

Michael let out a deep sigh. "She showed me a photograph once. I'm very sorry for your loss."

"Are you?" Lou Spaghazzi's face was twisted in a mixture of anguish and anger. He waved a handful of photographs in Michael's face. "I know all about you and Edie. You thought when you got rid of her phone, you got rid of the evidence. Ha! Lucky for me I told Edie I needed to check her phone battery before she left. I found these photographs and got them printed up. What do you have to say to that?"

From my vantage I couldn't see the details of the photos other than they seemed to be of two people at sunset near the lighthouse. Lou didn't wait for an answer. "Are you going to deny that's you? And that's her?" He held the prints right in front of Michael's face.

"I followed her up here this time. I was going to confront her and say she had to choose between us." Lou seemed to have no awareness that I was standing next to them.

Michael's posture slumped, and he let out a weary sigh. "She loved you. We were just friends who met up here. We had dinner and talked. Sometimes we watched the sunset," he said, indicating the prints Lou kept waving around. "It was all very teenage romantic stuff. She'd slip away after the activities of her retreat were done and we'd go for a walk in the moonlight, or more often, the fog."

Lou looked like someone who had been running full steam ahead toward something and then suddenly screeched to a halt. "That's all it was?" he said.

Michael insisted it was, but I had to wonder if he was

telling the truth. I remembered what Dr. Sammy had told me—Michael said he was going to break it off and that Edie had called him at his house.

"You were up here all along." I said to Lou Spaghazzi. It was as if they both noticed me for the first time. Lou's expression clouded.

"What's it to you?" Lou said.

"Lieutenant Borgnine said he reached you on your cell phone, didn't he?" I said. "What did you tell him—that you were in L.A.?"

"I never lied to the police," he said defiantly.

"But you didn't tell him exactly where you were, either."

Lou glared at me. "That cop doesn't need to know about any of this," Lou said. "Except maybe about him." He jerked his thumb toward Michael, poking him in the chest.

Michael reacted by pushing Lou's thumb away. I could feel the tension level between them growing and threatening to erupt. It made me uneasy.

What was I supposed to do? Distract them, maybe?

"I know Michael was going to tell Edie it was over between them," I said, thinking it might smooth things over, but it had the opposite effect.

"What?" Michael said. What little had been left of his formerly calm and easygoing manner went out the window. "How do you know that?" he demanded. Then he explained, "We had an agreement. Just the time we spent here with no interference in our regular lives. Edie broke the rules and called my house." He made a grab for the photographs.

"So, maybe you decided to make sure it was over," Lou said, jerking his thumb again.

The two men were glaring at each other, and I had no

idea what was going to happen, but whatever it was didn't seem good. Michael reached for the prints. This time he pulled them from Lou's hands and began to tear them up.

Lou tried to get them back, yelling that he was destroying evidence. Michael said something back. The words turned into flying punches. Neither one of them was much of a fighter, and most of the punches seemed to miss. Lou might have been a little shorter, but he was feistier and kept kicking out with his feet until he managed to trip Michael and both of them went down. The two of them kept pushing and shoving each other as they rolled around in all the pine needles.

The closest I'd come to dealing with anything like this was when I was substitute teaching and two first graders had gotten into a fight in the school yard. They'd been easy to break up. I just grabbed the backs of their shirts and pulled them apart. Would it work now? I watched them scuffling on the ground, trying to make a grab. It had been much easier with the first graders, because they were smaller and standing up. A moment came when the backs of both of their shirts were exposed, and I made my move. With a lunge, I grabbed both their shirts and pulled. Instead of getting them to stop, there was just a loud ripping sound and I ended up with two handfuls of fabric before joining them on the ground.

"Ms. Feldstein, what are you doing? Fighting with the guests now?" I recognized Kevin St. John's voice and the whine of a golf cart as he squeaked to a stop next to us.

"You better call Lieutenant Borgnine," I said.

27

"COFFEE," I SAID AND SANK INTO A CHAIR IN THE dining hall. Despite the fistfight in the parking lot, I had kept my word and found the group's table before the end of breakfast, although just barely. Lucinda jumped up and grabbed the thermal pot off the lazy Susan and filled my cup.

"What happened to you?" Kris said with concern. For the first time, I thought of my clothes and looked down. It was definitely the wrong day to have decided to wear a white shirt and khaki slacks. I quickly tucked in the shirttail that had come out and tried to brush the dirt off the front of my shirt. When I felt my hair, some pine needles fell on the table.

Bree gasped as I began to tell them about my encounter with Lou Spaghazzi and Michael. Melissa and Sissy both kept asking who they were.

"So, what happened?" Olivia said, very interested.

"Did you know that Kevin St. John carries plastic ties

you can use for handcuffs?" I said, mostly to Lucinda. "With my help he got them on both Lou and Michael as both men told Kevin that the other one had killed Edie. Then he shooed me away, saying he was in control, but I heard him on his cell calling Lieutenant Borgnine, claiming he'd caught Edie's killers."

There was a buzz of conversation as they all started to talk at once, but then silence fell over the group as Lieutenant Borgnine came in the door and made a beeline for our table. He pointed at me and gestured for me to go outside.

I still thought he looked like a bulldog with his round face and almost invisible neck, and he was wearing the same sports jacket with the lining peeking below the back. He pulled me away from the doorway, out of earshot of a couple exiting the dining hall.

"St. John said you were there when the victim's husband and the other guy started throwing punches. I took them in for fighting, but they both clammed up and asked for lawyers. You want to tell me what you know?"

Lieutenant Borgnine was very interested in hearing that Lou had been up here all along and suspected his wife was meeting someone. He was even more interested in hearing that Michael and Edie had been involved and that Michael was trying to break it off.

Lieutenant Borgnine grunted a thank-you and said he was going to scramble to gather evidence while he had them in custody.

"That's wonderful that they've caught Edie's killer or killers," Kris said, letting out a sigh of relief after I'd returned to the table and told them all what Lieutenant Borgnine had said.

Olivia seemed the most relieved. "Now maybe he'll leave me alone."

"So, I guess that's that," I said. It seemed a little anticlimactic. I noticed that Scott had watched all the proceedings from another table but figured out something was going on and joined the group as we walked toward the door. Bree latched onto him and started filling him in. Her version was a little cockeyed, but she did have the important part: Edie's killer had been caught.

As we joined the rest of the throng walking up the path toward the center of Vista Del Mar, I saw Dr. Sammy sitting on a bench doing coin tricks for a group of wide-eyed kids. I let my group go on ahead, and I stopped beside him.

The kids applauded when he finished pulling a coin out of a boy's ear. The wanted to see more, but he turned his attention to me.

"Later, guys," he said to them as he got up and joined me. When we were finally alone, Sammy stood facing me. I expected one of his goofy tricks like pulling scarves out of thin air, but for once there were none. "I heard the manager snagged the guy who killed your retreater."

I groaned. So Kevin St. John was taking all the credit. I told Sammy what really happened, and he seemed impressed as he brushed some pine needles off my shoulder. Before I could ask him what he was doing there, he explained.

"Your mother was going to come to help you pack up, but I suggested I come instead," he said. "I figured it would be easier for you."

"I didn't say I was taking them up on their offer," I said indignantly.

"C'mon, Case," he said. "You know you're going.

Everything is worked out. We all fly back to Chicago together and you leave for Paris on Wednesday. The new session of classes begins the following Monday."

I was stunned that my mother had gone ahead and set everything up when I hadn't officially said yes. Dr. Sammy knew all of the problems my mother and I had with each other, and it didn't seem to faze him in the least. He didn't take sides, just tried to work things out. And he was right. I was going to say yes, and packing things up with his help would be a lot more peaceful than with my mother's.

"Could you come back during lunch?" I said. "I want to be with my group for this morning's workshop."

"No problem. I'll hang out in the building with the table tennis." Sammy looked around at a cypress tree with its windblown horizontal shape and the dunes. The white sky was dissolving, and it seemed like we were in for some sun. "I can see why you like it here."

I felt like I had to do something, so I touched his hand before going on my way.

The group had already gathered in our meeting room. It felt cozy and intimate with the warming fire. I added the muffins to the coffee and tea service on the counter. Everyone was busy at work now, trying to make the most of the time. I watched them for a moment before joining in and was struck by the change in them since the beginning of the weekend. We'd all been just a group of strangers, and now we'd shared secrets, fears, and, sadly, the loss of one of our group. Just one more time together after lunch and then we'd all go our separate ways.

Olivia smoothed out the lacy shawl she was making out of the sparkly purple cashmere yarn. It was so delicate looking, I thought it might float in the air. Though she hadn't said it, I thought she was enjoying working with the luxury yarn.

Sissy held up her cabled scarf and checked her work. It wasn't finished, but the young woman was confident she could manage knitting the rest on her own. There was a definite look of pride in her eyes, and for once her mother wasn't adding her opinion. Melissa was too busy getting some help from Kris with the black-and-white houndstooth print scarf.

Scott had completed the most inches of anyone, but then he was working on huge needles. But I still hadn't seen him knit anywhere but in the privacy of this room or in the shadows of the Sand and Sea lobby. He might have been the most wistful about the end of the retreat, because it was also the end of his having so much freedom to knit.

I sat down next to Lucinda, who was happily doing her seed stitch. I admired the textured surface of her work as I picked up my needles. I was pleasantly surprised when my hands seemed to know what to do as I worked through another row.

It seemed like a perfect moment for us all.

But then Kevin St. John had to come in and ruin the mood. The dark suit and somber expression made him look more like an undertaker than the host of the conference center. His gaze went directly to me.

"Oh, you're here. I thought you'd be across the street packing." Then he ignored me and addressed the table.

"I'm already working on a wonderful retreat for you yarn lovers. It's going to be way beyond the scope of the current one or any that Joan Stone arranged. To keep it special, we're going to limit how many people can participate. I want to give you people the first chance to sign up."

I was shocked to see he had already made up a full color brochure, which he dropped at each person's place. "You'll note the last page has the sign-up. Just fill it out and give me a small deposit and your position is assured."

Of course, he didn't drop one in front of me. He continued to ignore me. Olivia seemed fixated on something out the window, and I took the opportunity to pick up her brochure and look at it.

There were a lot of pictures of Vista Del Mar, along with shots of Cadbury by the Sea and promises of a trip back to a simpler time, but no real substance. A whole page had been devoted to Cadbury Yarn. He must have made some kind of deal with Crystal and Gwen to handle the yarn craft part of the retreats. Maybe he'd convinced them they'd sell so much yarn, they were willing to throw in their skills for nothing.

"Good luck with the retreats," Kris said to him. "I've loved being the master teacher, but now it's time for me to move to a bigger arena. It looks like everything is working out. Casey is going off to Paris, you're taking over the retreats and I am going to be traveling around as spokesperson for the Retreat in a Box business."

"The losers are us," Bree said. "I was hoping to come to another weekend with you guys."

"Really?" Lucinda said. "I thought you were so lost being on your own and you were so upset about leaving your kids."

"Maybe at first," she said, looking sheepish, "or for most of the weekend, but then something kicked in. I was talking about things that interested me to people who shared that interest. When I'm home I kind of lose sight of who I am."

Kevin didn't miss a beat. "I'm planning to put some self-help workshops into the weekends." He was looking up at the ceiling, and I could see his eyes were darting from side to side. He was making it up as he went along. I shuddered to think of him running the yarn retreats. He certainly wouldn't have sat up with Bree the way I did. It was just business to him. My aunt must have made some money from them, but I knew her real motivation was that she loved yarn craft and the people who did it.

"You're all so busy talking about future retreats, but what about Edie?" Melissa said, directing her gaze at Kevin St. John. "Have the police figured out which of those two men did it?"

"Lieutenant Borgnine is handling the situation. He's an experienced investigator," Kevin said with pride in his voice as if the cop's abilities reflected on him. "Before he came to Cadbury, he was an investigator for the Los Angeles County Sheriff's Department." Kevin tried to reassure them that justice would be served, and nothing like that would ever happen again. "Not on my watch," he said, giving me a disparaging nod. How could it be my fault that Edie had been murdered?

I was happy when he finally left, and I had to bite my tongue to keep from saying anything bad about him. My feelings were based on my own dealings with him, and I didn't want to color theirs if they wanted to come back to his future retreats.

Kris looked at her watch and said it was time to stop. "Let's just leave everything the way it is. You can pick up where you left off this afternoon. It will be the last chance to get my help on anything, so think about it during lunch."

Kris left the room ahead of us, but the rest of us walked as a group down the path. As we got to the center of Vista Del Mar, we passed the small chapel just as the doors opened and a group came out. When I saw the woman in the white dress and the man in a suit, I realized it must be the wedding connected to the party I'd seen on the deck of the Lodge at the beginning of the weekend.

I was enjoying the happy sight when I heard someone bellow "no" followed by sobbing. It seemed to be coming from our group, and when I turned, I saw Olivia's face was squeezed in misery. I didn't want the wedding party's happy moment to be ruined, so I stepped close to Olivia and directed the rest of the group to follow.

En masse we moved away from the chapel to the board-walk and onto the beach as Olivia sobbed and wailed. Finally she collapsed on the sand as her sobs turned into hiccups. I knelt next to her and put my arm around her while smoothing her red-toned hair off her face.

Gradually she calmed down and then looked up at every-one with something new in her eyes. "Thank you all for your support just now," she said, clearly really meaning it. "I think I owe you all an explanation." It was as if the whole facade she'd had all weekend had suddenly melted and she became part of the group.

She glanced over us all with a sad smile. "My ex-husband got married this weekend. I've been trying not to think about it, but when I saw the happy couple coming out of the chapel, it was like I was seeing my ex and his new bride." There was a hum of sympathy from us all as arms reached out to touch her. "My son arranged this trip. He said it was a gift, but I think the plan was to get me out of town because they were afraid I might show up at the wedding and make a scene."

She had to take a moment to collect herself before she continued. "Can you imagine how hard it is to deal with their happiness when it is based on my misery? Both my daughter and son went to the wedding." Her little smile had faded, and she just looked sad. "I can't help it; I feel like they're traitors."

"Maybe your son did it so that you could be somewhere else and avoid the whole thing," Bree said. "It could have been out of compassion."

"It's kind of harsh thinking your kids are traitors," Sissy said. "He is their father."

Melissa gave her daughter a disapproving glance. "I understand completely," the mother said. "You feel left out in the cold by all of them. But you have us." Lucinda and Scott stepped closer and each put an arm around her and said they were glad she'd finally shared what was bothering her with us. The end result was that Olivia finally smiled.

"Thank heavens for all of you," she said as she got up. "You got me through this weekend."

When we were back on the hotel grounds, I let them all go on to get ready for lunch. I'd already told them I was skipping the meal.

"Don't worry, I'll act as host," Lucinda said, staying back as the others moved on. "You did a great job with Olivia's meltdown. Joan would be pleased." She took Kevin St. John's brochure from her pocket and, making a face, dropped it in a trash can. "He can count me out of his retreats." Lucinda chuckled in disbelief. "I'd rather spend the time with Tag, watching him measure how far the plates are set from the edge of the table." She looked at me. "You did a great job, you know."

"Really?" I said, surprised. "One of the members got killed. I was clueless about yarn crafts or how to run a retreat. The only thing I can say is that I did manage to stick it out to the end and Edie's killer seems to have been caught."

"Ah, but you put your heart into it. I think you have a natural talent. Maybe you inherited it from your aunt."

I thought I was going to cry.

28

MY EX, SAMMY, WAS IN DEEP CONCENTRATION
looking at a magazine when I found him in the seating area
of the main building. I stood behind him and glanced down
at the magazine, curious about what he was so interested in.
He must have sensed my presence, because he suddenly
looked up.

"I was just doing one of those puzzles while I waited."
He held up the page and showed me the two side-by-side
photos of some celebrity and his dog.

"Why did they put in two of the same photos?" I said,
and Sammy's face lit up.

"You just think they are the same," he said. He pointed
to the game directions that said there were eight things that
didn't match. With this information, I studied the photos
again. I was about to say I didn't see any differences when
Sammy pointed to the shorts the guy was wearing. In one

of the pictures, they were longer. How could I have missed that? Now I was hooked and stood over him until I'd found all eight things.

"And now when I look at it, the differences are so obvious," I said. Sammy got up and we walked to the door and then across to my place.

"You're really nice to help me pack," I said. He flinched at the words as we got to my door.

"Could you call me something besides *nice*?" he said. "It makes me sound about as exciting as a glass of warm milk."

"How about *thoughtful*?" I said as I opened the door.

He shook his head. "That might even be worse. *Thoughtful* sounds like something your ancient uncle would be when, frail as he was, he still opened the door for you."

I laughed and nudged Dr. Sammy. "Why don't you just pick your own word?"

He seemed to be considering things for a moment. "How about just *hot* across the board. Whatever I do, it's just hot. Or maybe even seriously hot." I'd forgotten how playful and fun he could be, and we both were chuckling as we went inside.

"This is where you've been living?" Sammy said, taking in the converted garage in one glance. "Well, at least you didn't have to spend a lot of time with housekeeping." He wiggled his eyebrows to show he was joking. Then he asked what he could do.

"I can just throw my clothes in a suitcase later. I'm more concerned with some things in my aunt's house." Sammy followed me as I walked across the driveway to the back door.

I was glad to have his company, because I still felt all emotional about my aunt's belongings.

He checked out the kitchen. "This is more like it." He touched the drying herbs that by now had become a little too dry. "Did you do this?" I explained it was all Joan's doing. "Then you left everything as is?" He opened the refrigerator at arm's length as if he was expecting something terrible. He seemed relieved when it was empty.

Sammy followed me as we went through the house. I kept pointing out all the things my aunt had made. "I want to take it all with me," I said, picking up the afghan on the end of the sofa and her shawl still hanging on the chair. When we got to her office, my arms were full and I dropped everything as I reached for the crocheted lion on her desk.

Sammy went to pick up the pile of handcrafted items. "Case, you can't take all this stuff with you." He set the armload of yarn-made items on the small love seat.

I knew he was right, but the thought of leaving all the things she'd made was making my lip quiver, and I could feel tears welling up. I brushed back the emotion and pulled myself together.

"You're right. I'll just take the lion and Joan's shawl," I said, gathering both. After that I just wanted to get out of there. On the way through the kitchen I saw the shopping bag with the things Joan had been wearing when she was hit. No way could I leave that. My hands were full, so Sammy got it for me.

We got back to my place and I set everything down. "Case, you'll probably be lonely in Paris. I found a great cooking school in Chicago," Sammy said as he went to put down the shopping bag. Somehow it got upended and I heard the clatter of things hitting the tile floor.

"Just leave it," I said, deciding to ignore his comment

about changing cooking schools. Sammy backed off with a shrug just as there was a knock at the door. I'd left it ajar, and after the knock, Dane, dressed in his midnight blue uniform, walked in.

Dr. Sammy made some kind of noise between a sigh and whine as I said hello.

"I wanted to apologize," he said. "I shouldn't have ignored your comment about the victim's boyfriend being a suspect."

"That's the guy I talked to, isn't it?" Dr. Sammy said. I nodded and he turned to Dane. "Casey and I were working as a team. I was her Dr. Watson, or more correctly Dr. Glickner," he said with a possessive smile as he stepped next to me.

"Did Lieutenant Borgnine figure out whether it was Lou or Michael who killed Edie?"

Dane totally ignored Dr. Sammy, focusing on me. "How about there's no evidence that it was either of them and both of them are insisting they didn't do it, but are trying to finger the other."

"I was hoping it had been settled. I don't like leaving with loose ends hanging."

"Then don't leave," Dane said. He seemed to have forgotten that Dr. Sammy was even there. "Cadbury needs your muffins." His radio squawked, and he attended to it as he went toward the door. He looked back before he walked out. "Think about it." Then he left.

"Geez, I didn't realize that guy was a cop. You like him, don't you?" Sammy said.

I tried to shrug off his comment. "He's just a neighbor. And let's say his lifestyle isn't my style."

Sammy had gotten mopey. "I wish I were different. Maybe some kind of CIA or Navy Seal type. You know, jumping into danger with only a pocketknife and my karate skills."

I looked to see if he was joking. I hoped he was joking. Actually, Sammy would probably make a good CIA guy. Nobody would ever suspect him.

"Or at least if I could be like one of those steamy doctors on television. They're having sex in a broom closet one minute and saving somebody's life the next." He sighed. "Everybody laughs when they hear my specialty, and then they say I bet you know a lot of bathroom jokes."

What could I do but stop thinking about my imminent departure. Call it for old times' sake or whatever, but I spent the next five minutes giving him a pep talk.

"You're a hero to your patients," I said. "And being a good guy these days is so rare, you should be proud. And being a magician," I added with a smile, "is the icing on the cake." When he still didn't seem completely cheered, I went on. "Besides, I heard those CIA and Navy Seal types are an unhappy bunch." I hoped he wouldn't ask where I'd gotten my information, because I didn't want to say from my own imagination.

He began to perk up a little, and his eyes were warm as he looked at me. "Case, you're the only one who gets me," he said.

I wanted to stop him before he said anything else. I pulled out the red bandana–covered box and opened it. "Sammy, I really need to look through this one more time. It's all my aunt's stuff for the retreat business. You've helped a lot already. I can do the rest myself." I gestured toward the door. "You should go and enjoy the scenery."

He didn't seem happy with my suggestion but finally took it.

I started to thumb through the paper. When I got to the back and the essay and knitting notes, I started to pass over them, then reconsidered. They seemed personal, and there was no reason to leave them for Kevin St. John. I took a moment and really read them this time, and as I did, an idea began to form in my mind. I pulled out the flash drive and fired up my laptop.

What had seemed like gobbledygook when I'd looked before now made sense. I went back to the photo of the group that Edie had sent me earlier in the retreat. I flashed on the pictures in Dr. Sammy's magazine—how they looked alike at first, but then there were subtle differences.

I left the computer on and dashed across the street. The grounds were quiet because everyone was at lunch. The inside of the Lodge seemed cavernous and empty. I found the wall of photos and began to study them. Then I saw it. Now when I looked it was so obvious. Edie must have seen it, too.

As I ran back to my place, I thought of what Crystal had told me about dye lots. I was still processing it all when I walked back inside my place. Now I understood that Edie's murder was connected to Amanda Proctor's death, which I didn't believe was an accident anymore.

My foot caught in the handle of the shopping bag that Sammy had dropped. I stopped and unhooked myself and then began to load everything back in the bag. The contents of the sweater pockets must have fallen out. I noticed the keys I'd felt before. As I picked them up, I discovered a plastic card twisted with the tissues. "How could I have missed this?" I said out loud as I examined it.

I stared at it for a long time, wondering why my aunt would have been carrying her auto club card when she went out walking that morning. Frank's training kicked in, and I picked up the phone.

By the time I clicked off, all I could do was shake my head with disbelief.

I was breathless as I called Frank.

"Feldstein, it's Sunday," Frank said with the usual exasperation in his voice. "What now?"

"I need your advice," I said quickly. He started to fuss about it being his day of rest, but I talked over him and told him it couldn't wait. At warp speed I explained about leaving, Paris and cooking school before presenting what I'd found out and most of all what I'd figured out. "How do I go to the cops with it?" I said.

"Hold on a minute, Feldstein. There's a problem. Everything you have is just conjecture. It's probably right, but before you go saying you've wrapped up the case, you might want to get some hard evidence. I told you, cops don't like it when amateurs do their jobs, and if you don't provide the goods, they'll just blow you off."

I started to say I didn't have a search warrant or any power to go looking for stuff. Frank laughed. "Feldstein, the fried chicken is getting cold, so I gotta go, but you don't need any of that warrant stuff. Just go get the goods. I never told you this, Feldstein, but I thought you had the makings of a pro." He started to go but stopped. "So, you're already bailing on that place? Cooking school in Paris?" He sounded doubtful. "Are you sure? I don't see you as one of those cooks where the garnish is bigger than the meal." He took a deep breath. "That's just my two cents." There was a long pause. "So, let me know what happens." There was no good-bye, just a click.

I knew Frank was right. I needed something solid to give the cops. And I knew what it was and most likely where it was. I threw down the phone and was out the door.

Everyone but our group had checked out or was at lunch, and the grounds were empty at Vista Del Mar. I went directly to the Lodge, and again it was deserted. There was a sign on the registration counter that said *Ring bell for service*. I slipped behind the counter and looked at the wall of pigeonholes, each marked with a room number. Each also had a hook for the room's keys. My eye went down the boxes for the rooms in Sand and Sea, grateful that only Edie had asked for two keys when she checked in.

My heart was beating wildly as I reached up and slipped off the one I was looking for. As I rushed outside, I glanced toward the dining hall and noticed lunch was still in progress. I needed to hurry.

I headed up the hill past the sea of golden grass. Sunday afternoon seemed to be the time for maintenance. There were housekeeper carts piled high with bedding along with the furniture from the lobby of Sand and Sea sitting outside of the building. A rug shampooer sat idly next to the clutter as it appeared whatever work was going on had stopped for lunch.

I saw a truck driving slowly up the narrow path toward the back of the building as I started up the stairs. Inside the living room area was empty and the fireplace appeared to be in the process of being cleaned out.

I rushed up to the second floor. The dark wood of the hall made it seem like I was heading into a tunnel of doom.

I could feel my pulse throbbing in my neck as my fingers fumbled with the key.

I shoved it in the lock and pushed the door open. Cautiously, I looked in and was relieved that the room was empty. I closed the door quietly behind me and felt a wave of cool air coming in through the open window. All the personal items were packed up, and the suitcase stood next to the bed, ready to go.

This was so not the way I was used to doing things, but there was no choice. My hands were shaking as I laid the soft-sided bag on the bed and unzipped it. I wanted to make it look like nothing had been moved, but the feeling of urgency made me dig deep into it, flinging the contents onto the bed. I was totally immersed in my search and didn't hear the door open just as I pulled out what I was looking for.

"What are you doing?" Kris said. She sounded wary, but not threatening. Her tone changed when she saw what I was holding.

"Give me that," she said, trying to snatch the cream-colored shawl away.

"Didn't Edie call this your trademark shawl?" I said, looking it over. "It's kind of strange that you stopped wearing it after the first night." She made another grab for it, and I took a step back to keep it out of her reach. I quickly examined it. "I might never have realized you'd changed it since the last retreat if I hadn't seen a game in a magazine where things looked almost the same except for subtle differences. It made me see the photograph in the Lodge and the one Edie sent me in a new light."

Seeing it close up, the strip of different stitches that had been added to each end in what seemed like a slightly different shade of the same color was more obvious. "Why would you want to change a shawl that you wore all the time? Unless something happened to it, like it got ripped. You must have wanted to fix it, but when you went to buy more yarn it was from a different dye lot, and the color wasn't quite the same. So, you added it to both ends, thinking it would look planned and no one would notice."

"You're making a big deal out of nothing. There isn't any crime in changing my shawl." She held out her hand and asked for it back. When I didn't give it up, she moved toward me.

"You're right, there is no crime in adding onto your shawl. But the question is, what happened to it?" I had it clutched under my arm now. I know that I should have stopped talking, but I was so proud of how I put all the pieces together, I wanted to show her I knew what she had done.

"Maybe someone tried to grab onto it before she was pushed off a cliff. Someone who was found with some off-white yarn still clutched in her hand. Amanda Proctor wasn't really knitting when she went for that last walk along the water, was she?"

It was as if a shade had passed over Kris's face and all the sunny perkiness had been replaced by a hard, somber expression.

"You don't understand. I was just going to talk to Amanda. She kept stepping backward, I tried to warn her, but she took a wrong step. I reached out to grab her, and she grasped onto my shawl. It ripped away before I could do anything, and she fell."

I didn't bother to bring up the fact that she hadn't gone for help. "What is it that you were talking about?" I said.

"Maybe something about Retreat in a Box?" I knew by Kris's look of consternation that I was right. I mentioned finding the flash drive in my aunt's box of papers, and that I hadn't realized what it was at first. "I didn't get what *RIB Test* meant at first, but when I checked it again, I saw there was another file on the drive. When I opened it, there was a note to my aunt from Amanda about the test version of the program Amanda had written for their project, Retreat in a Box. RIB. She wanted Joan to try it out and give her feedback." I looked directly at Kris. "There was no mention of you. When I went through some more of my aunt's papers, I understood why." I referred to the essay my aunt had written, which really was more like a mission statement for the Petit Retreats, and all her knitting notes, which made all the cryptic notations after the current group's names make sense.

"Joan's mission with the Petit Retreats was to give each of the participants a challenge and help them to meet it. With Amanda's help she was going to take it to retail. Amanda was a computer programmer and must have worked with Joan to develop the software. All those kits you brought to the first workshop weren't designed by you. Joan was the one who wrote the questionnaire and then used the information to come up with a project for each of the retreaters."

Kris shook her head in consternation. "We were supposed to be partners. Amanda, Joan and me. But when Amanda figured out that the whole Retreat in a Box thing was based on Joan's work, she wanted to cut me out." Kris looked at me for understanding. "Joan was fine with me being a partner and the front person."

I knew Kris was probably right about that. Joan was a generous soul. Before I could ask what happened, Kris continued. It was as if she'd been holding in all in and now it erupted.

"Amanda didn't understand. Joan wanted me to take the credit for the individualized projects. She told me to use the idea in other classes I taught. She even let me use the questionnaire she'd written. As for the Petit Retreats, she did all the behind-the-scenes work, but she thought it added to my cachet as a master teacher to let the retreaters think it was me. Joan liked to take part in the weekend with the other retreaters and made up her own."

Kris's voice grew in intensity. "Joan didn't want to be the face of Retreat in a Box. She thought having the former Tidy Soft toilet paper lady touting a yarn concept would seem weird anyway. Besides, I'm the one who had written patterns for yarn companies. I'm the one known as a master teacher around the Bay Area. I just wanted to explain that all to Amanda."

I took out the auto club card from my pocket and showed it to her. She didn't seem to make any connection with it.

"Joan was so good to you. Why did you kill her?"

The direct accusation caught her off guard, and she sputtered something about me being ridiculous.

"What did you do? Maybe call my aunt early that morning and tell her your car broke down and you didn't have an auto club card? And Joan being the sweetheart she was, she probably told you that she'd walk right over since it was only a few blocks from her house and she'd let you use her AAA membership."

"That's just ridiculous. I was as brokenhearted about your aunt's accident as anyone else. I was nowhere near Cadbury that day." She let out a huffy sound to punctuate the absurdity of what I'd said. "And I can prove it, not that I need to. I was in a silly accident in Seaside. My car rolled into a fast-food restaurant. Nobody was hurt, but my poor SUV." She took another step toward me, reaching again for the shawl, but I pulled it closer to me and moved away from her.

"That was just your way of covering up the damage from the hit-and-run you staged when my aunt showed up. You thought my aunt would call the auto club when she got to you, but Joan called it in before she left her house." All my telephone work for Frank had come in handy, and I'd been able to talk my way into getting the information I needed. "They asked for the license number of your car. Since Joan didn't have that or even the make, she gave them something else. The notes on the order gave the location and said the vehicle was a white SUV with a hand-painted design on the back window of a ball of yarn with the needles sticking out of it and KWRBK beneath it."

Kris swallowed hard at that bit of information, and I continued. "I can't imagine you would want to kill my aunt. What happened, did she figure out you were involved with Amanda's death?"

"I told her it was an accident, but she wouldn't let up. She wanted me to go to the cops and tell them what happened. We arranged to meet that morning. She said she would go with me for moral support. Though Joan never said it exactly, I knew she was going to tell the police if I didn't." Kris shook her head in dismay. "Why not just leave things as they were? It wasn't going to bring Amanda back."

"And it was going to land you in trouble. Because even if it was an accident, you didn't go for help. You left her there to die."

Kris gazed at the floor, and her body slumped. "If only I had called 911." Her regret sounded genuine.

She glanced up and regarded me directly. "I wasn't thinking clearly. All I could think of was that taking Retreat in a Box to retail was going to save me. I'm a single mother with no child support and two teenage kids. They need clothes, food and college. You don't get rich giving knitting classes. I couldn't let Amanda cut me out. And Joan didn't understand. Even if the police believed Amanda's fall was accidental, I would have gotten in trouble for not reporting it, for leaving her there."

"So then you ended up the sole partner," I said.

"Maybe I did, but the work Amanda and Joan had done was only a beginning. I took the concept to the yarn company I have a connection with. They redid the whole program and simplified Joan's concept, along with making all the instructional videos. Even so, I was planning to give some of the money to Amanda's family and, of course, to you."

I noticed a change in Kris. It was as though she'd made some kind of internal decision. Was she going to let it all out and give herself up?

"Edie had the old retreat photos on her cell phone, and when she compared it with the new photo she took of all of us, she noticed the difference in the shawl. That woman didn't miss a thing. She kept asking and asking me about it. Why had I made the change in the shawl I had said was my favorite? She guessed that it had gotten damaged somehow and then wanted to know what had happened. She was relentless. I made something up, but she poked holes in it and kept insisting on knowing the real story. When she brought up Amanda and the yarn in her hand, I had to do something.

"I thought the combination of the sleeping pills and the wine would shut Edie off for good. Accomplishing it was easy. I knew about Olivia's sleeping pills and had no problem lifting her purse at dinner. While everybody was looking for it, I had it at my feet and was transferring the pills to my bag and one to Edie's. Then I just said I'd found Olivia's. And the wine? I suggested the toast to Joan's memory. I had already crushed the pills when Kevin served the wine. I dropped the powder in my glass—"

"And you knocked over Edie's glass and gave her yours to replace it," I said, interrupting as I remembered the scene at the reception on the Lodge's deck. Kris gave me a terse nod.

"I knew Edie always got two keys to her room, and I'd taken one during our first meeting. I just went to check to make sure the wine and pills had done their job. But Edie had thrown up and was still breathing. I panicked and shoved the pillow over her face to finish her off.

"As soon as I added the pillow into the mix, it no longer would pass as an accident. I got the double-pointed needles from your aunt's and stuck them in Edie to make it look like it was the work of some kind of crazed knitter. I knew that Joan always left a key in the flower pot next to the door."

So, she hadn't been trying to frame me and apparently wasn't even concerned with adding something with fingerprints. But I suspected that Kris had other motives for going to Joan's. She probably had wanted to get the papers I'd seen that revealed that Joan was the real force behind Retreat in a Box. I realized if I hadn't taken that fabric-covered box to my place, Kris would have taken it and I would never have known about her deception.

"I'll take my shawl now," she said, reaching out for it. It didn't matter that she seemed to be ready to give herself up; the only hard evidence was the shawl, and I held it tighter.

I hadn't noticed it at first but now realized that Kris had been stepping closer and closer to me as we talked. Instinctively, I'd moved back each time. Now when she moved closer, I felt a cool breeze and the metal frame of the open window against my back. Before I could react and move away, she lunged toward me.

"If you're going to be that way," Kris said, ripping the shawl from my arms with one hand and giving me a hard shove with the other.

There was no chance to grab onto anything, and I sailed out of the second-story window backward.

29

"AN AMBULANCE IS ON THE WAY." I RECOGNIZED the voice as Dane's, but I was surrounded by darkness.

"Am I dead?" I said.

There was little surprised chuckle. "I'm pretty sure you're not."

"Then why can't I see anything?" I said, feeling a little panicky. I remembered falling and trying to squeeze myself into a ball and brace myself for the impact, but then there was a blank. Maybe it was a good thing. Did I really want remember hitting the ground with a thud? I was afraid to move. I only felt a dull ache, but I was sure if I moved all my broken bones would scream out with pain.

"You might want to try opening your eyes." Dane's voice was bordering on the teasing tone he'd used when he drove by my house. He wouldn't sound like that if I was in pieces, would he? I flickered my eyes then let them open fully and slowly moved my arms. There was no rip of pain. Instead I felt something soft. Dane was leaning over me, looking for damage. I saw the white undershirt and dark shirt and realized he was in uniform.

"This must be your lucky day." Dane held out his hand for assistance and asked if I could sit up.

I felt a little light-headed but was able to maneuver myself up. "What the . . ." I said, glancing at my surroundings.

"Sunday afternoon is when they do all the maintenance around here, like changing out the old mattresses." He showed me how they had been stacked three high next to each other, making a perfect landing spot for my backward dive.

"What are you doing here?" I said, swinging my feet over the side of the mattress pile.

"Cadbury PD got a call from Frank someone, who said he was some kind of detective and that you had worked for him and you might be in some kind of trouble." He pointed toward the fence and the street beyond. His cruiser was parked at the curb. "I saw you coming out the window and jumped the fence, but it was too late to try to catch you. But thanks to these it was okay." He gave the mattress a grateful thump. As he said that, what had happened before my fall came back to me.

"You have to stop Kris Garland."

"That's who did this to you?" The words were barely out of his mouth and he was off toward the front of the building. I didn't see it, but I was sure his gun was drawn.

I felt better and made an effort to stand up. As I moved around and checked everything to make sure I was okay, I saw Kris about to come through the back door. She must have heard Dane come in the front and thought she'd get out the other way. She froze in the doorway when she saw me. I don't think she'd expected to see me moving.

She clutched the shawl and her eyes had a panicked look.

Just then I noticed several deliverymen coming up the back path, each carrying a single-size mattress. "Stop her!" I yelled.

Both men had perplexed looks, but they didn't stop to ask questions. The closest one rushed to the door and blocked her exit with the mattress. A moment later Dane came through the building and nabbed her.

Dane was able to call off the ambulance before it roared in and drew a lot of attention with its lights and siren. Since his cruiser was parked outside the grounds, the peace of Vista Del Mar hadn't been broken. I told Dane a fast version of everything I'd learned and made sure he got the shawl as evidence. I told him they should check Kris's suitcase for the clothes Kris had been wearing that first night. Even if she'd tried to rinse them out, there was probably still some residue of Edie's throw up on them. I promised to stop by the police station and give Lieutenant Borgnine a complete statement.

"But for now, I have to get to my group," I said, feeling a heavy heart at the news I was going to share.

I tried to straighten out my appearance as I walked up the path to our meeting room. It seemed as though almost everyone but our group had left the hotel and conference center, and the walkway was empty. My heart had started thumping again as I tried to think of how I could possibly make this weekend turn out okay now.

Lunch had ended, and everyone but Kris had gone

directly to the Cypress meeting room. They were all working on their projects when I walked in. Melissa glanced up, and when she saw it was me, seemed concerned. "Kris isn't here yet. I can't imagine what's keeping her. She knows this is our last time together."

"She's not going to be able to make the workshop," I said in the understatement of the century. Everyone looked up suddenly, and I had their rapt attention.

"Is she all right?" Lucinda asked.

"Not exactly," I began. As I told them all that Kris had done, I noticed they seemed to huddle closer. When I got to my trip out the window, Lucinda flew out of her seat and rushed up to hug me and to examine me for damage. She found a nasty-looking bruise on the back of my arm, and I suspected there was a nice big one on my butt, too.

There was a long moment of silence as they dealt with the shock that their wonderful master teacher was a serial murderer. Then they looked at me with a bit of awe.

"You did it! You really did it," my friend said, starting to give me a pat on the back and then, realizing it might hurt, changed it to a soft touch. "You solved Edie's murder, your aunt's hit-and-run, and Amanda's supposed slip off the rocks." The group broke into spontaneous applause. I felt myself blushing as I took a mock bow.

"Thank heavens you're okay," Melissa said in a motherly tone. "I'm so shocked about Kris. It doesn't seem possible that she killed three people. And to think I was letting her give me advice on how to get along with my daughter." Melissa leaned in to Sissy and gave her a warm hug and kissed her on the cheek. "I know we fuss, but you have to know that I really love you and think you're wonderful."

Sissy's eyes filled with tears as she hugged her mother back. "You are the best mother in the world," she said. The mother and daughter showed off their projects to each other. I held my breath, wondering if Melissa would start critiquing her daughter's work, but instead she said she was doing a great job with the cables.

It was odd, but somehow the whole thing with Kris made everyone want to hug each other and say how much this time together meant to them. Lucinda waved the scarf she was making to show off that she had mastered the seed stitch. "I've gotten over my fear of purling," she said.

Now that we knew Olivia's problem, she got a group hug, along with a reassurance that she would get past her pain. "I know I wasn't very pleasant all weekend. Thank you all for including me anyway. Having this retreat really did help," Olivia said, giving us her first happy smile.

"And you will start a whole new chapter in your life. Believe me, I know about that," Lucinda said. I was glad she left it at that and didn't mention any of the pitfalls she had encountered.

Bree looked at her silent cell phone on the table and put it away. "This weekend has changed my life. I spend so much time with my kids or thinking about them, I forgot how to be by myself. Even staying in the room alone was good." She glanced down at the floor. "I know it sounds corny, but I got to know myself again." She held up the sari yarn scarf with all of its bright colors. "I wish I could have met Joan and thanked her for figuring out just the kind of project I needed to make. No computer program is ever going to be able to put in that human touch."

Only Scott still held back. He hadn't stopped knitting

and was listening to all that was going on but hadn't shown any reaction. I'm sure Joan hadn't always had a one hundred percent success rate.

"What about you?" Bree said, looking toward the spot where my work still sat. I fingered the swatches I'd made and the rows of the scarf I'd done. I felt my eyes fill with water now that I realized it had been Joan all along who had made up the project for me. I let out a big sigh as I picked up my project and began to work my needles. "I'm going to finish this in my aunt's memory." As I said it, I was really hoping it was going to be true. There seemed to be so much knitting to do.

For the rest of the workshop, we all focused on our work and enjoyed the comfort of being together.

There was another round of hugs at the end as everyone went back to their rooms for the last time and I headed across the street to the guesthouse. Well, I'd done it. I had stayed to the very end. I had finished something. While the group packed up their things and checked out, I made a quick trip to downtown Cadbury and stopped in at the police station. Lieutenant Borgnine was waiting for me.

As I followed him to his office, I glanced toward a hallway in the back. I'd never been back there but assumed that was where they had a jail cell. He saw where I was looking. "We're holding her on suspicion of attempted murder. She pushed you out the window, right?" I nodded, and he offered me a seat. He took out a pen and began to write as I told him the whole story.

"You should compare the yarn in the main part of Kris Garland's shawl with the yarn Amanda Proctor was holding. I'm sure the fibers will match," I said.

Betty Hechtman

"Ms. Feldstein, I know how to handle an investigation without any help," Lieutenant Borgnine said in a growly tone that matched his bulldog looks.

"What about Edie's husband and that guy Michael? You should let them go now that it's obvious neither one of them killed Edie," I said. The lieutenant appeared even more irritated.

"Not that I have to tell you, but they have both been released." Lieutenant Borgnine stood up.

He was true to his word. He did know how to run an investigation. They did still have the yarn from Amanda's fall in their evidence file. As I had predicted, the fibers did match, but there was no way to know for sure if Kris had pushed her or Amanda had really slipped in the midst of their argument, so Kris was charged with manslaughter for Amanda's death. The information I'd gotten from the auto club was enough reason for the cops to impound Kris's SUV as evidence. Even though she'd staged the accident to cover up any damage done when she hit my aunt, the cops found a strand of Joan's hair still sticking to the undercarriage. Again, there was no way to prove that it was premeditated, so she was charged with vehicular manslaughter.

Kris had been very careful in Edie's murder. She'd wiped the door handle clean, along with the needles she taken from my aunt's, so there were no prints, which meant all my worry and glass breaking was for nothing. But she hadn't wiped down Edie's second key before hanging it back in at the Lodge. And even though she'd tried to wash the throw up off her clothes, there was still some residue. The DA charged her with first-degree murder on that one. And finally, she was charged with attempted murder for my fall out the window.

She was moved to a prison to await trial. Any way you looked at it, she was going to be spending a long time in jail. The story was all over the Internet with headlines like *Master Teacher Masterminds Murders, Knitter is Needled to Death* and *Acclaimed Knitting Teacher is Serial Killer.*

Once the yarn company that was putting out the Retreat in a Box kiosks found out that Kris had stolen the idea from my aunt, they took her name off and called it Joan Stone's Retreat in a Box instead. They even offered to pay me the royalties due my aunt. I was glad for the extra income, but I felt bad for Kris's kids since they were just innocent bystanders, so I split the money with them.

But all of that was still to happen when Lieutenant Borgnine walked me to the front of the Cadbury police station and held the door open. "You're free to leave the area now," he said. Something in his tone made me believe he hoped I'd make a fast departure.

I drove home and went inside the guesthouse, knowing I couldn't put off packing my bag any longer. Sammy and my parents had no idea what had happened. They had just left me several messages on my cell phone, telling me what time they'd pick me up. There would be plenty of time to tell them about my afternoon on the trip back to Chicago. I tried to get myself excited about Paris and cooking school and wearing a starched white coat with my name embroidered on it.

I looked around my tiny abode, wondering why I seemed to be stalling. Wasn't this what I did best? Living my life as if everything was just a temporary arrangement before moving on? Why was I feeling such a bittersweet tug? I picked up the red fabric-covered box and held it close to me. I had taken out what Kevin really wanted, my aunt's list of previous clients and the file with retreat ideas. I knew Kevin was probably salivating behind the registration desk, waiting to get his hands on them. I don't know why, but I didn't want to leave them for him to find. I wanted to actually hand them over to him.

I picked up the file of papers and a set of keys and headed toward the door. I went across the street and up the driveway into Vista Del Mar. My retreat group was standing together outside the Lodge building waiting for the van to take some of them to the airport.

When I saw Scott, I stopped in surprise. He was back in his business attire of a sports jacket over slacks, and his briefcase was at his feet. But there he was in public with the giant red knitting needles, knitting as they waited. When one of the women who worked in the gift shop walked out, he held his hands high to make sure she saw.

"Yep, that's right, I'm knitting. I'm a knitter." His eyes were bright as he looked at me and made a little bow. "Thank you. I couldn't have done this without you."

"Without me?" I said, shrugging. "The big needles and the bright yarn were all my aunt's idea."

"Are you kidding? After what you did this weekend—just admitting to being a knitter seems like nothing compared with falling out a window and solving three murders." He pulled out his cell phone. "Watch this." He punched in a number and put the phone to his ear.

"Hi honey, it's Scott. I just wanted to tell you two things.

Number one, I'm a knitter, and number two, I didn't go on a business trip this weekend. I went on a yarn retreat."

Then there was silence as he listened to her response. Everyone tried to pretend they weren't paying attention, but we all were. He clicked off the phone and turned to face us with the happiest expression I'd seen all weekend.

"You want to know what my wife said?" He laughed and shook his head with disbelief. "She was thrilled to hear about the knitting. She knew something was fishy about this weekend and thought it was another woman. She can't wait for me to come home and show her my needles." He did a fist pump in the air and a little jump to punctuate it.

I was still holding the file of papers. Lucinda came and stood beside me. "Joan would be so proud of you. The way you stepped into her shoes and made this weekend meaningful for all of us even with Edie's murder. Are you sure you want to leave?"

Call me crazy, but when she said that, what I'd been feeling all along came to the forefront, and I knew I didn't. I didn't care about a starched white coat with my name on it. I wanted to stay in Cadbury by the Sea. So what if I couldn't bake croissants with my eyes closed. I liked the way I baked just fine. Poor Kevin wasn't going to be happy, because I decided at that moment that not only was I going to keep on with my baking, but I was going to use those lists of clients and projects myself to put on future retreats.

"I have something to say," I began. "This weekend has been a life changer for me. For the first time ever, I don't want to drop everything and take off." I hugged the file of papers. "I was just going to put on this retreat and end the business, but I've decided I want to look through my aunt's list of ideas for retreats and put them on myself." As I finished, they all began to cheer.

"Be sure and let Sissy and me know when you put on the next one," Melissa said. I told her I'd glanced through my aunt's ideas and they weren't all going to be about just knitting. "We don't care. As long as there is yarn in it, we're here," she said.

"Count me in, too, and next time I'm bringing my wife," Scott said.

"You can count on me, too, but no husband or kids," Bree said.

Lucinda hugged me tight and told me of course she was in, too.

Kevin St. John drove up in the van, and Scott and Bree went to get in. Olivia looked at the file in my hand and said, "We'll break the news that you're staying and continuing with the retreats to Mr. St. John on the way to the airport." With a final wave Melissa and Sissy headed toward their car.

Lucinda offered to wait with me until my parents showed up and act as moral support, but I told her it was something I had to do myself. This time when I went across the street to the guesthouse, the heaviness in my heart was gone. I looked inside the file I'd been holding so tight. I knew what the cryptic codes meant now. They had been my aunt's shorthand for our projects. The number for Lucinda referred to a scarf pattern. *S&SS* meant swatches and simple scarf for me. Scott's *BBB* was for big needles, bright color, bold pattern. I did start packing things up when I went back inside, but it was to move them across the driveway to what had been Joan's place. I was now ready to claim it as my own.

It was starting to get dark when my parents and Dr.

Sammy showed up. My mother took one look around the guesthouse and knew something was up. Before she had a chance to speak, I said I wasn't going to Paris.

"What?" my mother said, clearly upset. My father wasn't happy, either, and Sammy seemed my most disappointed. When I told them about the events of my afternoon, their mouths fell open, and then they started talking amongst themselves, convinced that I was just in some kind of shock and that's why I was being so ridiculous.

"All the things we want you to stick with, like law school and teaching, you drop by the wayside. But this baking at night in a closed restaurant and putting on some crazy craft weekends is what you hang on to," my mother said, shaking her head in very obvious disapproval.

I tried to explain what I felt there. I had an identity in Cadbury. People knew my baking, and the retreat I'd put on had changed the people's lives. And mine, too. I'd found my calling . . . at least for now.

Finally, they had to go or they'd miss their flight. My parents both hugged me and my mother said, "So, go on, try this for a while. I'll put your enrollment on hold. Paris will be there next month." I stood in the doorway and watched them drive off. I felt something soft touch my legs, and when I looked down, the black cat had returned and was doing figure eights between my ankles. He took one look at the open doorway and walked inside like he owned the place. I'd heard once that cats picked their humans instead of the other way around. Was he picking me? I remembered Kevin St. John's comment about the cat parading around the grounds like he was Julius Caesar. "I'll call you Julius," I said as I went inside and looked for something to feed him.

Before I resumed gathering my things, I picked up my phone and punched in Frank's number.

"So, Feldstein, it's you again," Frank said when I'd barely got the beginning of *hello* out. He sounded irritated as he went on about the time and that it was Sunday, but I knew him well enough to know it was all just a facade. "Are you going to tell me what happened?" he said when I didn't speak right away.

"First of all, thank you for calling Cadbury PD," I said.

"Feldstein, I could tell by the tone of your voice you were in over your head." I heard the squeak of his recliner chair.

"I hear your chair. Are you in the office?" I said, and Frank chuckled.

"I have recliners wherever I go. So spill the story." I gave him the whole rundown, ending with my change of plans.

"Good going, Feldstein. I taught you well. Glad you weren't hurt, and I didn't think Paris was for you." He was trying to sound businesslike and distant, but I could tell he meant it. "You know, if you get around to it, I wouldn't mind gettingt a box of those muffins."

I said I would send him some and was about to say goodbye. "I suppose I'll be hearing from you again," he said in the fake grumpy voice. "Now that you've had the high of solving those murders, it's in your blood." I started to disagree, but he just laughed and told me to wait and see before he finally hung up.

I began carrying things across the driveway to my aunt's—no, my house. Music blared from down the street. On a peaceful Sunday night, Dane had to be kidding.

I left everything and marched down the street to his so-called studio and pounded on the door. A moment later,

Dane opened it, and when he saw it was me, stepped outside. "Are you all right? Sometimes people get delayed reactions from a fall," he said.

I didn't let his concern dampen my annoyance. "I just want to let you know that I'm not leaving. I don't care if you have your orgies every night of the week, but how about closing down on Sunday?"

"Orgies?" he said.

"I know about the women's clothes you keep for your overnight guests and the industrial-size box of condoms. And you told me about your mattress-covered floor and ceiling full of mirrors." I suddenly felt embarrassed saying it all out loud, particularly when he began to laugh.

He grabbed my wrist and pulled me toward the door. I did my best to stay planted, but Dane was much stronger than I was and he pulled me inside.

I closed my eyes and put my hand over them. But even with my eyes closed and covered I could tell all the lights were on. Dane pulled my hand away from my face and ordered me to open my eyes.

"I don't want to see a bunch of naked people," I said. Dane seemed to find that very funny and told me again to open my eyes. Just as I'd done that afternoon, I flickered them first, as a test run. If I saw anything really offensive I could snap them shut.

But at the first flicker, my eyes opened all the way, wide. I thought the teenagers were dancing at first, but then the white pants and kimono-style jackets registered, along with their precise movements. "They're doing karate routines?" I said, and Dane nodded.

"And the mattresses," he said pointing with his toe, "are

mats so nobody gets hurt. And the mirrors, which are on the walls, not the ceiling, are so they can see their form."

He glanced at the group, who was paying no attention to us, but even so, he pulled me into a corner. "You don't know anything about me, but before I was a fine upstanding police officer, I was a messed-up kid. When I got my act together, I made a promise to myself that I would try to help other kids stay out of trouble. So I give them free karate lessons and let them hang out here. They like to do the karate to music. And the condoms? These kids are going to do what they're going to do when they're not here, and I want them to be safe. They know where they are and can help themselves."

Oh, was I embarrassed. I tried to edge toward the door. But Dane stuck to me like glue. "And the clothes you were so nosy about belong to my sister."

"Chloe is your sister?" I said, and he nodded with an impish smile.

"You look cute with egg on your face. But now that you mention it, this room would be good for an orgy," he teased.

When we got to the door, he leaned close. "I'm glad you decided to stay. The town would be lost without your muffins."

My muffins! I had been so intent on everything with Kris and then the idea of leaving, I'd forgotten all about baking desserts for the Blue Door. And I was way behind schedule.

"How do you feel about cobbler for monday?" i said when lucinda answered the phone.

"Casey, I didn't want to ask after all you've been through, but baking anything would be great." I heard her turn away from the phone and tell Tag what I'd said. He took the phone from her.

"Wonderful about the baking, and could you do me a favor and pull off the strips of tape I stuck on the menus over *homemade* when I thought you were leaving?"

I said I'd do it and hung up.

It had been a very, very long day, but I looked forward to the baking. The quiet restaurant looking out on the quiet street would be soothing. I drove the Mini Cooper down to the deserted downtown and parked next to the restaurant.

As I walked inside I felt like I was just where I belonged. I turned on some soft jazz and began to lay out ingredients, feeling the tensions of the day melting away. I was surprised to hear a tap at the door. I thought it was probably Lucinda, but when I looked out through the window on the door to the darkened porch, I saw tiny colored lights that kept changing hue. When I got closer, I saw that they were shaped like flowers.

Dr. Sammy smiled at me when I opened the door. "If I bring them inside, they'll go off," he said, referring to the bouquet he was holding. "It's nothing magic; they're solar lights." He stuck them in the flowerpots that hung from the railing, and the flowers continued their mesmerizing color dance.

"What are you doing here? Did your flight get canceled? Are my parents waiting in the car?"

"No, my flight didn't get canceled and your parents aren't in the car; they're probably flying over Denver by now. And as for your first question . . ." His eyes were warm, and he hesitated as though looking for the right words.

"After spending the weekend here, I knew I liked this area. I decided to stay a while longer and check it out. My partner was glad to take over my patients for the time being. A friend from med school has a practice in Monterey, and I heard he was looking for a new partner." Dr. Sammy shrugged his eyebrows in optimism. "Who knows, huh?" He looked inside. "Can I come in?"

I held my arms out, gesturing him in. He glanced around the restaurant's main dining room, which had once been the living room. "So, this is what you do at night." He stuck his head over the counter and looked in the kitchen. "Very nice."

I must have looked shocked and maybe a little upset. "Don't worry. I'm not stalking you." He pointed to the large yellow Victorian house on the corner I knew was a bed-and-breakfast. "I'm staying there for now. I looked out the window, and there you were. I just popped over to say hi."

"Did my parents put you up to this?" I said, eyeing him warily.

"No, Case, I'm just checking out the area. No strings between us, but we are friends, right?"

I nodded, not sure of how I felt.

"Your parents not only didn't put me up to this, they thought I was being irresponsible, illogical and reckless." He wiggled his eyebrows in an effort to look devilish and grinned. "In other words, I'm acting like an outlaw."

All I could do was roll my eyes and hand him the flour sifter.

Casey's It-Only-Looks-Complicated Scarf

U.S. size 13 (9mm) knitting needles
2 skeins Lion Brand Amazing yarn, worsted-weight, 53% wool, 47% acrylic, (147yards/1.75oz/50g)
Tapestry needle
Crochet hook (for fringe)
Piece of cardboard 5 inches wide
Scissors

Gauge is not important for this project.

Cast on 17 stitches.

Row 1: Knit across.

Repeat row 1 until the scarf is approximately 70 inches long. Bind off and weave in ends. Attach 5 evenly spaced fringes across each of the short ends. Trim the ends so the fringe is even.

Fringe: Wrap the yarn around the cardboard 20 times and cut across one end to yield 20 strands of yarn 10 inches long. Take two strands and fold in half. Working at one end of the scarf, bring the crochet hook from back to front. Keeping the yarn ends even, hang the folded yarn on the hook and pull the loop partway through to the back. Using the hook or your fingers, pull the tails of the yarn through the loop and tighten.

Heal the World with Chocolate Muffins

1 stick unsalted butter (4 ounces), melted and cooled
2 large eggs, well beaten
1 cup buttermilk
2 tsp vanilla extract
2 cups all-purpose flour
1 cup unsweetened cocoa powder
1 cup sugar
2½ tsp baking powder
½ tsp salt
1 cup semisweet chocolate chips

Preheat oven to 375 degrees F. Butter or line with paper inserts 14 muffin cups.

In a bowl, whisk together the melted butter, eggs, buttermilk and vanilla extract.

In a large bowl, mix together the flour, cocoa powder, sugar, baking powder and salt. Stir in the chocolate chips. Fold the wet ingredients into the dry ingredients. Stir just until the ingredients are combined. Do not overmix. There will be lumps in the batter.

Fill the muffin cups evenly with the batter.

Place in the oven and bake for approximately 25 minutes or until a toothpick stuck in the center comes out clean. Cool on a wire rack for 5 minutes before removing the muffins from the pan.

FROM NATIONAL BESTSELLING AUTHOR
Betty Hechtman

A STITCH IN CRIME
·A CROCHET MYSTERY·

*Molly Pink and her crochet group friends are packing up for a
creative weekend away. But with danger following them, trying
to solve the latest mystery might just prove trickier than a back
post double crochet stitch . . .*

Summer's wrapping up—and it's time for the annual creative
retreat hosted by the bookstore where Molly works. This year,
her boss has dropped out at the last minute, dumping the
responsibility all on Molly. But even with the stress of orga-
nizing, it should be an exhilarating weekend out on the Monterey Peninsula, complete with crochet classes and campfires.
Unfortunately for one teacher, though, the breathtaking scenery is where she'll take her last breath . . .

It's Molly who stumbles over the dead body of crochet teacher
Izabelle Landers. Now Molly will have to solve a murder *and*
find a replacement instructor. Fortunately her pals from her
crochet group, the Tarzana Hookers, are around to help her
untangle this tightly twisted yarn . . .

PRAISE FOR THE CROCHET MYSTERIES

"Get hooked on this great new author!" —Monica Ferris

"Readers couldn't ask for a more rollicking read."
—*Crochet Today!*

penguin.com